Devin's
Second Chance

A MORNING LAKE NOVEL

LORRAINE PATON

Visit Lorraine at **www.lorrainepaton.com**

DEDICATION

To my friends and family,
you made this possible!
Thank you.

ACKNOWLEDGMENTS

There are so many wonderful and supportive people in my life, and I want to thank them all for their help and belief in me.

My family has been urging me along this path for years. I knew I would get to this point eventually, and they did, too. Thank you to: my mom, who offered help in any way she could and listened patiently to me balancing my options; my nephew Dale, who always had ideas for my latest work-in-progress; my nephew Derrick, who offered to have his all-male work crew vote online for one of my romance writing contest entries; and my sister Brenda and brother-in-law Doug, who were always supportive and there for a camping weekend away when I needed to unplug from my computer for a while. And thank you to my friends Renee and Pati, whose entrepreneurial spirit made me think I could be an entrepreneur, too!

My local writing group, the Alberta Romance Writers' Association, has been a huge influence, and has taught me so much about the craft of writing. I think every writer in the world needs a fantastic group like ARWA! Thank you to all the members I've crossed paths with over the years—in your own ways, each of you has had a role in my writing path. It was here I met Judith Duncan, the first person I'd ever known who'd published multiple books. I was in awe, and probably still am. She's been wonderfully generous to me. Thank you, Judith. Through ARWA, I also met my fabulous critique partners, Deb Smith, Sarah Kades and June Baxter. Their thoughtful and knowledgeable feedback has had a huge impact on my writing and, in particular, this book. And perhaps without realizing it, they gave me the courage to jump into online social media, where I have met a whole bunch more wonderful writers and friends. The Six Sentence Sunday blog hop, which is now defunct, was a big influence, and I would like to thank the great people I met there who shared their Sundays with me. Watching everyone's publishing success stories unfold week to week inspired me to pursue publication. To my fearless beta readers, Pati, Jodi and Allyson, I would like to express my heartfelt appreciation—thank you so much for taking your spare time to read my book and give me feedback and comments. I would also like to thank my coworkers, particularly Allyson and Paul, who critiqued my various book cover options during their lunch breaks and listened to my day-to-day worries and excitement, and my boss, Doug, who has quietly supported this dream.

Lastly, thank you to my dear Joe, who just kept saying (in his sexy Scottish accent): "I don't know why you haven't done this already." He never had a doubt that I could or would; it was just a matter of when.

Thank you all for being a part of my journey.

CHAPTER 1

Summer in Morning Lake was disgusting—too many damn tourists, screaming children and shit hawks. As one of the largest and warmest lakes in landlocked Alberta, the town had become something of a destination to a certain type of people, and that type wasn't him. God, he hated going downtown this time of year. He avoided it whenever possible.

Today, it wasn't possible.

Devin Trent drove through the town's crowded streets for ten minutes, circling, looking for an empty parking stall, which was about as rare as pasty white skin in this town. The only open space was five blocks from the pub. Shirley, his wife's—his dead wife's—mother had chosen the place, so she shouldn't be surprised to have to wait.

The early July day was thick with the kind of heat that made you wonder how people survived before having an air-conditioned truck—the sky was clear, the air was still, and the sun blistered. Main Street snaked along Morning Lake's wide beach, so the whole town core was littered with half-naked sun worshippers. His scuffed leather boots, worn jeans and cowboy hat made him stick out like a bull in a chicken coop.

Not that he cared about fitting in, but their curious gazes still made him itch at the collar. By the time the pub's patio came into view, his temples throbbed.

God, Shirley was sitting in the sun in front of the Shining Whistle. Didn't she feel the heat? Perspiration rolled down the side of his face. He wiped his forehead. Mistaking his movement for a wave, Shirley lifted her hand, then dropped it to her lap again. He greeted her with a nod, knowing full well he was scowling.

Shirley smiled, seemingly unaware. How much had she had to drink already?

When Devin opened the gate to the outdoor patio, Shirley stood to hug him.

A moment later, they were seated at a table that could double as one of his living room's TV tables. His shirt was now stuck to his damp back from when she'd embraced him.

"I hope you don't mind, dear." Shirley motioned to the drinks on the table. "When I saw your truck pass a few minutes ago, I ordered you a lager. I don't remember which kind—something domestic."

Livy had never called a beer a beer either.

"Thanks." Damn, he wished Shirley hadn't dragged him here. He took a long draw from his beer, and the cool draught swished through his body. The throb in his head shifted down to a dull ache. When he set down his frosted glass, he watched Shirley poke at the ice cubes in her glass with a straw. The clear liquid was undoubtedly a double G and T. She was seldom without one clutched in her long thin fingers. Judging by the cluster of used straws beside the salt- and pepper-shakers, Shirley'd had a few before he'd arrived.

Under Devin's gaze, she pulled out the straw and set it on the table. She attempted a smile. He waited for her to speak, but she took a small sip instead. She seemed hesitant, which was odd for Shirley. She reached out to cover his hand with hers.

"What's going on?" he said.

"You say that like something's wrong." Shirley smiled as if to reassure. "I had a voicemail the other day." She paused again, before clearing her throat and looking up at him. "It was from the gallery here in town, The Red Door."

"Yeah, so?" Devin narrowed his eyes.

She slipped her other hand beneath his, so she was cradling his in both hers. "They phoned to ask about Olivia's art."

"I already said no." He withdrew his hand.

"They told me."

"Then it's done. They shouldn't be bothering you." The last thing Shirley needed was someone pestering her about Livy. The woman didn't need the constant reminders. She was a wreck as it was.

Shirley's gaze was soft and glassy. Was it caused by the booze or the talk of Livy? "It's been nearly three years—"

"I know exactly how long it's been." Devin shifted in his chair, trying to stretch his legs under the child-sized table. He patted his breast pocket looking for a pack of gum. He'd given up chew ages ago, but sometimes he still needed to gnaw on something. This was one of those times. He pulled out the pack. Damn, it was empty. He'd finished his last piece on his drive into town. He clenched his teeth. His foul mood was getting as heavy as the heat. Tossing the useless pack on the table, he looked out at the street.

"Devin," Shirley said, waiting for him to look at her again before she continued speaking. "It's hard. More than anyone else, I know how hard.

But it's…it's been time for a while now." Her voice broke, drawing his attention again. She dabbed at a trickle of tears. He was an ass for making her cry, but, damn it, they'd been down this road before and it wasn't time until he decided it was.

And it wasn't now.

"Put those stained glass pieces in a gallery and they'll be gone. For good. Livy isn't making any more."

Shirley cleared her throat again. "I know that, too. But you can't keep living how you have been, with all her work just sitting around you."

Devin picked up Shirley's straw and started chewing on the end of it. He'd heard it all before. Sweat slid down his neck. The woofer of a beat-up old hatchback thumped as the car rolled down the street.

He didn't respond.

"Let's go talk to the gallery owner. Maybe he'd be interested in highlighting local artisans, and he could show a few, without selling them."

Devin shook his head. "It isn't a museum. They work on commission. I'm not selling her stuff for the sole reason of getting it out of my space. I will not peddle her work as if we're holding some high-end garage sale." He hadn't sold them when he was hard up after Livy's death, so with his finances finally landing in the black, he wasn't about to hawk them now.

"That's not what I want either," Shirley snapped. Then she took a deep breath. "But Olivia was preparing for an event in Toronto when she got sick." Her voice was softer now. He used the same tone on spirited horses when they were being stubborn. "She was able to complete so many exquisite pieces. It would be a shame not to share it. She really was at her artistic peak."

Devin didn't know about that. It seemed to him no one much cared about Livy's art when she was alive, regardless of that supposed art show she had scheduled in Toronto.

"I often wonder if her illness gave her a special insight…"

They sat in silence for a few minutes. He didn't want to talk about this, but he did want another drink. Where was the waiter?

Shirley slapped the table, perhaps slamming down the memories with the gesture. "Olivia made the pieces with the expectation of selling them."

He leaned forward. "She hoped to make a living at her art. There is no need to do that now." He knew he was being a jerk, but she just wasn't getting it. How blunt did he need to be?

"I'm not suggesting you get rid of everything, but she didn't create those lovely pieces so they could collect dust in your house."

She'd called it his house. Not Livy's house. Not Livy's studio. Damn, he wished he had gum—the straw wasn't cutting it.

"For me?"

"Fine." He wasn't changing his mind, but he knew the gallery would not show without selling. That was how they made their money. Everything was about money.

Devin threw a few bills on the table. He was itching to leave town anyway. The sooner the gallery guy said no, the better. The instant he stood, Shirley had hold of him, gripping the crook of his arm, guiding him along the street toward the gallery. Her bony fingers bit into his flesh.

The gallery was along that same mobbed road he'd just walked and it was beside Livy's favorite trendy gift store. Neither of those things improved Devin's outlook.

To all outward appearances, they were two people out for a walk, taking in the tourist atmosphere. In reality, her hand on his arm felt more akin to a noose around his neck. He hated being told what to do. He'd usually do the opposite to prove he could, or he'd lose everything trying. That's what had gotten him on the rodeo circuit more than ten years ago—and that decision had almost cost him everything.

Shirley slowed as they approached the old wood building that housed the gallery. Its door had been freshened with a coat of red paint, making it stand out among its beige and white stucco neighbors. The gallery folk probably thought it was all chic and modern. It reminded him he still needed to paint the barn and the other outbuildings this summer.

She squeezed his arm—as encouragement, no doubt.

Devin glanced in the window. "What the—"

A life-sized image of Livy stared out at him from a poster in the gallery window. The photographer had captured the look Livy had "after"—*after* she had found out she had cancer, *after* she had confronted him about cheating and he hadn't denied it, *after* she realized she was dying…

His heart stopped. He couldn't move. He'd been sucker punched a few times in his life—this was worse. Then, in a rush, his blood blasted through his veins. "What the hell is going on?"

He motioned to the window. Shirley pivoted and her face paled at what she saw. "Olivia."

"What did you do?"

"I didn't know, I swear."

Devin shook her off before charging to the gallery. The door rattled on its hinges when he yanked it open. There were only three people inside the quiet, cavernous room. Their mouths all widened with surprise when he burst in. Devin glanced from one to another.

"Who's in charge here?"

The young couple closest to him shrugged. The man stepped between Devin and his companion and wrapped his arm over the girl's shoulders to guide her out of the gallery. Another woman averted her eyes and followed the couple. Then the place was empty.

Devin growled and marched to the back of the display room. Ahead, a door was ajar. A female voice carried from the room. Devin's boots rapped angrily against the polished hardwood. Shirley scurried behind him.

"Devin, it's a wonderful picture of Olivia. Did you see it? She is beautiful. They remember her, don't they? Everyone in town can see her. Remember her."

He ignored her.

When he arrived at the door, he pushed it open. It swung smoothly. A woman with very dark, very straight brown hair had her back to him and was murmuring into a telephone receiver. She had a nice voice, the kind you could imagine would be perfect for soothing a newborn with a lullaby.

Jesus, that beer must have gone straight to his head.

"Is there anything...anything I need to do ahead of time?" Her voice stumbled over the words.

When the doorknob banged against the wall, she jumped in her chair, then swiveled to face him.

"Excuse me a moment," she said into the phone. Then she covered the receiver and said, "I will only be a moment."

"Are you in charge?" Devin asked, crossing his arms.

"I said I will be with you in a moment. If you could wait in the gallery..." Her words trailed off when he leaned against the threshold.

"Fine, I'll wait." He stared at her. Shirley tugged on his shirt, trying to yank him into the gallery. He didn't move.

The woman let out a loud sigh. Devin expected her to hang up the phone, but she didn't. Behind him, Shirley was raving about some picture on the far wall, trying to lure him from the office. He stayed.

"I'm sorry," the woman said, turning her attention to the caller. Her words were barely more than a whisper. "What did you say again? The doctor needs me to—" She paused and scribbled on a notepad. "When is there an opening?"

She peeked at Devin, perhaps to confirm if he was still there. A faint blush had stolen over her pale cheeks. She scowled at him over her black-rimmed glasses, the artsy kind that Livy'd bought in three different colors. Other than the glasses, she didn't match his vision of a gallery person. And he'd had his share of gallery folk through Livy. This girl's clothes seemed more business and less art, but what the hell did he know?

"I...I would guess..." Her cheeks were bright red now. She traced her finger over a calendar on the desk. "Um...maybe fifteen days ago?"

Good God, was she making a woman's appointment? Why did his brain kick into calculating her ovulation cycle? Maybe he had spent too much time thinking about his mares' breeding schedules.

The woman was still trying to ignore him. She nodded as she listened to the speaker on the other end of the line.

"Yes." She turned from Devin then, and faced the far corner of the office. "All right, I'll be there. Thank you." She nodded. "I have your number if I have any questions."

She trembled when she replaced the receiver on its base. She took a deep breath. When she did turn to Devin, the blush that had crept over her white cheeks a few moments earlier was fading. Was she going to be ill? She looked as if she'd had a hell of a day, and he wasn't about to make it any easier. Then she met his gaze. Her eyes were the color of a clear blue sky in the morning. There was probably some fancy name to describe that color, but it all came down to the fact that they were stunning.

No, not stunning. He didn't find women stunning. Not any more.

"Is there a problem?" The woman circled the desk and walked toward him.

Now that he saw her move, he had the sense he had met her before. A long time ago.

"Devin Trent, correct?" She held out her hand to shake his. He kept his arms crossed. Realizing he wasn't going to shake, she frowned and withdrew.

"I want that poster removed." He pointed with his thumb toward the window where Livy's image faced the street. A billboard along the highway would be less visible.

"It's an advertisement for an upcoming event. Perhaps if you return then, you could purchase the original."

"No, I don't want to buy it. I don't want it. I don't want it hanging there."

The woman pushed her glasses up her nose. "I don't understand."

"That's my wife. I never gave anyone permission to—" Devin swallowed. "Take it down."

The red stain on her cheeks was returning. She was more attractive with a bit of flush on her skin. *What the hell was the matter with him today?* Devin shook his head. Maybe it was the heat that had gotten to him.

She straightened. Her lips pressed together. Her gaze took him in with a quick up and down. She didn't look pleased with what she saw. "I have the paperwork. Olivia Trent signed a model release form."

"Hi, dear." Shirley stepped between them. "Is this your work?" She motioned to the oil painting she'd been admiring. It was as if she'd forgotten the poster in the window. How long had she been drinking at the patio before he'd arrived?

The woman's gaze moved from Devin to Shirley. "No, this isn't my work, but I'll be having a show in a few weeks." Then she looked directly at Devin again. "The poster in the front is advertising it."

"Oh?" Shirley swayed toward the window. "That's yours? You've done an amazing job capturing my daughter's image. She really is beautiful." Her forehead creased. She pursed her lips for a moment and shook her head.

"Was. She *was* beautiful. Right to the end. Wasn't she, Devin?" Her voice sounded more wistful than grieving, but the last thing he'd want was for Shirley to start sobbing, so maybe it was better she'd numbed herself with drink. "So beautiful."

"Thank you," the girl said.

"You look familiar," Shirley said. "Have we met?"

"I knew Olivia. Actually, the show is a cancer fundraiser, in memory of people in our community, like Olivia, who've…" Her voice faltered. She cleared her throat. "People who've had to confront cancer. I had hoped to display some of your daughter's pieces with her portrait, but when there was no response to the letter or the phone messages I left for Mr. Trent…" The woman tilted her head, as if with her short stature she could pull off peering down her nose at him.

He had at least a foot on her.

Devin shrugged when Shirley shot a questioning look his way. There may have been a letter, he didn't remember. The minute anything came in with the word "gallery" on it, he'd tossed it. Voicemails were erased. Sooner or later people got the idea. Evidently, this woman wasn't overly bright.

"What a lovely idea. My daughter's name will be out in the public again. Her talent was so great, I knew she wouldn't be forgotten. Devin, dear, we were just discussing that very idea, weren't we? I knew when I heard your message I had to bring Devin here today, and I was right." Shirley clapped in a short and rare burst of enthusiasm. "What is your name, dear?"

"Claire Best." She shook the older woman's hand. She didn't offer her hand to Devin again.

"Was that why you called the other day? That was you, yes?" Shirley was focused on Claire.

Claire nodded.

"What a lovely idea," Shirley repeated. "Devin, don't you agree?"

"I want the poster down," he said.

"Devin, dear." Shirley touched his forearm. "It's to raise money for cancer."

"So?"

"Perhaps in this instance…"

Devin gritted his teeth. The last thing he wanted was to have the world remember Livy that way, with *that* look on her face. It was the one he'd put there and couldn't erase. It'd haunted him, and now it was on display for everyone in God's creation to see.

"Devin, dear, perhaps you need some fresh air?"

He scowled.

"No?" Shirley shrugged. "Okay, let's chat about how to proceed. I'm sure the gallery will be very accommodating with Olivia's work and whatever concessions you might want. Right, Claire?"

7

He growled.

Claire raised her eyebrows.

"Go on now, Devin. We'll talk about this tomorrow. I'm sure we can work it out." Shirley's eyes pleaded with him silently as she spoke. They begged him to let this be.

Devin pivoted toward the poster. The display area wasn't obviously accessible, or he'd have ripped the damn thing out himself. "There is nothing to talk about, except getting rid of that picture."

"Devin, perhaps you should leave. We can talk about this again once you are calmer."

He fought the urge to hit something. Maybe it'd be better if he left. An instant later, he was walking down the street to the convenience store. A bell jingled when he entered.

He didn't like being sideswiped. And if Shirley thought just because he felt sorry for her he'd give in to this gallery girl's demands, well, perhaps even Shirley couldn't push him that far. Sure, she could manipulate him into going to the gallery, but this was a whole other situation.

He grabbed six packs of cinnamon flavored gum on his way to the checkout counter.

CHAPTER 2

Claire stood beside her sedan on Devin's furrowed gravel driveway. It was amazing how muted a farm in the middle of the bare prairie could be. The hot afternoon air hummed softly with the mooing of a distant cow, the buzzing of a bee and the far away drone of a tractor in a neighboring field.

Where was Shirley? She'd promised Devin had changed his mind. She'd also promised to be here, but the drive was empty. There was no evidence of Shirley or Devin. Claire hadn't thought to ask for the woman's cell phone number.

Should she wait? The place was hardly intimidating, and not what she would have expected for Devin. She'd expected the plants to have been removed and weeds to have choked out the grass in the years since Livy's death, but instead it appeared there were more shrubs now, and the lawn could rival any golf course.

Squat potentillas and robust lilacs skirted the two-story white farmhouse. The driveway continued past the house, weaving through short grass for another hundred meters or so, ultimately leading to a big red barn.

The barn appeared equally abandoned. Its two large doors were open, a dark gaping entrance. Was he in there? If he was close, he should have heard her arrival. Claire waited, but no one came out to investigate.

She wiped her palms on her pants and trudged to the front door. Shirley wouldn't have lied, would she? Claire didn't want to confront Devin on her own about the decision to take a few of Livy's pieces to the gallery—especially if Shirley hadn't discussed it with him yet. She really didn't need to be yelled at again either. What was the harm in displaying a few things anyway?

The fundraiser would benefit from having Livy's work displayed. That was the important thing—the show. Sure, it'd be okay without Livy's art, but it'd be better with her work there. Livy had such a talent for stained glass—so Claire's boss, Peter, and the Toronto critics had said. Admittedly, sunlight energized the stained glass, even if Claire thought the subjects were trite.

What could be more important than raising money for cancer survivors?

Devin's front porch was clean. One tiny pot of purple geraniums was tucked into the corner. Again, not what she'd have expected. The screen door was open, so she knocked on the inside door's curtained window.

Her heart beat faster as she waited. There was no sign of movement inside, but there was a faint murmuring. Was he ignoring her the way he would some door-to-door salesman? He seemed to have a knack for that. How many letters had she sent? Six?

Having visited the farm a few years earlier to take Livy's portrait, Claire could remember the house's layout. Livy's studio was an extension added to the back, with big windows facing a meadow. She'd heard he hadn't moved a thing in the studio since Livy was taken to the hospital for her final weeks, but that didn't make any sense. Livy'd complained he'd hated her work, so why would he keep it intact?

It didn't fit. Besides, rumors had also said he'd returned from the rodeo circuit flat broke. So it was probable he'd sold every bit of Livy's art. That was a more likely reason for why he hadn't answered her messages—he didn't have anything left.

Claire knocked again. Still no answer. What an ass.

Well, at least she could find out if the studio was empty. She walked around the building toward the studio, which would undoubtedly piss off Devin if he saw her, but Shirley should be there any minute and then they'd be digging through the studio anyway.

Claire stepped through the shrub bed and leaned in to the window of the studio. It appeared full. Wait. Was that just the reflection on the glass? As she raised her hands to shield the glare on the windowpane, she heard a sound. She jumped.

To her left, a window opened. The figure was hidden from view by a gauzy curtain. She scrambled out of the shrub bed, but it was too late. She'd been caught. The figure paused, then pushed aside the curtain.

Claire expected Devin's angry face. Instead an older woman waved at her. Claire waved back as she moved farther away from the studio. Through the opened window, she could hear the laugh track from a television sitcom.

The woman cranked the window wider and leaned out. "You must be Claire."

She nodded, willing her heart to slow to a normal rate. "I'm supposed to meet Shirley."

"I've been waiting for you. Did you knock?"

Claire nodded again. "Is Shirley here?"

"Oh, dear." The woman shook her head. "I suppose I had the television too loud. Well, good that I saw you here so I could let you know Shirley couldn't come today. She called a little bit ago, though, to say you'd be around."

Shirley wasn't coming? Now what? Here she was snooping in Devin's windows for nothing. Heat rushed over her face. "I'm sorry to have troubled you."

"Go on out to the barn. Devin's out there."

"Oh, I don't want to bother him."

"No bother at all. He's due to come in shortly anyway. I'm sure he'd be happy to see you." The woman winked at her. "It's not often pretty young girls come around here."

Claire doubted Devin would be happy, but the woman in the window had told her to go, so how could she refuse? Besides, maybe she'd been too harsh with him the other day—it probably hadn't been easy seeing his dead wife's picture on a poster. But Claire hadn't been in the mood to try to soothe him then, particularly after he'd tried to intimidate her by listening to her conversation with the doctor's office.

Her stomach fluttered at the memory. She swallowed. She'd been setting up an appointment with a specialist. To investigate abnormal cells. On her cervix. The doctor didn't say she had cancer, but this procedure, a colposcopy—now there was a word that didn't roll off your tongue—would be a more thorough test for it. She was being tested for cancer. And Devin had stood there a few feet away when the nurse had asked when her last period had been.

"Are you okay, dear?" the woman asked. "You look ill."

"No. I mean, yes," Claire replied quickly. "I mean, of course, I'm fine. Devin's in the barn, you say?"

Maybe she should try to talk to him again, though she'd already tried to warn him. If he'd returned her calls or replied to her letters, he would have known about the show and the poster. Then it wouldn't have been a surprise. She wasn't about to take the poster down now because he couldn't be bothered to read his mail. It was her best advertising for the event. They'd received more inquiries from that poster than any other piece of advertising.

She needed to get the word out. This was important. She had Shirley's full support, and if Livy's mother had agreed, why should her husband have concerns?

Claire grudgingly hiked to the barn.

She'd heard through the Morning Lake grapevine Devin would do anything to help a friend, but every time she'd seen him, he was just an arrogant bastard. No wonder Livy had been unhappy—even before she'd been diagnosed with cancer. Claire'd always expected to hear Livy was divorcing him. After all, if Livy had hinted at it with Claire, who was hardly more than a passing acquaintance, it had to have been bad. But it hadn't happened like that. Livy had died of cancer instead.

Reaching the dark doorway, Claire peered inside. She wanted to assess Devin's mood before barging in. If he was intently working on something, anything, she'd turn around and come back later, when Shirley could be there, too.

Claire crossed into the barn and fought the urge to sneeze. Motes of dust and the sweet musky smell of hay hung in the air. Sweat beaded across her forehead and the skin on her arms tingled. Barns didn't usually bother her, unless—

Oh God, what had she climbed through to look in that stupid window? Claire inched back to the door, but then she saw Devin. He was reaching to a low rafter over by some stalls, facing the other direction. His T-shirt's thin gray material stretched tautly over his wide shoulders and back. Each well-developed muscle was defined and clear. And look at his hair! Devin's dark hair looked nearly black in the shadowy barn.

Why did cowboys have to look so good in a pair of Wrangler jeans? Or was that just Devin?

Damn it, why did *he* have to be the epitome of what she found attractive in a man?

She really needed fresh air. Her surging allergies were making her light-headed.

CHAPTER 3

"Come on, you beast."

What was he talking about? Claire turned back, and looked up to where Devin's gaze was fixated. A wide-eyed orange cat complained from its perch and twitched its tail. Oh good, he hadn't been calling her a beast!

"You got up there," Devin continued, "so we both know you can get down. Don't be scared, I'll catch you. Be a man and jump."

The cat cried out to him, as if it understood what he'd said.

Devin's voice enticed and soothed—completely unlike what it had been when he had visited the gallery a few days earlier. "You were only trying to do your job. It's the mouse's fault, right? No need to blame yourself."

Claire couldn't stand it any longer. She sneezed.

Devin stayed focused on his task, while the cat's yellow eyes glared warily at her. Its orange tail switched back and forth ominously, hitting the rafter with a thump. Now *that* sentiment was familiar—like owner, like cat.

Looking up irritated Claire's nose again. She let go another sneeze.

Perhaps scared at the noise, a bird she hadn't noticed scratched at a rafter high above her, before swooping down and sailing from the barn.

With the rush of flapping wings, a shower of pigeon droppings and filth cascaded down, straight on Claire's head. The cat must have jumped at Devin at that moment, because when Claire opened her eyes, she saw Devin toss the animal to a small hay bale.

"Jesus, George," Devin cursed. "Why the hell did you do that?" He studied his thumb before wiping blood across the front of his work shirt.

"Making friends everywhere, I see," Claire said. It was an attempt to lighten the mood, but even to her ears, the tone was flat. She brushed her fingers through her hair. Dirt fluttered to the ground. She sneezed again, and part of her realized he hadn't said bless you once. That figured. He'd probably wish her straight to the devil if he had the chance.

"Ms. Best," he greeted her in an equally flat tone. A scowl crossed his

13

face. What a surprise. Then he turned his back to her, as if to continue what he'd been doing before George started complaining about being stuck in the rafters. His thumb must have bugged him, though, because he put it in his mouth to suck off some of the blood before wiping it on his shirt again.

"That'll stain," Claire warned.

Devin's frown suggested he had no idea what she meant.

"The blood, on your shirt." She pointed to the two rust-colored streaks on his gray T-shirt.

He shrugged. "What did you want, Ms. Best? I'm going to take a wild guess and say it wasn't to give me laundry advice."

He was looking at her now, and she averted her eyes. Stupid. *Don't show a sign of weakness*, her dad had always said. Claire braced her shoulders and forced herself to meet his gaze. "Shirley thought it might be good to—"

"No."

"No what?"

Silence. He'd gone back to ignoring her. Swell.

Claire stepped closer to him. "I was supposed to meet Shirley here today, but I guess she called to say she wasn't coming."

That got his attention. "You've been up to the house?"

Claire held her hand to the bridge of her nose to suppress another rise of pressure. "Can we talk outside?" Through her tearing eyes, she saw Devin smile for the first time. "It isn't funny."

"All right, Ms. Best, I'll follow you."

As she exited the allergen haven, Claire fumbled in her purse for a tissue, something pure that hadn't been contaminated by the barn or her scramble through the shrubs. She needed to wipe her nose and eyes. She stopped for a moment and peered into her bag. Nothing. Claire fought the urge to sweep her face with her hand, which would undoubtedly be covered with the annoying allergens.

"Livy's work wouldn't be sold," Claire continued as she clawed through her bag again. "Not if you don't want that. We would showcase a few pieces—" She sneezed again. This time she followed it with an impatient groan. How was she supposed to enter into a serious conversation when all she could think about were her burning eyes and her mucous-filled nose? This was ridiculous.

"Are you okay?" Devin stepped closer. Even through her bleary sight, he didn't seem as amused as he had been a minute ago. God, she must look dreadful to make him concerned.

Know your limits, her father also used to say. And this was it. "I'm sorry to be a bother, but I really need to wash my hands and face."

He hesitated. Her increasingly blurry vision meant she could only see a blob, which she knew to be his head, nod. "Let me help you." He came toward her, and before she knew what he was going to do, he put one hand gently on her waist and another on her elbow.

His hands were large. They were strong. Claire stiffened, but resisted the urge to pull from him.

He guided her to the house. "Have you always been this allergic?"

"No, actually." Claire tried to laugh. "I think most people would sneeze after getting all that *stuff* dumped on them." She shuddered and some of the filth shook out of her hair. She closed her eyes. "I suppose I'm a little sensitive to hay, but my allergies were triggered by something else. Do you have—"

Claire froze, and Devin stopped with her. Another explosion was building in her nose. Gah—at what point would her nasal passages just accept defeat, too?

"Look up," Devin said.

"Why?"

"It's supposed to help."

When Claire tilted her head to the sky and took a deep breath, the bomb inside her nose stopped for a moment, but an explosion of a different kind was being energized.

Devin's touch was light, but she was hyper-aware of his movements. When he lifted one hand to her head, all the oxygen seemed to disappear, which was ridiculous, because they were outside, surrounded by nothing but air.

"You really got covered, didn't you?" He brushed something from her hair.

Reel it back in, Best.

She swallowed, but her throat could have been blanketed in dust and hay for the relief it gave. When she straightened, Devin returned his hand to her arm.

They started walking again.

It was a strange process, this dance across the farmyard, and she felt huge empathy in that moment for Grandpa English, who'd been nearly blind when he died. The poor man refused to learn how to use a walking stick to guide him—he must have had bruises everywhere. Why had she never thought about that before?

If it weren't for Devin, she'd probably stumble over a clump of grass and end up crawling, which would only bring her up close and personal to a million different pollens—maybe even a wayward evil shrub. Then she'd be in even more trouble.

"You were saying? Asking if I have something?"

Claire shook her head, sending dust fluttering to her cheeks. Then that temporarily postponed sneeze exploded with no warning.

"God, I've never had my allergies react so strongly." She moaned. "Are there junipers here?"

"I think so, around the back of the house."

Claire sighed. It served her right for snooping. How had she missed seeing the nasty shrubs? She'd been so focused on Livy's studio, she'd climbed straight into them.

Ahead, she heard a door creak open. She blinked rapidly to clear her eyes. Tears streamed down her cheeks.

"What's happened?"

"She'll be okay, Mom. Ms. Best has some allergies, that's all."

Devin's mother gasped. "Will she need an EpiPen, like what's-his-name on my two o'clock show? Should we take her to Emergency?"

In spite of feeling like her skin was being reshaped by coarse sandpaper, Claire smiled. "I'll be fine. I just need to wash my hands and face. And I'd love a glass of water."

"We're coming up to the steps," Devin said beside her. His voice was close to her ear. His breath tickled her neck. Her skin tingled in an entirely wrong and sensuous way. How could her body respond to him? Devin Trent? At a time like this?

Claire strained to see the wooden stairs. She tried so hard, her eyes were probably bugged out like a cartoon character, but everything in front of her seemed to blend into the sidewalk.

"Step up, now," Devin said as he nudged her with his hands, like a skilled dancer leading her around the ballroom.

She'd obviously read too many historical romances in her life, since she half-expected Devin to hoist her up into his arms and carry her to safety. He didn't—and she couldn't deny the small sense of disappointment when he continued to lead her into the house and through to the bathroom without picking her up once.

She scolded herself for wanting to be picked up in his muscular arms. Saved by this tall, brooding man, a cowboy even. A strong, capable cowboy.

Claire groaned again.

"There, there, Ms. Best," Devin's mother said softly somewhere to Claire's left. "We'll get you all fixed up in no time. Now sit down on the toilet and I'll fetch a clean washcloth. Devin, you go pour the poor girl a cold drink."

As soon as she heard them leave, Claire fumbled toward the sink. Finding the taps, she turned on the water. She took off her glasses and set them down. A soft clatter told her she'd missed the ledge around the sink. She hoped they weren't scratched. Her main concern, though, was alleviating the itchy, burning ache in her eyes.

"Let me help you," Devin's mother said as she reentered the room. "It'll be easier that way. Why don't you splash your face first and then we'll go from there?"

Claire leaned over, cupped her hands under the cool water and splashed her eyes. Heavenly. "What a mess," Claire said. "I'm so sorry."

"Don't you worry about a thing, Ms. Best."

"Please, call me Claire."

"Okay, Claire. I'm Helen, Devin's mother."

"Nice to meet you, Helen," Claire said, pausing from throwing water at her face for a moment. She blinked at the mirror and tried to focus on the reflection of the woman standing behind her, but her eyes were still too sensitive.

"Here, let me help you now." Helen touched Claire's shoulder lightly. Claire turned toward the other woman, keeping her eyes closed, letting the tears clear away the irritants. While Helen dabbed a wet cloth over her face, Claire felt cared for as if she were a little girl again...or an invalid. That was probably closer to the truth.

"Now, don't be thinking Devin is one of those men who can't live without his momma. He was my change-of-life baby. I thought it was too late, but, well, sometimes God just has other plans." Helen nodded. "A true blessing, that boy. Now he's looking after me, not the other way around. I've got bad arthritis—it has me all tied up some days."

"Um, I..." Devin's mother couldn't think Devin and she could ever be interested in one another, could she? No, of course not, she was making conversation. "My grandmother had arthritis, too. It is a terrible thing."

"Yes, well, God doesn't give us anything we can't handle." Helen took Claire's one hand in her own and then the other, and gently lathered and washed each with soap and water. Then she pressed a cloth into Claire's palm. "Wash your face with this. I've put a drop of soap on it."

Claire lathered and rinsed.

"Okay, dear, I'll leave you to it. My next show is about to start—it should be good today. Janey just found out she's pregnant with her boss's baby. She's supposed to tell her boyfriend this episode...but holler if you need anything."

Claire scrubbed her face and hands again. Once she began to feel a touch more normal, the heat of her embarrassment rushed over her. She rinsed the cloth under cold water and pressed it against her eyes. What would Devin think? This whole afternoon had been a disaster—not exactly the way to win friends and influence angry cowboys.

"Better?" Devin's voice shot through her like an electrical charge.

"Yes. Thank you." Claire reluctantly removed the cloth. Her sight was blurry yet, but at least the tearing had calmed to a mild dribble. She wiped her face again, before blinking at the floor.

"Lose something?"

"My glasses. I think they fell." Claire shifted and tried to focus. Where were they?

Devin put his hands on her waist, holding her in place. They were warm.

Her nerves zinged. She hadn't been touched so much in years. And this man didn't even like her.

"Don't move, or you'll step on them." Then his hands left her. He bent down beside her and picked up her glasses. "Here."

"Thanks." Claire rinsed them under the tap and wiped them on a towel she saw folded beside the sink. After pulling on her glasses, she brushed at her bangs. They were a damp mess. "I'm sorry," she said to both Helen and Devin, "for all of the inconvenience."

But Helen was already gone. Claire was alone in this tiny room with Devin. Her pulse jumped, and she swayed toward him.

His forehead creased and he grabbed her elbow to steady her. "Are you okay? Are you sure you can see?"

Claire nodded. *She was not attracted to Devin. She was not attracted to Devin. She was—* Why did she need to remind herself of the obvious?

"Let's go to the kitchen, so you can sit for a bit and grab that water."

Devin stepped out and motioned for Claire to walk in front of him. The darkness in the dimly lit corridor was divine on her aching eyes. There were two other doors along the hallway. She wasn't sure where they led, but she did know the kitchen was ahead at the end.

Entering the country kitchen, Claire heard the television blaring from an adjoining room.

"Mom's gone back to her soaps," Devin said as he followed her into the room. He indicated she should sit at the table, then he grabbed a glass from a cupboard by the sink.

"I've already imposed too much."

"Did you want me to drive you home?"

"No." The word came fast, perhaps too fast.

"Then let's make sure you can see before we send you out driving, okay?"

A clear pitcher of water was already on the table. Condensation dripped from the smooth glass container when he picked it up, soaking through the cheery cotton tablecloth. Ha! Devin had a peony-patterned tablecloth! Ice clanged against the lip of the ewer as he filled the tumbler. "Water," he said as he set the glass in front of a chair at the table and motioned for her to take a seat.

He was being nice to her. In the limited experience she'd had with him, it was out of character. She sat on the edge of the wooden kitchen chair. Devin stayed standing. She sipped the water and resisted the urge to squirm under his watchful gaze.

"You were talking about Shirley?" he said finally.

Claire nodded. "She asked me to meet her here to look through some of Livy's things." She rushed to add, "We don't have to sell anything."

"So you already said." Devin leaned against the counter, thumbs hooked in his belt. He was smiling at her again. He seemed almost normal and not the heated, angry man she knew him to be.

"Oh, did I? Well, it's true." Claire paused, then took a deep breath. "I'm sorry how this has come about."

"I'm not surprised." Devin's voice sounded weary. "Shirley can't keep many promises these days."

What was it like to have a troubled mother-in-law? He seemed involved in her life, still concerned about her, even after all this time. His interest in Shirley didn't fit what Livy had suggested about his character.

"I'm not sure I understand that comment, but I wasn't thinking about Shirley in particular. I mean all of it." Claire wiped her nose. "I tried to call and tell you, but I never caught you."

"Well, I guess it's my fault, isn't it?"

"You're twisting my words. I'm trying to apologize. I imagine it must have been a bit of a surprise to...um..." What? See your dead wife on display downtown?

A little tick along his jaw throbbed. "Something like that."

"And I wasn't much help that day. I was a little preoccupied with... Never mind." She met his gaze then. "Anyway, I'm sorry."

They let her apology linger between them for a moment. Why didn't he say something?

"Okay then." Claire nodded when she couldn't handle the silence any more. "Would you think about my idea? I promise the gallery will take extreme care when handling any of Livy's pieces. Well, they take care with everyone's—oh, you know what I mean. That is, if you decide to let us show some of Livy's work."

Devin pulled a pack of gum from his shirt pocket. "Want a piece?"

"No, thanks," Claire said as he popped two pieces in his mouth. Had that been a peace offering? "We wouldn't sell anything if you didn't want us to— Right, I said that already."

Devin chewed vigorously on the gum and watched her.

"It is for a good cause." She was grasping for things now.

"You knew Livy?"

Claire nodded.

"I don't remember you. Well, maybe a bit, but I can't place where we met."

She averted her eyes. "I didn't know her well. I just came here a few times, when you were at rodeo events. I met you at—"

"At the funeral?" Devin nodded. "You didn't come to the hospital at the end, though, did you?"

Claire didn't want to answer his questions. There were some things she didn't have to justify—to anyone. "I'm surprised you remember the funeral."

"Answering with a jab? Is this a sensitive topic, Ms. Best?" Devin was watching her closely now. "Why are all of the proceeds going to cancer survivors or support or whatever it was you said?"

"It is a good cause, like I said."

Devin nodded. "There are lots of good causes. What makes it a good cause for you? Perhaps if you explained, I'd understand."

"Isn't it enough that your wife died of cancer?"

"Apparently not."

"Everyone has reasons," Claire said. "My reasons are my reasons. If your reasons aren't strong enough to convince you this is a good and decent thing, then there is nothing I can say to change that."

She got up from the table and pressed her fingers gently against her eyelids. They were still swollen, but she had to get out of here. "I'm sure I can drive now. I'm feeling much better." She extended her hand to shake his.

"I probably have hay and grit all over me. It's best if we don't touch."

Devin crossed his arms. Then he smiled again. "We agree, then? My reasons are my reasons, and I don't need to explain them to you any more than you need to explain yours to me."

Claire's mouth dropped, then she snapped it closed. "You've made your point. Thank you again for your hospitality this afternoon. I didn't mean to be such a bother. Please thank your mother for me, too." She summoned her best smile to shoot back at him. "And do think about showing some of Livy's things, will you?"

"There are lots of things to think about," Devin said as he saw her to her car.

Why, oh why, hadn't she stayed in her car and waited for Shirley? After fifteen minutes, she could have left and no one would have been the wiser or the worse for it.

As Claire pulled out of the driveway, she refused to glance in her rearview mirror. She knew Devin was standing at the porch watching her. She just knew it.

CHAPTER 4

After watching Claire's car disappear from view, Devin stepped inside. He stroked his chin. Yep, there were things to think about. Why couldn't he remember more about Claire? He'd met her before, he knew that, but the memory was a blur. Of course, it didn't help that the day of Livy's funeral he'd been three sheets to the wind. It hadn't been one of his better moments.

A lot about his marriage to Livy would be classified under the same category. He'd long ago acknowledged it hadn't been the best marriage, but it had been *his* marriage—his one and only. Women and he didn't mix quite right. But damn it, seeing Claire all proud and feisty, even with red eyes and sniffling... Well, there was no denying she tempted him—tempted him more than she should.

He walked to the living room where he could hear someone on television declaring forgiveness.

"I'm going to the barn," he said to his mom, raising his voice so she'd hear him over the melodramatic dialogue.

"Is she gone?" Helen looked at him.

He nodded and started to leave.

"Devin, wait a minute." His mom turned down the volume on her program. He couldn't remember the last time she'd done that during one of her daytime shows. "Claire is a sweet girl."

He shrugged.

"Don't give me that attitude," Helen scolded. Devin knew this particular expression well, though he hadn't seen it in a long time.

He raised his eyebrows. "I'm sure she's a nice person."

"What did she want? What was she going to do with Shirley?" His mom's gaze darted repeatedly back to the big screen as she spoke.

"Nothing important." He crossed his arms and chewed harder on his gum. "You're missing your show."

Helen grimaced and plucked up the remote from the corduroy couch. Then she turned off the TV, another unprecedented move. This wasn't going to be good. "What was she going to do here with Shirley? Shirley hasn't been here in ages."

"It doesn't matter. It's nothing."

Helen crossed her arms, holding the remote control in one hand. Her forefinger traced a pattern between the buttons. "You heard the car come in, didn't you?"

Devin sighed, and leaned against the threshold.

"Did you know they were coming? It would have been nice if you'd told me, so my hair wasn't all up in curlers. And I could've made cookies or a date square." Helen patted her head. "After Shirley called, I had to run to the bedroom and pull out my curlers. They're in a heap on my dresser now, and my hair is probably a frightful mess."

"I heard the car, but I didn't know the two of them were coming out today. I thought it was probably a holy roller or someone here to sell encyclopedias."

"People don't buy encyclopedias anymore." Helen rolled her eyes, then her face creased with concern. "Was Ms. Best okay to drive?"

"She said she was fine. Listen, I need to get back to the barn."

Helen held his gaze, then she said softly, "They want to look at Livy's artwork, don't they?"

"I suppose they do, but it isn't going to happen."

"Why not? I've kept my mouth shut about this for a long while, but I agree with them. Maybe it is time."

"Not you, too." Devin straightened. "It's time when I say it's time." He pushed away from the doorjamb and left the room.

"Devin Archibald Trent," his mother said sternly. "Don't take that tone with me. We are having a conversation, and this talk is long overdue."

He shoved his hands in his pockets and returned to the living room. His mother was his mother, and there was no ignoring her. She didn't often get stern with him nowadays, and at his age, it didn't really matter if she did. He was an adult, for Pete's sake, and she was living in *his* house. On the other hand, he'd been raised to respect his parents, so he couldn't leave now and she knew it. That tone combined with the use of his full name was the ace up her sleeve, and there'd be hell to pay later if he left after she slapped it on the table. "This isn't a good time," he said.

"Maybe there isn't a better time. What do they want?"

"They want to display Livy's work in town."

"Show it or sell it?"

"Show it. It's to raise money for cancer research or something, so they say."

"Oh, Devin, that sounds perfect. What's holding you back? It's high

22

time you dealt with what happened. It can be difficult, but..." Helen stopped without finishing her sentence. "They keep asking, don't they? Think about it. If you give Shirley this one showing, maybe it'll appease her."

"I doubt it."

"Well, she hasn't given up yet, has she? And I know you hate to see her, well, you know..."

"What? I hate to see her what? Drunk? Crying? Is that what happened today? Claire said Shirley was supposed to meet her here. Why did she cancel?"

"Shirley has her cross to bear," Helen said, shaking her head. "Maybe it would help if she had a few more of Livy's things?"

"Why are you pushing this?" He needed another piece of gum. Two weren't enough.

Helen set the remote on the sofa. She stood and walked to Devin. "It can't be healthy—you living like this." She waved in the direction of Livy's studio. He hadn't been in there for months now, but he knew it was the same as it had been when they'd called the ambulance to take Livy to the hospital. She'd never returned to their home after that day. Hell, she'd never left the hospital.

"I have my reasons."

"Son, I know how I was when your father passed on. It's a hell of a thing losing your spouse and lover—" God, had his mother really just used the word *lover*? "—but you've got to pick yourself up. Devin, I know you could if you let yourself, but there's something gnawing at you. What happened before Livy died? You never did—"

She stopped speaking and pursed her lips. "Nope. That's none of my business, but I know it wasn't all roses."

"Why are you saying this?"

"You'll remember in time, I suppose. I just hope it isn't too late."

"What's that supposed to mean?" He remembered everything: every tear Livy'd shed when he'd left her to go to the rodeo, every kiss or embrace she refused him when he returned, every accusation she threw at him from her death bed...

"I want you to put a few of Livy's things in this show." Helen nodded. "That girl Claire seems so nice. It must have been hard on her with her grandmother and all."

"What do you know about Claire? I didn't know you knew her." Devin hated his curiosity. He hated that he asked, especially since his mother seemed a touch too interested in getting him and Claire together in a room again.

"Oh sure," his mother said. "She came out to the farm a time or two, but I always stayed up at the barn when Livy had people over and I was here for the chores. I remember her mostly from Livy's funeral. She wore the same dress she wore to her grandmother's funeral less than a year earlier—" Helen's voice broke. "Poor girl, she's up at the big Underwood residence all by herself now." Devin must have looked confused, because his mother continued, "Claire is Janet Underwood's granddaughter."

Mrs. Underwood had been a substitute teacher when he was growing up. They had been pretty rough on her a time or two, but she was always there with a kind smile and warm heart. He remembered hearing she'd died of cancer a few years earlier. Memories of his former teacher weren't going to sway his decision, but it did explain why Claire had a burr under her saddle about this whole cancer thing.

"What is the worst that could happen if you let them display a piece or two of Livy's?"

"I don't know." Devin rubbed his neck.

Helen stared at him and waited.

"They'll want more."

Silence.

"It'll be a bother and I don't have time for any of that."

"I can help Shirley and Claire." Helen smiled. "You don't have to bother about it at all. You go call that girl and tell her to come back."

Devin didn't budge.

"It's the right thing to do, for everyone: Livy, Shirley, Claire and perhaps you, too."

She was wrong. This was the last thing he needed, but if he didn't say something close to what she wanted to hear, he'd never get back to the barn. "I'll think about it."

"Tell me when they're coming so I can make a sweet."

"I didn't say yes," he said, but his mother was already settled back on the sofa with the TV blaring.

Devin let the screen door swing shut on its own. Why was everyone pushing this at him? Why now? He had a dozen or more things to do to get the yearling ready for sale, and the stables ready for the next wave of summer boarders. He had fences to fix, buildings to paint, and the damn grass to mow. He didn't need this, too.

Would everyone leave him alone if he let them show a few things? What *would* be the worst that could happen? They'd badger him for more, probably. They'd push him to sell. Then again, he'd rejected this kind of thing before and he could again.

He should just say no.

Devin spit out his gum before entering the barn.

It was for cancer something or other—not for profit. That was something good. Maybe it would help Shirley. Devin doubted it, but he suddenly wondered if that possibility alone was enough of a reason to call

Claire. Besides, he'd forgotten to talk to her about that damn poster.

Christ, he had to quit thinking about her.

His hands still tingled with the memory of her body as he guided her to the house. She'd followed wherever he led, which he chalked up to her desperation. In all other things, she'd shown she was a strong woman with strong ideas of her own. He doubted very many people had the opportunity to see her vulnerable.

In those moments, he'd felt a strange protectiveness swell through him. Luckily, that impulse passed quickly enough.

For the next half-hour, Devin did chores around the barn as he mulled over the last few days. Shirley was a mess. There was no denying it, but it wasn't unusual either. Claire believed in what she was doing, and although he suspected she didn't much care for him personally, she did seem to be trying to bridge the gap between them so she could display Livy's things in the show. Now his mom had joined with them.

Devin crossed to the barn's modest office, where he kept the medicine and records for the animals. It was clean, organized, and exactly the way it should be. He sat on the chair he'd stolen from the kitchen a few years earlier. He drummed his fingers on the edge of the desk. Patting his chest to locate his pack of gum with one hand, Devin pulled out the phone book with the other. He found Claire's number and drew an arrow beside it, then leaned back in his chair.

Was this really what he wanted to do?

It couldn't hurt, he supposed. It wasn't as if his life would change by showing a few of Livy's things. His mom could be right, perhaps it could give peace where it was needed—not that he needed any peace. He'd get enough of that when he was dead. But it could possibly help Shirley.

He pulled the phone to the center of the desk and punched in Claire's number.

CHAPTER 5

Claire let loose three raucous sneezes as her car rounded the corner to her driveway, but luckily she recovered quickly enough to see two cars parked in front of her. Who was here?

Oh no, her renters! How could she have forgotten her summer renters? The same ones who hadn't bargained over her suggested rental rate, and who she'd promised herself to keep happy so they'd return next year. Their money was the difference between keeping her home and having to sell it. They were Peter's relatives, and he'd arranged everything. All Claire had to do was be there to give them the key, but here it was their first day at Morning Lake—their first day at the house—and Claire had kept them waiting.

She was too preoccupied with the show. That was her only excuse.

After parking her car behind theirs, Claire scrambled out. She didn't see her renters, but their luggage was resting on the front porch. She dashed around the side of house to the back yard, where she found them lounging in the chairs her great-grandfather had made, enjoying the view of the lake.

"I'm so sorry to keep you waiting," she said. She rushed forward with her hand extended. "You must be Bob Gregory. I'm Claire."

Bob, a short round man wearing socks with his sandals, rose from the chair. "How nice to meet you," he said as they shook hands. "Of course, Peter has told us all about you."

He introduced Claire to his wife Anne, who was at least a foot taller than him and apparently also fond of socks with sandals. Then they collectively pointed to their teenage son, Jay, who was sitting at the picnic table, tapping on his phone's screen.

The boy didn't look up. Claire couldn't tell from here how old he was, but even from this angle he looked the type to attract many a teenage girl's attention. Maybe it was the purposely messy look to his brown hair, and his strong jaw. Yep, all she could really see was that he was wearing too much black for a hot July afternoon, but she was sure he'd broken more than a few hearts.

"I got held up," Claire said quickly.

"In a barn. Yes, I can see that." Bob laughed.

Claire combed her fingers through her hair, wondering what she had missed. A clump of straw came out in her hands. Just the sight of it made her sneeze again. "Yes, well, sort of," she agreed. Her eyes itched at the memory. "I'll grab you a set of keys, then I'll show you inside."

"We'll be here," Bob said with a smile on his face. He seemed like a nice man and whatever misgivings she'd had about renting for the summer faded. Peter had assured her as much, but it helped to ease her worries now that she'd met them. She was confident Bob and Anne would be responsible and respectful of her grandmother's home.

Claire darted across the lawn to a set of steps at the side of the garage. Taking them two at a time, she leapt up the stairs. At the top, she fumbled in her pocket for her keys.

After entering her studio apartment, she glanced around. Man, she'd love to jump in the shower, but she'd already kept them waiting. Oh for heavens' sakes, where had she put the extra set of keys?

She looked through all the hooks and all the kitchen drawers. Aha! The keys were on her bedside table in front of a family photo. She paused to consider her parents' smiling faces. God, they'd hate it if they knew she was staying in the suite while renting out the main house. Claire took a deep breath. There was nothing to be done about it though—at least not as long as she wanted to keep both the house and her newfound career.

Of course, they wouldn't understand that either. Abandoning a respectable career as an engineer for the unpredictable one of a photographer, well, that wasn't something they'd accepted. Yet. Every week, she spoke with them, and every week, it was the same conversation. *When are you coming back and picking up where you left your life?* But Grandma would've understood, and more importantly, she would have approved.

"Sorry, Mom and Dad," she whispered to the picture, "but it has to be done."

Grabbing the keys, Claire spun around, anxious to return to her renters as quickly as possible. She was at the door when the phone rang.

She froze. She couldn't keep the renters waiting any longer—she'd already been rude by being late—but no one ever called. What if something had happened?

She dove for the phone.

"Claire? This is Devin Trent."

She was so surprised she didn't respond immediately.

"Did I catch you at a bad time?" he asked before she could formulate a sentence.

Man, his voice was deep over the phone. Sexy. God, she had to stop thinking about him that way.

"Um…" Claire glanced out the door toward the lawn. The Gregory family seemed to be amusing themselves, pointing at the boats on the lake. "I really need to attend to something." Then her curiosity overwhelmed her etiquette. "But I can spare a minute."

"I've been thinking perhaps a few of Livy's pieces might be appropriate for your show. Remember, though, they are not for sale."

"Of course. Thank you. Wow, that's—" Claire scrambled for the right word, "—a surprise. What made you reconsider?"

"Reasons are reasons, right, Ms. Best?"

"When would you like me to come by and pick them up?"

"How about tomorrow?"

"Thank you. Yes, great," Claire said. She had quit spying on her renters and was flipping through the to-do list she kept by the telephone. Drawing a line through the task for Livy's art felt darned good.

"Claire?" Peter's voice filled the apartment.

Claire jumped. What was he doing here? "Just a minute."

"I called and you didn't answer."

She held her finger up to him to stay him for a minute. Wow, how had he managed to enter her apartment without her noticing?

She turned her attention to Devin. "Should I call Shirley?"

"I'm sorry if I've taken you from something important," Devin said, the tone of his voice hinting of curiosity. "Don't worry about calling anyone. Mom will set it up. How about nine?"

"Great. See you tomorrow." Claire hung up the telephone and twirled to see Peter coming toward her. His tall, gaunt form, dressed all in black like his nephew, looked wrong in her studio apartment. He was part of her work world, and now he was in her home. It didn't feel right.

Peter gasped when he saw her. "Claire, oh my God, what's happened to you? You've been crying." Peter held out his hands to her, as if inviting her into his arms. His straight sandy hair fell over his face, hiding his left eye. He wiped the hair back quickly before extending his arms to her again.

"You'll never believe this," Claire said, bubbling with excitement.

"You look upset. Your eyes are so red. Jesus, you look like you could cry blood. Let's get my sister settled in, then we can talk."

"Your sister! Right, I've got the keys." Claire sniffled as she moved toward the door. "You'll never guess where I've been or what's happened. Livy Trent's work is going to be in the cancer show. Can you believe it?" She almost hooted, but Peter would've been mortified if she had.

"Olivia Patterson?"

"Who?" Claire paused. "Oh, right, Patterson was her maiden name. You know I didn't grow up here. I don't remember those things. But seriously, can you believe it?"

"You were at the Trent farm today?" He stopped her by touching her shoulder and turned her so she faced him. "Did he hurt you?" His eyes flashed, but his voice was soft. "Did he make you cry? What happened?"

If she found his presence in her home bizarre, this was downright alien—like something from Mars. He'd never shown such interest in her before.

"It isn't a very exciting story, Peter." Claire laughed as she stepped away from him. She suppressed the shudder threatening to snake up her spine. "Some of my allergies acted up, that's all."

His nostrils flared like he didn't believe her.

Claire tried to force another laugh. "Relax."

"Oh, Claire." He pulled her into his arms.

Claire stiffened. "Peter? What are you doing?" They worked together—he was the gallery owner. Bosses didn't grab employees for hugs, at least not bosses like Peter.

"Devin can be a scary person." He loosened his hold on Claire and peered into her eyes. "Promise me you won't go out there alone again."

"He doesn't seem so bad," she said, surprising herself. Now that he had agreed to let her collect a few pieces of Livy's work, Devin Trent had grown in her estimation. "Besides, we were hardly alone. His—"

"Promise me," Peter said. He raised his hand as if he was going to touch the side of her cheek. Claire ducked and charged toward the door.

She shook her head. Peter was missing the whole point. Sure, she remembered the things Livy had said about Devin. Obviously, Peter remembered them, too. Who wouldn't? Devin had left Livy isolated and trapped on that farm while he went off and played at being a cowboy. He'd wasted all of their money on his horses and his traveling, cheated on Livy with God-only-knew how many Wrangler-clad cowgirls, and left her to do all of the day-to-day work of running the ranch. But Devin was going to put Livy's work in the show. Today had been a huge success.

"I won't go by myself," she said, "but really, I think you are being a bit odd about this."

She didn't tell him she was going to Devin's the next day, because under his rules, technically it wouldn't count. She wouldn't be by herself—Shirley and Helen would be there, too.

"Good," he said.

"I need to go see to your sister and her family."

CHAPTER 6

Claire was relieved to find another car already parked in Devin's driveway the next day. George was stretched across the trunk of the other vehicle, basking in the morning sunlight. The orange tabby seemed more relaxed today than he had the day before.

"Where are we? Green Acres?" Jay yawned.

"How do you even know about Green Acres?" Claire asked. The old TV show had been cancelled long before she was born. There was no way Jay should know about it.

"Late night reruns."

"You watch it?"

"Sure, you take a drink every time they say—"

"Never mind, I don't want to know." Why hadn't she deposited the seventeen-year-old at the house before coming out to Devin's place? He was going to be in the way, and things were already awkward with Shirley and Devin. Jay wasn't going to help make any of that easier.

Peter wasn't a stupid man, she'd give him that—but perhaps eavesdropping wasn't an indication of intelligence. He had heard when she made the appointment with Devin. What was it with men listening in on her conversations lately? And he'd thrown out the whole "you're my employee, you need to listen to me" thing, announcing it loudly in the gallery until it became simpler to take Jay with her. Evidently Peter saw a need to send his nephew as her protector. The kid looked as interested in art as she was in hockey, video games or whatever it was teenage boys liked.

"I'm not sure what you're going to do." Claire parked her car and turned off the ignition. "And I really don't know how long this'll take."

Jay grunted in response.

What did that mean?

He climbed out of the car and slammed the door.

Claire cringed and resisted the urge to explain how the door would close properly with half the force he'd used. When had she turned into her father? She led him to the house. "Come on, then."

Jay trudged behind her. She could hear the scraping of his shoes against the ground. Now she understood why her grandmother had always told her to pick up her feet—the noise *was* annoying. God, she needed to relax about this. Jay didn't want to be there any more than she wanted him there.

Claire had brought her camera and equipment with her, just in case Devin had suddenly changed his mind about actually letting them leave with the pieces. That way, she could at least take some more photos of Livy's work. If that happened, Jay could be useful and help her haul in the equipment.

And what if she took her fundraising endeavors to the next level? She had been developing an idea for what she could do with these photos. She had to give it more thought before she approached anyone with it— whether Peter or Devin.

When they arrived at the front porch, with its shingled roof and sturdy white posts, Helen greeted her. This was the first time she'd seen the woman clearly and was surprised to realize how much older she looked. She reminded Claire of her grandmother. The memory brought with it a pang of nostalgia.

"You look so much better today, dear."

"Let's just keep me clear of the junipers." Claire laughed. "How are you?"

"Fine, fine." Helen peered around Claire at Jay, who was at least a foot and a half taller than the elderly woman. "Who's this with you?"

Claire stopped on the porch to make the introductions.

"So, you are staying at Morning Lake for the summer?"

Jay shrugged.

"Well, this art business will probably be a bit dull for you. Why don't you go and see if you can find out what the men are up to? They're out in the barn, I think. Some men are down from the rodeo to check on the horses. It's quite the thing, I suppose. Listen for the curses, and you'll be able to find them, I'm sure."

Jay looked at Claire, shrugging again.

"Oh," Helen said, "unless you are allergic like Claire here, then you'd best sit right here."

"No, I'll be fine," Jay said. His attention was already on the barn.

"Go on, then," Helen said again, shooing the boy in that direction.

As Jay jumped off the porch, bypassing all the steps, Claire said, "Are you sure Devin won't mind? If they are doing business out there—"

"It'll be good for the boy," Helen said, dismissing whatever fears Claire might have on Devin's behalf. "Come on in, dear. Shirley and I were just about to tackle the studio."

Claire followed Helen through to Livy's studio. The east facing room was part of an older addition. She imagined the space might have served as a sunroom at some point before Livy started using it as a studio. It would be a great workspace. You couldn't feel anything but happy in this room—it was bright, spacious and had a view of rolling hills draped in fields.

If only she had a place similar to this. She resisted the urge to sigh. Envy was such a useless emotion. Besides, the morning sunlight cascading through the large floor-to-ceiling windows wouldn't be suitable for a photography studio.

"Shirley is already busy at work, I see," Claire said when she entered the room.

"Look, Claire." Shirley held a piece for them to see. The woman's crisply pressed linen suit looked out of place in the messy studio. "This one is lovely."

Claire walked through the maze of tables and stained glass to where Shirley was perched on a stool. Finished and partly finished pieces cluttered every surface and space of the studio. Some pieces were stacked on the floor, others were leaning three or four deep against the wall. Glass shards, soldering tools, glass cutters, grinders, and sketches were strewn haphazardly across the scarred worktables.

It really did seem as if Livy would float into the studio any minute, flamboyantly declaring her exasperation at trying to meet the deadline for the show. Claire remembered Livy'd said it took one to four months to complete a project, depending on the complexity of the design. Sure, Livy had worked at her art full-time for several years, but there were still so many pieces. It didn't make sense. Had Livy ever sold anything? She had so much inventory here, and yet every time Claire had talked to her, it seemed Livy was still scrambling to fill the walls for the big Toronto show. Had Livy ever slept? That Toronto gallery must be huge.

Shirley's hand shook with strain as she pulled up a framed piece from the others.

"Here, let me help you," Claire said. She leaned over quickly to steady the piece. A faint odor of alcohol mixed with spearmint floated in the air around Shirley.

"Thank you, dear."

"Oh, I remember this one." Claire held it up to the afternoon light streaming through the large windows. "Livy had me photograph it for her portfolio."

"You own photos of her work?" Shirley's face lit like it had its own sunbeam shining on it.

"I thought I had mentioned that in the gallery the other day. I'm sorry, it must have slipped my mind." Claire set the glasswork on the desk, keeping it aside as a potential piece to exhibit. "The colors are so brilliant. She really captured the elegance of the orchid, didn't she?"

"My girl had such a special talent." Shirley pulled out a tissue from her sleeve and wiped her nose. "It shouldn't all be gathering dust out here like some abandoned mausoleum."

Shirley slid her finger through a film of dust on the piece in her lap. "Filthy."

Helen crossed her arms.

"Her work needs light to live. Not—" Then Shirley sneezed. "Oh, the dust is—"

"I'm sorry if the dust is getting the better of you," Helen said, with a chill in her voice.

Claire raised her eyebrows at Helen's defensiveness. By Claire's standards the place was clean, but perhaps it wasn't quite as spotless as the rest of the house. Helen was obviously sensitive about the different standard here. "I clean, of course, but there are so many nooks and crannies. It is hard to reach all the spots."

"No, no." Shirley shook her head. "You've kept it exactly as Olivia had it. The place is perfect. It's just her art is languishing." Shirley peered about the room, as if seeing something the others didn't. She dabbed her nose again with the rumpled tissue.

Helen nodded and some of the tension slipped from her shoulders.

Shirley wandered through the studio, brushing her fingers over the table and the smooth surface of the glass in Livy's work. "Her scent is here, isn't it?"

Claire doubted Livy would've been happy to discover she smelled faintly of dust and lemon-scented cleaner. Helen and Claire exchanged glances, but Shirley continued her way through the room until she reached a small desk tucked in the corner.

"Oh, she always sat here, didn't she, Helen?" Shirley slipped into the chair and stroked the wood. "She'd sketch here, in the sunlight. Her last sketches must be—" Shirley yanked at the desk drawer but it didn't move. She pulled the handle again.

"I think it might be locked," Helen said.

"Locked? No, it can't be. She didn't keep anything from me." The desk wobbled as she jerked at the drawer. "It's stuck, that's all. I'll have it open in a moment. Her last work is there. Her last ideas. Her last thoughts…" The words ended on a soft, gasping sob.

Helen went to Shirley.

"Oh, my Olivia." Shirley covered her face with her hands. "My beautiful girl." Her pain was so vivid and fresh, even after all these years.

Helen squeezed Shirley's trembling shoulder.

"I miss her." Shirley grabbed Helen's hand. "Some days I…I don't… How am I here and she's not?" Tears streamed down Shirley's face.

Claire wiped away a tear of her own. She turned from them to give Shirley some privacy and tried to concentrate on the stained glass she was holding.

After a few minutes, Shirley rose abruptly from the desk. The chair scraped against the floor, and banged against the wall. She walked to the other side of the room, grabbing her go-mug as she went. Claire doubted there was a drop of coffee in that cup.

Hoping to steer their thoughts to less emotional waters, Claire grappled for a change of topic. "What types of pieces do you think we should highlight? There is so much to choose from, perhaps if we had a theme it would be easier?"

"Flowers are good, I think." Helen held up a small piece of a daisy. The petals were rendered in a milky opaque glass, and the green of the leaves had some kind of crackle effect. It wasn't the most original rendition of a daisy, but it was pretty enough.

"Or butterflies." Shirley slammed her mug on the workbench. "Do you think she did one of a butterfly? She knew they were my favorite. I'm sure she must have a butterfly in here." Wood frames clapped together as Shirley flipped through her stack of stained glass pieces with renewed vigor.

Claire worried she should have left well enough alone. What if there wasn't a butterfly in the lot? Would Shirley be more upset? Claire sat on the floor and started to carefully sort through a pile.

After an hour of sifting and re-sifting through the collection, they had chosen five pieces. Thankfully, one was a butterfly. It was one of the largest pieces, and Shirley blubbered incoherently for two minutes after she found it. She'd wrenched it from the pile with such force Claire was worried she was going to break one of the other pieces. God, how would they have explained that to Devin?

Helen pointed out where Livy kept the packing supplies, so Claire could carefully wrap the pieces in bubble wrap and cardboard. It was only a fifteen-minute drive to the gallery, but she could not let anything happen to one of the pieces. What would Devin do if something broke while in her care? She shuddered and put an extra layer of bubble wrap around the piece she was holding.

Helen left Claire to pack the pieces, but Shirley stayed at her side. "Do you think you could take pictures of these, too?"

"Um, maybe," she said, thinking again about her idea. She was about to explain it to Shirley when she paused. Devin would probably appreciate being asked first, before Shirley got all gung-ho. "I'm going to haul these out to my car, and I think we're done."

"Thank you, Claire." Shirley laid a shaking hand on her arm. "I don't know what you said to convince Devin, but it worked. I'm so grateful."

"It'll be a strong display of her work." Claire tried to give Shirley a reassuring nod. The dark creases under her pale green eyes looked almost painful.

Claire smiled and hoped she looked encouraging. Witnessing Shirley's obvious pain made Claire's heart ache—the hurt was too intense. Memories of her grandmother's passing and of missing her own mother, who was miles away, swamped her, and she had to turn away.

What a terrible thing it must be to lose child. In the deep recesses of her mind, she wondered if her own mother would be as determined to have her work shown under similar circumstances.

Her test with the cancer specialist was coming up soon. Then she'd know. A sharp pain flashed through her chest. She tried to ignore it. No need to be afraid. Yet. Besides, it really wouldn't help to worry about something she couldn't control. But she did have control over the show, and with these pieces and the work she was collecting from other local artisans who were affected by cancer, it was going to be a success—at least as successful as she could make it.

Tears welled in Shirley's eyes, as if she could hear Claire's thoughts. "It'll be a good show."

Claire lifted two of the pieces and left Shirley in the studio by herself while she took them out to the car. As she passed the kitchen, she could hear the clink of dishes and smell the sweet, warm scent of steeping Earl Grey.

Putting the two pieces in the back seat, Claire looked toward the barn. The door was gaping open, just as it had the previous day. It beckoned to her. Not because she wanted to see Devin. No, that wasn't it at all. Jay was lost somewhere in its depths. She should go check on him. Even though the dust and hay shouldn't bother her on a typical day, her eyes started to sting with just the memory of her reaction the day before.

She sighed and tried to listen over the calm summer air for voices. Nothing. Not even the curses Helen had promised. If Devin had been angry about Jay's unexpected presence, the kid would have returned by now.

After another moment of lingering and hoping to see or hear something, Claire returned to the studio to retrieve the remaining pieces of stained glass.

She loaded the final packages into the car and paused in the drive. She knew it wouldn't be possible to leave without a cup of tea and a piece of some freshly baked cake. Perhaps she should call the men to join them.

Claire glanced at the barn again. It seemed as vacant as always. Was Devin rescuing another cat? She smiled at the memory of how gently he had coaxed George from the rafters, but she suspected her string of sneezes had more to do with the cat's final jump than Devin's soothing tones.

If only she could hear the men, then she could call out to them. Pretend it was a casual coincidence that she'd heard them. Claire listened again. Nothing.

She turned to the house. Women were in the house and men in the barn—how clichéd. Still, she was better off in the kitchen, so she couldn't quarrel with the division of roles too much.

When Claire let herself in, she was surprised to hear Shirley and Helen arguing in the kitchen. "It's only three o'clock, Shirley. There is no reason to have a drink."

"But it is a celebration, don't you think? Olivia's work is finally going to be seen."

"We can celebrate without spiking the drinks." Helen's tone was hard.

"You're no fun. We need to have a toast."

"I'm sure there will be a toast on the night of the showing."

Claire quietly moved to the doorway to watch Shirley and Helen. She didn't want to interrupt, and she didn't want to get involved. What could she do? Going out to the barn had more appeal with every second, even with its haze of pollen and dust. Hell, she could roll in that juniper out back if it would ease the tension in the room.

Helen had her hands on her hips.

"Fine." Shirley scowled. "I'll just have a splash in mine, but it would be better if you joined me." She went to the cupboard above the fridge and extracted a green liquor bottle. Was that gin? When she turned, she saw Claire. "Claire! There you are. Come, we're celebrating."

"I'd love to, Shirley, but I have to drive Jay back into town, and I have to unpack Livy's pieces at the gallery today, too."

"Hosh posh. One drink won't hurt."

Claire felt heat rush over her cheeks. How could she say no without offending Shirley? "I want to be at my best when I'm working with Livy's stuff. I'd never forgive myself if something went wrong."

Shirley sighed. "I suppose you are right." Then she set the bottle on the table. "I'll have a drink for both of us, then."

Helen pulled out a cake pan from the pantry and motioned for Shirley and Claire to have a seat. "Cake?"

"You didn't have to go to such fuss," Claire said. Her mouth watered at the smell of the spice cake. "But, of course, I'd love a piece."

"No fuss at all." Helen grinned as she carefully cut the cake into squares.

CHAPTER 7

Devin stormed into the art gallery for the second time in one week. Again, the hinges jingled. Again, the few patrons there opened their eyes wide with surprise. This time he didn't need to ask who was in charge or where to find them, he walked straight to the office. How could they have picked out the pieces, packed them up and hauled them off without finding out what his thoughts were? Unbelievable.

Some kind of somber operatic music was whispering from the office. Devin paused when he heard Claire's soft, feminine voice mingling with the deep, throaty notes of the song. He knocked before entering this time.

Claire opened the door. The surprise on her face was evident. "Devin?"

"I didn't know you were taking the stuff yesterday. I thought I'd see it first."

"I'm so sorry. Here, come in. I can unpack them for you to see. If you want anything changed, it is easy to do."

She seemed so eager and accommodating, Devin was starting to feel stupid now, but he was there so he might as well make her unpack them. "Mom said you took five?"

"They're over here." They were still wrapped. Claire gingerly brought over each piece and set it on the desk. Then she opened up the various drawers a couple of times before pulling out a pair of scissors. They appeared to be nail scissors, but Claire used them to snip and pick at the packing tape.

In the end, Devin couldn't quarrel with their choices, not that he had any real idea of what had artistic value or not, but he knew what he liked and didn't like. The pieces Claire revealed were well chosen.

"When are they going up?"

"Well, these will be in the front display case as a precursor to the show as of tomorrow. That's the best light in the gallery, so they should show beautifully. The show's official opening will be in about a month and a half.

You are invited, you know, to the opening. I left an invitation with your mom."

"A wine and cheese?" Devin raised his eyebrow skeptically. He hadn't seen the invitation, but he couldn't imagine Claire organizing a kegger for her little show. "How long will you have Livy's stuff up?"

"I've been badgering Peter for more time, but for now we're scheduled for three weeks."

"Peter? Peter Neilson?"

"Have you met him?" Claire asked, but the tone in her voice suggested she knew they were acquainted already. "He's the gallery owner. Actually, Jay, the boy who was out at the farm yesterday, he's Peter's nephew."

"You might say I've seen Peter a time or two." Devin clenched his hand into a fist. He should have remembered this was Peter's place. In Devin's opinion, there was no one scummier than Peter, but Devin had already made an agreement with Claire, so he wouldn't renege now. He needed to get a grip on his anger, so he forced his hand to relax. "Known him for long?"

"A few years or so, I guess."

Devin wanted to warn her about the creep, but if she'd worked with him for years, she probably knew everything already. Livy had gone on and on about Peter, his roaming hands and his not-so-subtle propositions. Devin suspected the stories she'd told were watered down so Devin didn't go and beat the living daylights out of the man, which meant the jerk really shouldn't be close to women. Devin studied Claire. She seemed so naïve, maybe she didn't know. She was nothing like Livy, so it could just be that she wasn't Peter's type.

Nothing like Livy at all. If only he'd married someone like Claire.

Devin swept his gaze over Claire as covertly as he could. She had smooth, pale skin that begged to be caressed, straight hair that swung with each movement she made, and a nice, trim little body that was way too tantalizing in her skirt and high-heels.

Heels? That made him laugh. Even with the extra inches under her feet, she was still so damn petite. When he'd first seen her, he'd thought she might be intimidated by his size, but she wasn't a pushover. God, why had he even thought about intimidating her? She was independent, which was crazy appealing all on its own. Yep—Claire was smart, beautiful and dedicated. How could she have stayed under Peter's radar for so long?

"Is something wrong?"

Then again, if Peter and Claire were involved, and it was Peter's voice he'd heard on the phone the other day… No, that didn't seem likely. On the other hand, he barely knew Claire, and she was obviously well acquainted with Peter. It was probably better he stayed out of their business. "No. I just wanted to see what was here. Good luck with your show."

"Devin, before you go." Claire braced her shoulders. "I have an idea I want to run past you."

Devin crossed his arms. "What?"

"I've been thinking about Livy's work and the fundraiser and everything. And, well, a few years ago I took some photos of Livy's work. They turned out very nice. She used them for her portfolio. Do you remember?"

Devin shook his head. Livy hadn't shared her art with him.

"Did you want to see?" Claire turned and walked up to a bookshelf that lined one wall. She pulled out a binder.

"I'm sure they're great." It was probably good Claire was talking about Livy. He shouldn't have let himself look at Claire like that. Like a man who wanted to slip his fingers under her snug little sweater.

Claire looked at him with a question on her face.

"I don't think I need to see them. I get the idea."

"Well, I was thinking a three week show really isn't very long, and there isn't a lot of traffic in Morning Lake. Sure, there are the locals and the summer tourists, but no one really wants to think about cancer on their summer holidays."

"I suppose," Devin said, wondering where Claire was going with the long preamble.

"So, what if I put a book together? A coffee table book perhaps, with photos of Livy's work and other people's work, too…but I'd want to include Livy's for sure."

"A book?"

"Wouldn't it be great? We could market it online and it'd reach a huge audience—the world even. Part of the proceeds from the book sales would go to the same cancer organizations. Have I told you about that? We're dividing the proceeds from the show between local non-profit organizations that help people with cancer, and their families."

Devin nodded. "And this book, it'd be full of your photos?"

Claire's cheeks went red in a flash. "You hate the idea."

"I never said that." Why was she talking to him about this? Was she seeking investors for her side-project? "You haven't asked, but I'll say it anyway, I don't have money to invest in this type of thing."

Confusion crinkled her forehead for a moment. Then she gaped as if offended. "No, I didn't ask and I wasn't going to." She cut her hand through the air as if to brush aside the thought. "There is so much opportunity, that's all—opportunity we wouldn't have in the gallery. And to highlight the work of local artisans at the same time—"

"Do you take pictures of your own, too? Or do you only take pictures of other peoples' work?"

"I…I do portraiture." Claire stood straighter.

How could he forget? The haunting image of Livy's face remained hanging in the gallery window. That photo had started this whole fiasco.

There was a knock at the office.

"Hello? Anyone in there?"

"Yes?" Claire said, as she crossed the office to greet the person. The office had a small window facing into the gallery, but the blinds were pulled, so neither he nor Claire had seen the person approach.

"Hi. My wife and I are in town for the summer. And, well, we saw this." The man waved a postcard at Claire's face. "Nice photos, we think."

"Thank you."

"Are you acquainted with the photographer?" Claire smiled, but before she could answer, the man continued to talk. "Because we were thinking it'd be a great thing to hire a professional photographer for our daughter's wedding. Not really the frou-frou stuff you see nowadays in wedding photos with chain link fences and rust in the background and all that." The man tapped the card. "But, you know, proper wedding photos. Their day is coming fast, so we would want to contact the photographer sooner rather than later."

The disappointment on Claire's face was quickly hidden, but Devin was sure he'd seen it. "Of course. I am the photographer, but I don't do too many weddings these days. I can meet your daughter and her fiancé, though. They can review my portfolio, then decide if I'm a good fit for them."

She gave the man her business card.

"Thank you," the man said. Then he left.

"Portraiture?" Devin asked.

"Portraiture, yes, but very few weddings anymore. I've done my share of them, but they make me want to scream." Claire groaned. "I suppose I shouldn't have said that. Everyone has their bread-and-butter work, I guess."

"Weddings are romantic," Devin said with a smile. Then he realized what he'd said. What the hell was he talking about? His wedding had been a disaster. The flower girl stepped on Livy's train and tore the gown. His best man showed up in blue jeans. The maid of honor refused to give a speech at the last minute. The priest got pickled and started debating theology with Devin's atheist cousin. And, perhaps most memorably, Shirley passed out, face down, on Livy's bouquet. In retrospect, the wedding had been a harbinger of what was to come. They should have annulled it en route to the hotel.

Claire's attitude suggested she had her own story—a story she wasn't going to tell him, at least not today. Had some man hurt her so badly she hated weddings? An unfamiliar surge of anger rushed through his blood. He took a deep breath.

Claire rolled her eyes at his wedding comment. "They aren't so romantic when you've been to as many as I have. Usually, I hear about their separation before I can even offer an anniversary photo package."

"Cynic."

Claire crossed her arms before responding to his taunt. "Some things are more important than others. A big wedding with a four-tier cake and five attendants on each side—that's not as important to me as working toward a cancer-free world."

Devin nodded and thought about what his mother had told him about Claire's grandmother. Her death must have been hard on her. Did she have any family to help her through it?

He remembered all too well what it was like to watch someone wither and die. Livy had given up. She had let the tumors course through her body. She hadn't put up a fight—at least not that he saw. She'd blamed him, he knew.

But for what? He couldn't be sure exactly. He knew what he blamed himself for, though. If only he'd been with her when she had first been diagnosed, if only he'd been able to give her something to hope for, if only he hadn't been talking to a divorce lawyer a few short hours before she'd broken the news to him...

He'd failed. At marriage. At being a husband. At being a decent man.

Maybe if he hadn't been so derelict in his spousal duties, Livy would have stood up to the breast cancer. People survived breast cancer all the time. Then she would have been the one standing in the art gallery talking about her work instead of him.

By the time Livy had told him, it was too little, too late. Sure, he had quit the rodeo immediately, but by then there was nothing he could do but watch her die.

CHAPTER 8

For a full week, Devin had ignored his mother's expression—that one with the raised eyebrow and half smirk. It'd been especially obvious at breakfast this morning. He could only guess it had to do with Claire coming today to start taking photos of Livy's work.

He needed to get the hell out of here before she arrived.

What was that sound?

Devin paused to listen. Shit, it was a car engine. He was too late. Why was she out here at eight in the morning? Devin peered out the window as he pulled on his cap. Sure enough, her pint-sized sedan was in his drive.

He would just say hello on his way to the barn.

Claire had already started unpacking her equipment, piling it on the gravel drive, when he stepped outside.

"You're at it early," he said.

She jumped, as if he had startled her. Then she smiled at him. Damn it, but she did have a nice smile. How had he not noticed the dimple in her cheek before now? "There is a lot to do," she said. "Have you seen how many stained glass works are in there?"

"What is all this?"

"Flashes, flash stands, collapsible reflection screens, background drop cloths, a folding table, a tripod, and two cameras." She pointed at each thing as she listed it.

"How'd you fit everything into your car?"

"The back seat folds down." Claire grinned.

"Here, let me help you move your equipment."

"I don't want to disturb you from your work."

"You already have," Devin muttered. She disturbed him more than he would have liked. "Is that the kid in the front seat?" He pointed to a dormant figure in the car leaning against the front passenger door. He couldn't be sure it was the teenager because the kid's hood hid his face.

"Yes." Claire glanced at the kid. "Jay came along to…um… help."

That was a lie, nothing but a lie. "So you're a photographer and a babysitter?"

"Something like that." Claire shrugged. "He's supposed to be working at the gallery this summer. Peter thought it would be good for him to get out in the fresh air a bit."

Peter. The man's name grated on Devin like wiping out on your dirt bike on a gravel road. There was a reason he liked horses.

Claire glanced in the car again, presumably to see if there was any other equipment to unpack. She pulled out one last small bag, then closed the trunk.

"The kid fell asleep on the ride out here?"

She nodded.

Devin walked over to the car and yanked the passenger door open. Jay fell out, reaching blindly to catch himself. Dust billowed up around him.

"Up and at 'em," Devin said. "You're going to help us take this gear into the house."

Behind him, Claire sighed. "I was going to let him sleep."

Jay blinked at Devin from his spot on the ground, before peering around as if trying to figure out where he was. Then Jay stretched leisurely and pulled himself up to a standing position, not bothering to brush the dirt from his jeans. It appeared to take considerable effort. He looked too groggy to get angry about his rude awakening.

As soon as Jay was upright, Devin shoved a tripod in the kid's paw, then he grabbed a plastic tote box and led them inside. Jay yawned, but followed Devin without complaint.

When all the equipment was in, Claire started to shoo Devin away in the mildest possible way. When he didn't run straight away, she turned her attention to Jay. It was easy to see she had no idea what to do with the kid. He might be there as a photographer's assistant, but Devin doubted this photographer wanted him.

"Come on, Jay," he said. "Let's head to the barn. It's getting late."

The kid's face lit up.

"Are you sure?" Claire started to protest. "He can stay—"

"I'm sure."

"Thanks." There was that little dimple again. Now that he had seen it, he figured he'd probably wait for a glimpse of it each time he saw her. He might try to make her smile just to see it.

Devin grinned. God, she was sweet.

Jay didn't say anything until they got to the barn. "The last time I was here… Well, I'd never been close to a horse before." The boy's brown eyes were wide as he peered around the barn.

"Well, kid, you're about to get a whole lot closer." Devin patted Jay on the shoulder. A week ago, the kid had just leaned on the fence and watched the horses. He wasn't going to get off so easy this time. "Let's get to work."

The morning went quickly, but a sense of unease had settled over Devin early and he couldn't kick it. Claire was up at the house, poking around in Livy's studio. One minute he wanted to march up there and tell her to pack up her cameras and leave. Then the next, he wanted to peek in the studio window and make sure she was still there. It made no sense. He hated it. This woman was constantly making him question his sanity.

He tried to concentrate on his chores, but his daily routine did little to distract him. They fed the horses, gave the old mare her medicine, and cleaned out most of the stalls. All the stalls should have been cleaned by this time of day, but it was surprising how much time it had taken to teach the kid how to hold a pitchfork and work so he didn't throw out his back.

Just before noon, Devin couldn't stand it anymore.

"Time for lunch," he called to Jay.

"You go on," Jay said. The kid wiped his brow. "I'm almost done this and then I'll come."

Well, what a surprise. The kid wanted to stay and work, did he? Cleaning a stall nonetheless. Okay. Devin wasn't about to say no.

When he walked to the house, he saw the truck was gone. His mother must have gone into town. Good. If he was caught up at the house this time of day, she would think he'd come in from the barn early to talk with Claire—not that he wasn't going to talk to her, but that wasn't why he was coming in. He was coming in because he needed to see what she was doing. He needed to satisfy himself she wasn't disturbing too much.

Well, that was stupid, wasn't it? Of course she was moving things. The whole studio would be in upheaval before the end of this project.

Devin walked through the house to the studio with his boots still on. There would be hell to pay for that. When he arrived at Livy's studio, he paused. Claire was talking. What the hell?

He stepped into the room. Claire was alone, and he realized she'd been talking to herself. She didn't acknowledge him. She was obviously deep in thought. Devin doubted she'd noticed he'd arrived. She peered into the miniature window on her camera. When she stood, he could see her profile again. She wrinkled her forehead and bit her bottom lip. Her lips were pink, as if she had been licking and biting them all morning long.

Devin stared at her mouth. So damn tempting. He wanted to taste her. Shit, her tongue ducked out, leaving a moist sheen on her lips. Lust shot through him. For Christ's sake, she almost had him staggering with it.

She moved around her camera, adjusting the light on her left, turning away from him.

Devin swallowed. He needed to calm down.

Crossing his arms, he stepped back until he could lean against the doorjamb. He glanced around the room—anywhere but at her. She'd been busy. It must have taken her most of the morning to clear a space and rig up her backdrop, lights and camera. That was a lot of heavy lifting and moving. He should have stayed and helped her, except she was the one who had sent him and the kid away.

She murmured again as she peered into the camera. Again, he couldn't understand what she'd said. He remembered his first impression of her voice, soft and soothing. It was the kind of voice that belonged in a home full of children, used to settle little squabbles with love and patience. Then she started to hum, very softly. He didn't recognize the song, but the sound was as lovely as he had imagined it would be. It was so much nicer to come into a house with that sound rather than the tinny drone of the television shows his mother usually watched.

What was wrong with him? She was here to document his wife's things, for Pete's sake. And she didn't like him.

He cleared his throat.

Claire jumped in surprise. She laughed at her reaction, then she smiled and a faint pink stole over her cheeks—filling that damn dimple.

"We'll eat in a few minutes. Jay's finishing up in the barn." His voice was gruff. He spun on his heel and left the room. He had to get the hell away from her.

45

CHAPTER 9

Devin glanced down at the tiny camera gizmo, no bigger than his thumbnail, lying on the seat beside him.

Claire had forgotten her camera memory card thing, and that was the only reason he was going to town. Sure, she hadn't asked him to bring it in for her—he wasn't sure she knew it was missing yet—but coming into town to drop it off for her had to be easier on his peace of mind than having her at the farm again. She had already been there every morning for four days.

He hadn't found the thing. His mom had, and she'd seemed as pleased as George did when he delivered a fresh mouse to the porch step. True, seeing the twinkle in his mother's eye had probably influenced his decision to come in, too. His reasoning was sound: if Claire had no reason to return to the farm and she quit coming around, then his mother's inclination to matchmake would eventually fade. That'd be healthier for all of them.

At lunch the day before, Claire had said she wasn't going to the gallery today, so Devin drove straight out to the old Underwood place. Massive cottonwoods lined the drive to the big heritage house. In the spring, he bet the cotton would drive Claire's allergies crazy—or was it only junipers she couldn't handle? Devin shook his head. Her allergies were none of his business.

He stopped his truck beside Claire's car. At least it appeared she was home. He'd run in, give her the card, and be on his way.

A moment later, he'd knocked and was waiting on the front step. It wasn't too early, was it? Devin glanced at his watch. No, she had to be awake and up by now. God forbid if she answered the door in her housecoat. What if she didn't have a housecoat? What if—

Stop it.

He rapped his knuckles on the door again.

A shadow crossed over the window, then the door creaked open.

Jay's brown eyes were bloodshot. He kept blinking as if he couldn't focus.

"Hey, kid, where's Claire?"

Jay shrugged and yawned. "Dunno."

"This is her place, isn't it?" He glanced up at the house number. His mom must have been mistaken.

"Ye—" His word was cut off by another yawn. "I guess. She's in the garage." Jay pointed to a two-story building across the driveway, then shut the door.

In the garage? Devin crossed to the garage and banged on the side door. Nothing. Well, why would she be in the garage anyway? He was returning to the house for more answers, when he glimpsed Claire through the hedge separating the front yard from the back.

Clutching the memory thing, he walked through the clipped opening in the hedge. Wow, the view of Morning Lake was beautiful from here. Claire's home was separated from the water by a square of lawn, a ribbon of sand and that was it. It seemed the yard had one foot in the lake.

But he only gave the grounds a passing glance. Claire was so much more stunning. Even in the cool morning, she was already wearing little jean shorts and a baggy T-shirt. She'd always worn pants and conservative shirts when he'd seen her before. Seeing her in the comfort of her home, dressed in what his mother would call "I'm-not-leaving-the-house clothes" was something new. She looked a hell of a lot more natural. And look at her legs. A man could spend a lot of time learning the sweet spots on just that stretch of skin alone. That baggy T-shirt was equally enticing. His fingers curled just imagining what it'd be like to draw it up…

Devin swallowed. He had to stop that.

She still hadn't noticed him. He called out to her, not wanting to surprise her as he had yesterday. He wasn't sure he'd be able to keep from kissing her if he saw her pink tongue slip between her moist lips again.

Claire was sitting on a stool, bent over, examining a pile of wood. She glanced up when she heard him.

He expected that dimple. He didn't get it.

She crossed her arms over her chest. "Devin, what are you doing here? This…this isn't a good time." She didn't stand.

"I'm sorry I didn't call, but—"

"I set a bad precedent, didn't I? I showed up at your place without calling. Sorry about that."

Devin stopped. What else had he expected? That she'd open her arms to him? That she'd want to kiss him as much as he wanted to kiss her?

"Did I catch you at a bad time?"

She swallowed, then stared at the pile of painted wood. Perhaps they'd formed some kind of furniture in the recent past. Whatever it had been, it was painted to match the stool she was sitting on.

"What's this?"

"I…I can't…" Tears pooled in her beautiful eyes. Well, damn, now what?

"What's happened? You're upset."

"It's stupid. You'll think I'm stupid for—" She pulled her glasses off and wiped the tears with the heel of her hand. After she'd replaced her glasses and straightened her shoulders, she considered him again. "Why are you here, Devin?"

He waited a moment, hoping she'd tell him why she was so upset, but she needed to calm down first. "Mom found your camera thing." He held it out to her.

She rose and took it from him. Her fingers licked over his palm. Her touch was the strangest thing—like fire and feathers. It was hot, soft and sent tingling ripples up his arm. He swallowed.

"You didn't have to bring it in."

"No, I guess I didn't have to. I wanted to." Shit. As soon as the words were out, he knew it was true. He liked her laughter in his home, her humming, and especially the soft way she touched his arm when she got excited talking about her progress and her ideas. He'd been restless from the moment he woke that morning—knowing she'd finished her work and wouldn't be back at the farm. He'd wanted to see her, but it was obvious she was less than thrilled to see him.

Claire's gaze met his. She was surprised by his admission. Hell, *he* was surprised. Her mouth appeared so soft and it was almost as if she was leaning toward him. Damn it, he wanted to kiss her.

Devin fisted his hand before he reached for her. "Now tell me what's happened."

Claire stepped back and took a deep breath. "There was a party last night…"

"You had a party?" Well, if that didn't kick him in the guts. She was entertaining—probably getting all cozy with the guy he'd heard when he'd called the other day. Was she in a relationship? How could he find out?

No. He didn't need to know.

"Of course I didn't have a party." Claire rolled her eyes. "Jay's parents returned to Calgary and left him here so he can keep working in the gallery." The tone in Claire's voice made it clear she didn't think much of the kid's contribution to her workplace. "He's obviously made some friends—probably summer folk. I've already filled two bags with empties."

Devin raised his eyebrows. "What did you do?"

"What could I do? I turned out the light and tried to sleep."

Devin glanced at the house.

"I stay in the apartment over the garage."

She'd given up her home to Jay. Looking at how sentimental she was over the old patio furniture, he couldn't imagine this decision had been easy.

Devin understood what it was to make tough decisions. He wanted to offer to help, but it wasn't as if he could pay her bills for her and oust the renters. He didn't have that kind of coin at his disposal. Besides, he doubted she'd let him even if he offered. She was independent, proud, and he respected that about her, but there was at least one thing he could do.

He started walking toward the house.

"Where are you going?"

"To talk to the kid."

Claire darted in front of him and put her hands up. "Oh, no, you don't."

He stopped.

She grabbed his elbow and pulled him around. Her touch was light but he followed her lead anyway. She guided him from the house, back to where they'd been standing. "Jay is my problem."

"And have you?" His tone was rougher than he'd expected. Devin jerked his arm from her touch. It was distracting. "Talked to him?"

She rubbed her forehead. "I know I have to, but I need these renters. I have to, but…" She worried at her hands. "This has to be tactfully taken care of."

Obviously she figured he wasn't diplomatic enough. She was probably right. He wanted to yank the kid out here and make him apologize. Then the kid would clean up this mess. Jesus, was that puke he could smell now? The kid should be out here scrubbing the place down.

Claire touched his arm again. "I can do this. It isn't any of your concern."

Devin wanted to argue, but she was right. He hadn't even known she had renters until a moment ago. There was a lot about Claire he didn't know.

"And what's this?" He nodded to the heap of wood.

"That—" Claire choked on the words. "Shit," she muttered. "Why am I so upset by this? It's just a thing, isn't it? An object. An inconsequential bit of wood—" She turned toward the lake.

Devin waited.

"My great-grandfather made that chair. It's been in the family for…well, for a long time. He made it the first year they moved here. It's one of those things you think will always be there. Do you know what I mean? God, I must sound ridiculous. No, I know I do." She waved her hand through the air to stop him from speaking. "It's a chair—an old wood chair that has probably rotted."

She paused. Her lips trembled. "Yes, it was likely rotting and diseased on the inside where no one could see. I bet it would have fallen apart if anyone had sat on it. It just happened to be Jay and his friends. I probably should have thrown it in the garbage two summers ago." She was tearing up again.

Damn it.

A wave of protective instincts clamored through him, itching to be free. He wanted to slay her dragons, even if it was just to get the kid out here cleaning up his mess. If he didn't think it'd upset her more, he'd ignore her request to stay out of it and he'd drag the kid out here to teach him some respect. That kid was a lucky SOB today.

Devin stepped forward and pulled her into an embrace. She might say the chair getting broken upset her, but he didn't think that was all of it. Something else was at work here. What wasn't she telling him? Was she protecting the kid? Or was it something else? He couldn't tell. All he knew was she'd had a passionate response to the destruction of an old chair. The cancer fundraiser was obviously wearing away at her perspective. It couldn't be easy to be surrounded by cancer stories every day, triumphant or otherwise.

At least she didn't resist when he put his arms around her. She didn't hug him back, but she leaned into him. She let him hold her. God, how he'd wanted to have her in his arms. Her cheek was resting against his chest, directly over his heart.

Thank God she didn't break into a weeping fit.

He wanted to squeeze her tight—hold her until he'd absorbed all her pain—but she was so small, fragile really. He needed to soothe her. *Gentle, be gentle.* He rubbed her back. Then his fingers brushed against her bra strap. He jerked his hand away, slipping lower until he found a safe zone on the small of her back.

Her hair was damp and smelled of lavender, probably from a morning shower. Damn. His brain kept circling to the worst things. The last thing he needed to think about was Claire naked, with water slipping over her skin—

Oh, for f—

Claire pulled away. She smiled, more of a thank-you smile than a let's-go-up-to-my-bedroom smile. Then she stepped out of his embrace and focused on the wood at their feet. "I suppose I should toss it out."

Devin knelt and examined the wood. "A few pieces are broken, but the rest just looks pulled apart." He picked up a couple of pieces and tested them. The boards weren't soft, nor did they break or crumble. "Not that I know a lot about this kind of thing, but the wood seems fine."

Claire's eyes brightened. "Are you saying you could fix it?"

Devin would never be a master carpenter, but he could fix a fence. Would this be that different? "I can't promise it'll be exactly—"

"Thank you, thank you, thank you." Claire clapped her hands. "Just for saying you'd try. I didn't think it'd be possible."

Devin wanted to gather her in his arms again. He didn't. This one little dragon was slain, and he felt victorious.

Besides, there was that dimple again.

CHAPTER 10

The day of her appointment with the specialist had finally arrived, but all Claire could do was gape at her car's mangled bumper and flat tire. How could that have happened? She hadn't driven the car for a week, not since going to Devin's to take photos.

Crap, crap, crap to the nth. She had to leave. She didn't have time for this. A strap of panic tightened over her chest.

Jay. It had to have been him. Who else would have taken her car for a joyride and returned it? She needed to get his skinny butt down here and have him fix—

No, Jay had already left to work in the gallery. She'd seen him leave twenty minutes ago.

Now what?

She glanced at her watch. So much for grabbing a bite to eat in Red Deer before her appointment. If she changed the tire now, she could still make it on time.

A moment later, all the contents of the trunk were stacked beside the car. Everything except a tire, that is. The trunk was bare. How could she not have a spare tire? All cars had one, didn't they? Then again, she had purchased hers secondhand, and she'd never had the need for a tire before.

A litany of curse words swirled through her mind.

Should she phone Peter? Ever since he'd discovered she'd been at Devin's place, he'd been overly attentive. He brushed by her, touched her. He smiled too long. He kept looking at her, and not in a friend sort of way. It was more like I-want-to-see-you-naked kind of way. She'd have to talk to him about it eventually. She had to make it clear there would never ever be anything between them.

But that wasn't going to happen today. Today, she needed to get to the city. Pronto.

Against her better judgment, Claire punched in the gallery's number on her cell. It rang six times before connecting with voicemail. She disconnected without leaving a message.

The pain in her chest spiked. Shit. She didn't need a panic attack now. She hadn't had one since she moved to Morning Lake. Why didn't she have anyone else to call? How had she not realized before now she didn't have anyone to call in an emergency?

Should she call Devin?

Her heart raced.

Why did it have to be today? A doctor was going to be waiting for her. An authority on abnormal cells. A cancer specialist. She grabbed the car to steady herself.

Breathe, Claire.

She really needed to get a grip on this situation, then go to her appointment, which was going to be simple. It wasn't a big procedure today—just a more thorough exam.

Okay, first step: call Devin.

Devin would be in the barn or a field or somewhere. He wouldn't be hanging out waiting for her call, but she had to try.

No answer.

What was the matter with everyone today? Was there some national holiday she'd forgotten about?

Five minutes gone and she was still standing in her driveway.

Claire took a deep breath and hoisted her bag higher on her shoulder. The answer was there in front of her—her bike. She was going to have to bike to the city.

At least she'd inflated her tires recently. Not that she biked a lot, but each spring she'd lie to herself about exercising every weekend. Every May she made sure her bike was ready to go, and then it loitered, all alone, in the garage until the next year.

Yes, today was her exercise day.

How long would it take to bike into the city? She should have time, right?

Sweat trickled down her spine within a few blocks. Her legs tingled. This was depressing. How out of shape was she?

As soon as she broke free from the town limits, she saw the gloomy matte of gray clouds. They were the color of asphalt.

No. Claire shook her head. No rain would fall on her. She'd dealt with enough already today.

CHAPTER 11

Devin eased up on the gas as he guided his truck around a bend. It was probably better his mom hadn't come with him today. She'd be squealing at him about driving slower, hydroplaning or some such nonsense.

The rain slammed into the highway's asphalt so hard it bounced two feet in the air. The windshield wipers flew over the glass so fast they seemed to be trying to take flight. Yes, it was a good day to check out the auction. There was nothing else to do.

Devin punched up the volume on the radio so he could hear the country music station over the noise of the hard rain on the cab of his truck.

The day was gray. It suited his mood. He'd been hard pressed not to turn into town to see Claire, but he hadn't figured out how to piece her chair together yet. The answer would come to him eventually. And other than the chair, he had no reason to see her. God knew she hadn't been eager to see him last time.

If only he could forget her scent or the feel of her body when he'd held her, then he'd take that damn chair back to her in pieces and tell her he couldn't fix it. Then he'd never see her again. That'd probably be better.

But he couldn't make himself.

Even today, he'd almost driven by her place instead of going to the auction. Hell, he was worse than his horny teenage self. It was an unsettling realization. He knew damn well he hadn't been this consumed with Ginger Anderson, even after she'd given him the first ride of his life.

Through the pelting rain, a figure on the side of the road became visible. Devin slowed down. Some idiot was out on a bike today. He bet that son of a bitch was sorry about that decision. What the—

The form wobbled, and the bike glided into the drive lane.

Devin swerved. They'd find themselves dead if they kept riding that way. He guided his truck to the side of the road in front of the biker. It was obvious they could use a ride, and he could use a distraction. Besides, the auction wasn't going to be interesting. It was an estate sale—some old person's junk.

He flicked on his hazards, then rolled down his window and waited for the biker. Rain smacked his arm where he rested it on the door. The person stopped and climbed off their bike. They pushed the bike toward the truck with their head down, huddling against the elements. He'd be damned if it didn't look like Claire.

Great, now he was imagining her stranded on the side of the road—a damsel in distress he could rescue. He was an idiot.

He shook his head and glanced back at the mirror.

Shit—it really was Claire.

He hopped out of the truck.

"What the hell are you doing?" He grabbed the bike and tossed it into his truck. The bike clattered across the bed and hit the side. "Get in the truck."

Claire didn't look at him. She didn't nod. Was she sick? Was she hurt? His stomach clenched. He approached her, but she walked around him to the side of the truck and climbed into the passenger seat.

Devin got in the truck and slammed the door. He rolled up the window. The windshield wipers swished. The rain pounded. Condensation fogged the windows. He waited.

"Wow," Claire exclaimed after a minute. "That's quite the storm, hey?"

Devin bit his lip, and cranked up the heat. When the windows cleared, he turned off the pulsing click of the hazard lights and shifted into drive. He looked up and down the road before swinging the truck in a U-turn.

"Wait, what are you doing?" She put her hand on his arm. He wanted to throw it off and he wanted to cover it in his own and warm it up, all at the same time. Shit, he was messed up. Instead, he left it where it was.

"Taking you home."

"I'm not ten. You can't convince me I'll catch my death from a bit of rain. I'm a little wet."

Devin looked at her for the first time since getting in the truck. She was soaked. Her clothing was plastered to her body. Outlining every curve—

Not again.

He scowled. Claire grinned at him. "Seriously, I'm fine. I need to get into Red Deer. Is that where you were going?"

Her grin seemed a bit off. He realized then that it was forced. Why was she putting on a show for him? "Pretty sure your trip can wait."

He glanced at her. She was staring out the window. Her mouth was trying to smile, but the skin around her eyes was pinched. "I promised a friend I'd visit her...at the hospital." Her voice was bright, happy...and false. "Would you be able to take me in?"

He pulled the truck over. "Hospital?"

"Yep." Claire directed her smile at him. "Oh, don't worry. My friend will be okay. She's…anxious for company. I did…um…promise."

She was lying to him. But why?

"Okay," he said. "I'll drive you in, but you don't have to lie to me."

Her eyes widened. "No, I'm not—"

"If you don't want to tell me what's going on, that's fine. Reasons and all that" Devin said. He pulled the truck around in another U-turn, back toward the city. "Just don't lie."

CHAPTER 12

Claire shivered and rubbed her hands together. Devin had insisted she wear his jacket and for about two seconds she'd considered refusing, but thank God she hadn't. Now that she was sitting in the air-conditioned waiting room, her wet clothes were freezing. Would she be able to peel the clothing off her body for the exam and then pull everything on again after the appointment? At least she hadn't worn jeans today—they would have been impossible to pull on wet.

Hands folded in her lap, she leaned back in her chair and studied the people around her. Her fellow waiting room inmates sat in twos around the perimeter—everyone except Claire. One couple held hands. One friend was distracting her companion with pictures on her phone. Everyone else was motionless and quiet. The few, random spoken words were whispered. Even the phone at the desk had a soft tone when it rang. Still it was easy to pick out who the sickly bunch were. She'd seen the same pinched look around her eyes and pursed lips when she'd peered in the mirror every morning for the last week.

She took a deep breath and tried to steady her racing pulse.

The jacket smelled of Devin. Spicy. Masculine. She was probably imagining it, but she was sure she could also feel some remnant of his body heat lingering in the fabric.

Obviously her brain was playing tricks on her—imagining he was somehow there with her.

The office door opened. Everyone in the waiting room looked. It was true—misery did love company. Another couple entered. The man had his hand at the woman's lower back while she spoke with the nurses. A gentle reminder, Claire supposed, that the woman wasn't facing this alone.

She crossed her arms. She was an independent, capable person. She didn't need someone to hold her hand or rub her back. The abnormal cells could be anything. Well, not exactly *anything*, but they did *not* mean she had cancer. They were just…abnormal.

Claire shifted in her seat. The soft vinyl chair squeaked against her wet trousers. A man across the room frowned at her.

Who was she kidding? The colposcopy procedure was a biopsy. *Biopsy.* As in checking for cancer.

Her stomach tightened.

Of course, she'd searched on the internet every night since the doctor's office had called. High-grade squamous intraepithelial lesions, aka abnormal cells, were precancerous—*carcinoma in situ.* Sure, everyone said they weren't cancer, but they could be morphing into some malignant monster this very moment. Had they already done that since she had her Pap test? How long ago was that? A few weeks? How long did it take? What if the one spot the doctor had sampled was still abnormal, but another lesion was already all out cancerous? Oozing, omnivorous cancer.

Bile shot up to the back of her throat.

She hugged Devin's jacket tighter. Maybe she should have asked him to come in with her. No, then he'd have confirmation she'd been lying. Moreover, they hardly knew one another. You didn't invite acquaintances with you to doctor's appointments. What could she say? *Yep, my cervix is growing a nice little crop of lesions—abnormal, mutating lesions. So don't even think about having sex with me.*

She clenched her teeth. She should not be thinking about sex with Devin.

When were they going to call her name?

She had to think of something else. The wedding was coming up. Claire closed her eyes and tried to run through the pictures she planned to take of the happy couple. God, she didn't want to do that function. The only thing keeping her from bowing out was that the money she could earn from that one wedding would pay her property taxes for the year. Okay, bride and groom alone in front of the church, bride with her parents at the park…

The nurse called her name.

When Claire stood, she was unsteady. Her muscles were rubbery from her morning bike ride.

The nurse smiled at her. She seemed friendly, not pitying, thank God.

Claire returned the smile and followed the nurse down a short corridor. The second last door on the left was open. The nurse motioned her inside.

The nurse described the procedure. The woman probably went into more detail, but all Claire heard was—Doctor—metal speculum—special solution to show the abnormal cells—tissue sampling, which will cause bleeding—followed by an application of paste, which will stop the bleeding. There may or may not be pain.

Did she have any questions? The nurse's expression suggested Claire *should* have questions. She didn't.

The nurse left her to change.

A few minutes later, she was in a hospital gown in a hospital. Healthy people didn't go to hospitals. They didn't need pastel hospital gowns. Healthy people spent their days sitting on the beach.

Claire folded her clothes and placed them on a chair in the corner. A few minutes later, an older male doctor came in with a nurse and another younger woman.

"Good morning, Ms. Best," the doctor said. Why couldn't it have been a female doctor? "I have an intern with me today. Is it okay if she stays for your colposcopy?"

A whole troop of people was going to study her cervix. Excellent. What more could she ask of this day? Claire nodded.

The doctor motioned his intern toward the foot of the bed. "And the nurse? She's explained the procedure to you? Good. Do you have any questions?"

"No." Why did everyone think she should have questions? She cleared her throat. "No questions."

"Lie on the table. Now, put your feet in the stirrups. Just so. Bring your bottom a little closer to the end of the bed. Yes, like that."

Her heart pounded.

The bottom of her gown was lifted. Three sets of eyes were now focused on her. Down there. She stared at the ceiling. Her cheeks were on fire.

The procedure was really no different than getting a Pap.

Claire waited, fists clenched. The intern was asking whispered questions. She wished she could hear what they were saying. Or maybe she didn't.

Every so often, the doctor would speak loud enough for her to hear. He described slowly and evenly what he was doing as he examined her.

For her benefit or the intern's? Couldn't he hurry up?

Her fingernails bit into her palm.

"All right, Ms. Best, we're all done." The doctor pulled the gown down. "Now, you might feel a pinch of pain, and that's normal. If the pain gets worse, though, or if you have heavy bleeding, call the clinic."

Claire sat up. She nodded.

"All we have to do now is schedule you for a procedure to remove the abnormal cells."

She forced herself to keep breathing.

"It'll be a L.E.E.P."

The intern was scribbling in her notebook. The nurse was attaching labels to the sample containers. Claire stared at the doctor.

"Now then, for that procedure an electrical current passes through a little wire loop, which will be used to remove the abnormal cells. The nurse will give you a pamphlet describing everything."

Then it hit her. She hadn't really expected the doctor to find anything. She'd thought it had been a mistake—a random, one-off thing—but it wasn't. God, the doctor had seen something when he'd put that stuff on her. She had abnormal cells, not just one or two. There were enough to be visible. There were so many she was going to have to come back so they could deal with them.

Claire swallowed. Her mouth, her throat, everything was so dry. Parched. She wouldn't be able to drink water though, even if she had brought some. Nausea was sweeping through her in waves—white-capped waves.

It wasn't over.

CHAPTER 13

Two days after her colposcopy, Claire could finally look at herself in the mirror over the bathroom sink without thinking she appeared pale, haggard or dying.

There was no sense brooding over it. Everything that could be taken care of was taken care of. The next procedure was booked. At this point, no amount of healthy living, vitamin pills or fresh vegetables was going to scrub off the abnormal cells. Waiting for the appointment was all she could do.

Mind you, it was one thing to tell herself all that, but it was another to deal with the reality. Her world was submerged in reminders.

Everywhere she sat in her studio apartment, she could see the calendar on the fridge with the big red circle noting her appointment. Her apartment was too small. She couldn't escape. Her one attempt to hide in the gallery was worse. The fundraiser's flyers, inventory, invitations and final planning filled the office and her every moment. She needed to escape, to think about something different...*do* something different.

Her car was at the shop. It'd been there for ages and the mechanic had yet to start the work. She hoped he would begin tomorrow, but that didn't help her today. She needed to take action.

What to do? She could hop on her bike for the second time in a week. That would be different. The twinges of pain that'd stabbed at her abdomen after her procedure had faded. Compared to her last attempt at biking, the weather was much better this time. In fact, the weather was great and she had nowhere she had to be. She could glide leisurely over the land and soak up the sunlight and fresh air.

She hadn't taken flowers to her grandmother's gravesite since Mother's Day, so she was due for a visit. The cemetery was a few miles outside the town limits, and within easy biking distance. It'd be a beautiful way to spend the afternoon. Her bicycle was propped in the driveway, exactly where

Devin had left it when he'd dropped her off after her appointment.

No, she wasn't going to think about Devin today. Today was all about forgetting things.

She knew the crops in the countryside were starting to ripen. The yellow fields would be vibrant against the bright sky, great for pictures. The perfume from the canola filled the air in town, so the sweet pollen would clog the air in the country. Definitely something different.

A few minutes later, she was packed up with a handful of yellow lilies and blue salvia from her grandmother's perennial beds. She tucked her camera bag into the basket on her bike, strapped on her helmet, and peddled away from everything.

Stopping at the entrance to the cemetery, Claire could see it was empty. Headstones, all in straight and tidy lines, stood guard like a silent military troop. Just inside the gate, there was a freshly dug spot. The newly laid sod was yellowing around the edges, not established yet. It didn't even have a marker. Beneath that bit of half-dead turf, there would be a body. A person who had been alive last week was now…down there. Claire trembled, and forced herself to look away.

She counted the headstones—three down and one over from the rutted dirt lane—there was her grandmother's plot. She could see the rectangular limestone marker from the entrance, but she couldn't make her legs carry her onto the sacred ground.

She might be spending plenty of time there soon enough. Just like the other new person…and all those already placed there. Maybe she'd be next.

Perspiration trickled down her spine. She wiped her forehead.

Nope, she couldn't do it. Not today.

She tucked her flowers next to the pillar marking the entrance, before hopping on her bike and continuing down the road.

When she steered off the asphalt highway onto a secondary road, Claire gave up trying to deceive herself. She was going to see Devin. If he wasn't home, she'd watch his horses for a bit. Somehow she knew Devin wouldn't mind.

When he'd driven her back from her appointment the other day, he'd been patient. He hadn't prodded. He'd let her sit in silence, and it hadn't been awkward. When she'd first exited the hospital, she'd recognized that expression in his eyes. He'd wanted to ask why she was there, but he didn't. It'd been oddly reassuring to know he'd listen if she wanted to talk. She'd never have suspected she'd find comfort in his presence.

Her narrow bike tires plowed through the freshly graded gravel. She was probably the only idiot to try to ride a bike on this road, but she kept pushing forward.

Claire's legs were burning and the bike was weaving like a drunk at three in the morning when she finally arrived at the ranch. The place appeared deserted, but she wasn't worried this time. The place always looked empty. They must hide their own trucks behind the buildings somewhere, out of sight from the entrance.

She propped the bike against the garage and grabbed her camera bag. She could take some photos of the horses now that she was here. According to some blogs she'd read, stock photography looked like a viable opportunity to make a bit of money. People liked horses, so they might buy photos of them.

It was unlikely that Devin would be in the house, but Claire started there anyway. When a few knocks on the door produced neither Helen nor Devin, she swung her bag over her shoulder and headed for the barn. Today, having avoided all contact with junipers, she'd be safe. She'd be able to see the world where Devin lived, because although his name was on the house's deed, the barn was his real home.

Her heart felt lighter than it had in—no, she wasn't going to think about that. She was just going to enjoy. She lifted her face to the sunlight. This was exactly what she needed. Big white clouds plumed in the sapphire sky. How long had it been since she'd watched clouds glide through the heavens?

What would it be like to live outdoors every day? Sure, Devin may rest his head on a pillow every night, but his life was out here, with animals at his side and the earth under his feet. Did he realize the connection he had to nature? Or was it so much of who he was that he didn't know? He probably couldn't even imagine anything different.

The barn door didn't seem as much like a gaping mouth today. Instead, it was a secret entrance to a hidden and magical world. Claire stepped inside. No one was in sight.

"Devin? Helen?"

The smell of oats, hay and animals crowded over her. It smelled of history, too. It was hard to imagine a time when this was the norm for everyone, whether they lived in the city or the country. Most of the modern world didn't experience this anymore.

A few pegs on the far wall held horse gear. She figured they were bridles, reins and bits, but with one equine experience to her resume, she'd be hard pressed to figure out how to use them. She had ridden a horse once, years ago, when she was at a summer camp. It had been a miserable experience. All Peanuts—now why did she remember the stupid horse's name after twenty years?—had wanted to do was eat the grass on the side of the trail. The trail guide had been irritated with her for not keeping the mare on the path and plodding along with the rest of the group. Claire had tried to urge the horse back to the trail. She tugged the reins this way and that, but the beast ignored her. Maybe it had been hungry, or lazy, or could simply recognize that she was at a loss about how to control it.

At the far end of the barn was another door. It was ajar. Sunlight pierced around it, as if it was yet another magical entrance to yet another magical world. Dust motes glittered in the sunrays like fairy dust.

Claire had just reached the door when it swung open.

There, framed with sunlight, was Devin. The air around him glowed like a halo around a Greek god. Did Greek gods have haloes? It didn't matter. The point was he was magnificent. Big. Powerful.

Then she knew why she was here, why she'd struggled to drive her bike over that awful gravel road. She wanted Devin to spirit her away from everything.

CHAPTER 14

Devin froze. Jesus, his mind was really getting creative now. It wasn't enough that she plagued his dreams and his every waking thought, now he was hallucinating Claire was standing in his barn, with a lacy bra outlined through her white T-shirt and a pair of khaki shorts that showed off her spectacular legs. He blinked—twice.

She was still there.

"Devin? Are you okay?"

She was real. Devin dropped the bridle he'd been holding. "What are you doing here? What's wrong?"

He approached her cautiously. That lavender scent of hers swirled through the air—a teasing scent in this world of horses and feed. When he'd dropped her off at her place the other day, he was sure she was done with him. He'd called her a liar to her face. People didn't usually get warm and fuzzy with you when you did that.

He probably should have apologized when she'd come out of the hospital after her so-called visit with her imaginary friend. Jesus, he could still see her face. She'd been as white as the mountain peaks in the distance. Yet he hadn't said sorry. She'd lied.

Why was she here?

"I decided to go for a bike ride and…well…I happened to be passing by, so I thought I'd stop in." Claire shrugged.

There she went lying again. She was clearly not here because she was in the neighborhood. It was two miles to the next farmhouse and the space in between was filled with nothing but cows and fields. "I haven't had a chance to fix your chair yet."

"Oh, I'm not here because of the chair," Claire said.

"Well then, why are you here?"

Her long, thin fingers wove in and out of a strap dangling from the backpack she had swung over her shoulder. Was she nervous? Had *he* made her nervous? Devin drew closer to her. He moved on instinct, bridging the distance between them.

His midnight fantasies played through his mind unbidden.

"Couldn't stay away?"

She tilted her face to look at him. The long stretch of her creamy throat tempted him. He watched the thrum of her pulse quicken under her skin. Damn it, a man could only deny himself for so long. He needed to taste her.

"Did you long to see me, Claire?"

"I went for a bike ride." Her words were barely audible. Her gaze rested on his mouth. She leaned toward him, just a little. The silky whisper of her breath teased his lips. "I thought I'd stop by and say thank you for driving me into the city the other day." She moistened her sweet lips.

The control he'd been reining in for weeks now broke. He crossed the gap between them and grabbed her.

Her surprised, feminine gasp only fueled the fervor exploding through him. He forced her tight against his body. Her delicate, warm curves crushed against him. He looked into her eyes. The whites of her eyes framed her irises, but she didn't protest. Her mouth opened in a small "o" and that was invitation enough.

Her mouth yielded against his. She tasted of cinnamon. A groan vibrated from the back of his throat. He'd dreamed of savoring her. This was everything he'd imagined and more. Her arms slid up over his chest, not to shove him away but to draw him nearer. Desire spiked through him. God, please let her feel it, too. Although his shirt stopped their flesh from meeting, his pulse throbbed with her every touch.

Claire moaned.

Had he hurt her? She was so small in his arms. God, he hadn't harmed her, had he?

Devin scrambled for control and dragged himself away. Her breath was coming fast. Her lips were pinker now—and wet—from his kisses. Her eyes were dark and soft with need. God, she was beautiful.

He wanted more.

She tugged on his shoulders, trying to bring his mouth back to hers. When her fingers met the bare flesh at the back of his neck, Devin reeled with hope. He saw passion in her eyes. This was no murmur of yearning. No, it was loud, screaming, and unruly.

He'd never thought she'd want him. That she welcomed his embrace was a crazy surprise. He ached to be in her, but he needed to confirm. "Claire?" Her name alone carried the question.

"Devin, please—" Claire's voice quavered.

His heart swelled with the trust she was giving him. He gathered her in his arms and carried her to the office. He set her on the desk and wrenched the camera bag off her shoulder. She pulled her glasses from her face. They clattered against the desk when she dropped them. She smiled shyly. A faint blush swept over her fair face.

"I've dreamed of you," he said, "of this." It was the truth. This moment was all about truth for him. He could not deny his need of her anymore, his desire for her. It nearly crippled him. And it empowered him.

He needed her to understand how much he wanted her. She needed to know what she did to him. Devin set his hips between her legs and pressed his erection against her. She flushed and moved against him. Inviting more.

He groaned her name and dug his fingers into her hips.

She wrapped her legs around him. *Oh, God.* She squirmed, urging him to do more. They had too many clothes on. There were too many barriers.

"Kiss me," Claire demanded. Her voice was huskier than it had been a moment ago. Had his kisses done that? She grabbed his shirt and jerked him down.

Their mouths collided. Hunger roared under her rough caress. All thought stopped.

Their bodies crashed together. Claire surrendered to him. Or had he surrendered to her? She clutched at him, driving him to go faster. He stroked her, feeling her shape through her clothes. The curve of her breast was a soft weight in his hand, but he wanted more. He wanted to feel her heat when he drove himself deep inside her. He wanted to watch her eyes when he filled her.

Devin tugged at the button on her shorts.

He just needed to hang on. Just…a…little…longer… He slid the zipper down. *So close.* His fingers slipped under the silky barrier of her panties. Claire's moan vibrated against him.

His body tightened. *Slow down.* He could—

He dipped his thumb into the mass of her curls. *There.* She was swollen and silky with need. Already. God, she was so ready for him. He kneaded her, savoring the feel of her until she gasped his name and she shattered beneath him. When she flung her head back, he nibbled her neck. She quivered against him, hot and sweaty. He thrust his fingers deep inside her. She was so tight. He groaned as her body shuddered and squeezed him. He wanted to thrust inside her *now*, to feel that tremor of her release convulse over him.

Soon. He had to give her every pleasure he could first. He would not deny her anything. He stroked her, teasing out every bit of her orgasm.

When she lay quiet beneath him, he brushed a kiss over her mouth. Her eyes fluttered open. The intimacy in her face made his heart stagger. An instant later, she had shuttered her emotions, but he'd seen it. That she trusted him with her body was an incredible gift.

Jesus, what was he thinking? He froze. She was beautiful, and he was honored she let him touch her, but he didn't deserve her.

She jerked him closer with her legs. Caught off guard, his thoughts scattered and he fought for balance. He snatched his hand from her sweet treasure in time to balance himself. Bracing on the desk, he peered down at her.

Her chest heaved with her every panting breath. Where her skin peeked out above her shirt collar, it was flushed pink. He wanted to see more. Did the blush cover her breasts? Did it curl around her nipples?

His fingers were wet with her juices and he breathed in the intoxicating perfume of her sex. His heart pounded. He hadn't been overcome so fast since he was a teenager. She rubbed against him again. Her nipples jutted out against her T-shirt, beckoning him. Her gaze met his.

Then she writhed against him recklessly. She demanded more. She clung to his hips and held him firmly. It was so close to where he wanted to be. Her heat burned through their clothes, igniting him. He couldn't stop. He couldn't wait.

He rocked against her.

The release crashed through him. His arms gave out and he fell over her. His face pressed against her smooth throat. The dainty aroma of lavender and the heady scent that was uniquely Claire filled him.

His body shook.

For Christ's sake, she'd made him come in his pants.

CHAPTER 15

Claire grinned. She'd made Devin—her big strong cowboy—tremble with need and lose control. His body burned against hers. He shivered again and her heart skipped in response. Her limbs were loose and delightfully relaxed for the first time in—

Oh, no. What had she done? Fully clothed make-out sessions with men like Devin led to fully naked sex, didn't they?

She couldn't have sex yet, could she? She hadn't really listened when the doctor talked about sex. Why would she? She hadn't had sex for years—some days it felt as if centuries had passed—so she'd figured the chances were slim to zilch.

And that paste stuff the doctor had used on her—what if it wasn't all gone yet? Did she smell like medicine? Claire sniffed. The air smelled of sex, thank God, but she couldn't be sure that awful goop was all expelled from her yet. No, this was as far as they could go. It was done. No more. Not today.

Not today?

Was she really thinking this was going to happen again?

Devin propped himself up on his elbows and bent to spread kisses along her neck. *So good.* Every inch of her tingled and rejoiced. His tongue teased that sensitive spot below her ear. Claire stretched to expose more to him. He licked her. She moaned and felt his lips change. Was he smiling? She sank her fingers into his hair.

No, she couldn't do this. She had to—

His calloused fingers slid under her shirt. He caressed the underside of her breast. The heat of his touch through her bra sent her nerves sizzling. He nudged the satin down, then traced her areola. He pinched her nipple. Claire cried out his name and arched her back.

"I want to see you," Devin murmured against her skin. "All of you."

This had to stop.

"No, I—" Claire pushed against his shoulders.

Devin raised his head. Confusion shadowed his eyes.

She shoved him again.

He lifted himself off her and stepped back. He looked hurt. No, that couldn't be correct—he was disappointed, sexually frustrated.

Claire glanced down to her hands. "I...I don't know what happened," she stammered. She zipped and buttoned her shorts closed. She adjusted her shirt. Where were her glasses? There they were—lenses down against the desk, probably scratched all to hell. She scooped them up and rammed them on her face. Then she dared to peek at Devin again.

He appeared fine, maybe a touch flushed, but his clothes were all in place.

"I'm so sorry," she said.

"You're sorry that I want you?" Did he really just growl?

"I..." Claire wrung her hands. She couldn't think straight when her every nerve still thrummed in post-orgasmic joy. "I...can't." She leapt off the desk, away from him. She needed to get out of here, but he was standing in the only doorway.

He crossed his arms over his chest. "You could have said no."

"Oh, God, no. That's not what I meant. I liked it." *Like* probably didn't do that justice. When *was* the last time she'd had an orgasm?

A whisper of a grin, filled with masculine arrogance, teased Devin's mouth. "Liked?"

"You know what I mean." She closed her eyes and shook her head. "I just can't...well...you know." She eyed the door again. She didn't dare approach him, in case she lost her mind and forgot everything again. He had a crazy effect on her thinking. "Would you move? I need to—"

The grin died. "I wouldn't force you. You realize that, don't you?"

Claire gaped. "Oh, I didn't mean to imply... No, that's not it at all."

Devin raised his eyebrows and studied her for a moment. What was he thinking? The tension in his face was grim. "Okay, Ms. Best. You are here, so why don't we make you useful? Do you take photos of horses?"

"What?" Claire's mind spun at the sudden change of topic. His calling her Ms. Best stung. "Horses?"

"I have a yearling to sell. I need a picture."

He hadn't really just dismissed everything that had happened and asked her to take a picture of his horse, had he? Would she break her wrist if she slapped him?

CHAPTER 16

He didn't need to be a psychiatrist to realize he'd spooked her. And what did you do when someone was spooked and you didn't fancy being trampled? You made them comfortable again. Claire was a photographer, so it made sense that taking pictures would calm her, right?

The murderous expression in her eyes suggested his assumption had been wrong.

What else could he do? The tumble of emotions he'd seen in her over the last few minutes was nerve wracking. Now she seemed even more uncomfortable than she had a moment ago.

He was probably no more composed. How had she turned everything off? One minute she was urging him on, demanding more and making him lose it. Now, she was testing his control in a whole other way.

Damn it. He needed to clean himself up. He hadn't been so damn uncomfortable in years. If he shucked his jeans to deal with it, she'd bolt faster than a cat with a dog on its tail.

"I'll meet you outside." He pivoted and made for the washroom at the back of the barn. Until this moment, he'd never understood the need for the toilet out here.

Five minutes later, he stepped into the sunlight. Well, now, wasn't this interesting? He'd expected her to run as soon as he was out of sight, but Claire was leaning against the fence, camera bag slung over her shoulder. Some of the heat from their embrace still tinted her cheeks.

When she saw him, her blush deepened. She quickly glanced back to the horses. The look of her, flustered and shy, sent another jolt of lust straight through him. There was no way she was going to convince him that she was unaffected by his touch, that she didn't want more. If he could kiss her again, he was positive she would melt against him.

"I saw your mom." Claire's voice wavered. "She's going to take me to town." She cleared her throat and lifted her chin. "If you want pictures of your horse, I'll arrange to come out another day. I'll call Helen."

Devin rocked on his heels. Any lingering thoughts of seducing her were crushed like a cigarette under the heel of his boot. What was there to say? "Don't bother."

She gaped at him.

"With the pictures." He bent and grabbed the bridle he'd dropped when he'd first seen her. "Don't bother."

Then he went into the shadowy depths of the barn, leaving her in the sunlight. He didn't look back. There was nothing to see or do. She'd made her decision.

She was right to pull back from him. All he had to do was let her go.

CHAPTER 17

Claire hoisted her bike into Helen's pickup truck.

Her tears, which she refused to let free, had nothing to do with Devin and his dismissal of her. No, she would not cry. Orgasms released emotions. It was nothing more than that. Or it could be her allergies kicking in again, though she hadn't been close to any junipers today.

And if she could believe that, she could believe anything. Maybe she could even make herself believe she didn't have abnormal cells.

Why didn't he trust her? For that matter, why didn't she trust him? She couldn't tell him she was in the midst of a cancer scare. She just couldn't. What would he say? What would he do? She couldn't handle that pitying look people got when they heard that kind of news—not from Devin. Every time her grandmother went out in public after her diagnosis, it was always: *How are you feeling today? When do you start chemo? You look so much better today.* No one ever just said: *Hi, Janet, how are your tomatoes growing this year* or *did you see the latest action movie*—Grandma loved shoot 'em up movies with car chases— or any other mundane, normal thing.

It was always about the cancer. So wasn't it better that he thought she was a tease instead of on her deathbed?

What had she been thinking, making out with her dead friend's widower anyway? And why was she thinking about high school phrases like "making out"?

She blinked away the tears and forced a smile on her face before stepping back. Helen was standing beside her but didn't peep at her, thank God. Instead, she slammed the tailgate closed.

Claire jumped. If Helen noticed, she didn't say anything.

"I'm glad you came out to the farm today," Helen said as she wiped her hands on her pants. "We have so few visitors, but you're always welcome."

"I'm such a nuisance, bumming a ride to town," Claire said after they'd climbed into the cab of the truck. Her legs would not have pushed through the gravel roads again. She shouldn't have come out here without thinking about how she was going to return home.

Correction—she shouldn't have come out here at all.

"Sandy, that's my horse, she can wait a little longer for her ride. I needed to run to town today anyway. We're out of bread and milk, and I can't make breakfast tomorrow without them." Helen smiled.

"You ride horses?" Claire had always imagined the horses were Devin's.

"Oh, sure," Helen said as she popped the truck into gear and flew out of the driveway with hardly a peek up or down the road for oncoming traffic. Claire snapped her seatbelt into place. "My Jack and I, we loved horses. With the pair of us raising the poor boy, Devin never did have much of a chance to be a lawyer or some such."

"I guess Livy liked horses, too," Claire said.

Helen laughed. "Heavens, no. We couldn't get that girl out to the barn for anything."

"But—" Claire stopped. She didn't need to pry into this. She tapped her fingers on her leg. Screw it, she was going to ask anyway. "But Livy took care of the animals when Devin was at the rodeo, didn't she?"

Helen's laughter filled the truck for a good mile. She snorted twice, without apology. "Whatever gave you that idea? Livy, bless her heart, couldn't tell the difference between a scoop of oats and a bale of hay." Helen chuckled again. "When Devin was gone, I'd drive out to the farm and do the chores. I lived with my sister in town back then. Sometimes, when my arthritis was acting up, I'd ask the Jenkins boy from up the road to help me. Good kid, that Jenkins boy. He'll do his daddy proud by taking over their tree nursery some day."

Claire bit her lip. Why would Livy have lied? It was such a silly thing to fake.

"Livy was an interesting sort of girl. My Devin would have done anything for her." Helen kept her eyes straight ahead. "The first big check he ever got from the rodeo, he gave it all to her so she could purchase her fancy art supplies. She started by ordering a bunch of glass from around the world, some from China and Italy and other places I can't pronounce."

Claire knew she should stop Helen from saying anything more. She didn't want to hear about Livy and Devin. She didn't need to know about how much he loved her, and how his world continued to revolve around his dead wife. Claire looked out the window, but no words came out of her mouth to turn the topic of conversation.

"But that was our Livy," Helen continued. "You know, Claire, I was thinking I'd like to go to the rodeo in Bannister next weekend."

"Hmm? What?" *Rodeo?* What was she talking about?

"The rodeo."

"That's nice, I'm sure you'll—"

"You should come with me," Helen said. "I'll pick you up at ten."

"Oh, no." Claire's heart leapt her in her chest. She couldn't go. Devin would think she was stalking him. "I couldn't—"

"Nonsense." Helen stopped talking to blast the horn at a scrawny gopher scampering over the road. It darted away in the knick of time. "I want to go and have no one to go with me. My sister is off to Vancouver to visit her daughter."

Claire scrambled for an excuse.

"And Devin can't take me," Helen continued. "I've already asked him and he said he couldn't." She reached over and patted Claire on the knee. "Really, dear, it'll be fun. You could bring that fancy camera of yours and take some pictures."

Devin wasn't going. Claire felt an odd mix of emotions. She could go and find out about rodeos, get a glimpse into Devin's world, and he wouldn't be there.

"I don't think—"

Helen smiled. "Of course you do. I'll pick you up at ten, okay?"

Claire's heart thumped in her chest. "Okay."

Devin wouldn't be there, so why did she feel like she'd be spying on him?

CHAPTER 18

At the rodeo grounds, Claire and Helen paid their admission fee to a clean-cut teenager standing at the entry gate before they'd even parked their truck. The gravel parking lot was filling and people were already starting to park their vehicles on the grass. A couple of teenagers tried to direct Helen to park amid the other pickup trucks, but she had her own idea about what was best and parked close to the entrance. The kids shrugged and waved at the next vehicle.

"We'll leave the folding chairs in the truck for now," Helen said when they left the truck and walked toward the event facilities. There'd been a bit of mist earlier that morning, so the air hadn't warmed yet. Claire shivered as the coolness sank through her thin cotton T-shirt. "We might need them later, depending on how they've got things set up this year. Me, I like to be close to the action. Smell the animals, see the sweat, and hear the bones crack."

"Bones? Crack?" Claire shivered again, but this time it had nothing to do with the temperature.

"Don't worry, honey," Helen said. "Those EMTs aren't used much."

Claire hadn't seen the first aid truck at the end of the drive aisle, but, now that she had, her stomach nosedived. Thank God Devin didn't do this anymore. She pulled her camera bag higher on her shoulder and followed Helen.

Claire had driven by the Bannister rodeo grounds a few times over the years, and it had always seemed to be a lonesome place with its bleachers, empty pens, and acres of grass. Today the place was filled with people, vehicles and animals. It was far from forlorn, and it appeared much larger than she'd imagined.

The parking lot and main entrance were on higher ground to the north of the competition area, so Claire had a good view as they walked toward the facilities. At the center of everything was the rodeo itself. A small tractor zipped around the arena, and Claire supposed someone was doing last minute maintenance before the events started. The viewing stands faced east, and a few spectators were already staking out their seats. To the west, behind the stands, a cluster of tents and portable food trailers were arranged in rows. There were even a few small carnival rides.

She would never have guessed this was such a big event. To the east, the pens were filled with farm animals. To the south, there appeared to be an RV sales lot with trailers and campers of every description tucked in close to one another. That must be where the competitors stayed, but there were lots of RVs there. Other people must camp out for these types of events, too. Did rodeo cowboys have groupies like rock stars? Had Devin been blessed with some?

Everywhere Claire turned, there were people dressed in cowboy hats, colorful buttoned shirts, and jeans. She didn't have the full unofficial uniform, but no one really spared a glance in her direction. She may not have the right shirt, the boots or the hat, but at least she'd opted to wear jeans that morning, though her decision had been purely practical. She had thought about wearing khaki shorts, but she had no idea what she'd be sitting on.

"Now let's grab us some pancakes." Helen winked at her. "We have about a half hour before they pack up breakfast and turn the place into a beer tent."

When they sat at a long table with their paper plates full of food, an older man—all cowboy—approached them. His silver and gold belt buckle was the size of Claire's pancake. He was an attractive man, maybe in his early fifties. He had a swagger in his step that'd probably set more than one girl's heart tripping over itself.

"Helen, how the devil are you?" He gave Helen a peck on the cheek.

"As good as ever, Roy." Helen blushed. "I'll bet you haven't met Claire," she said. "She's a friend of the family and a photographer. We're going to try for a good spot for the rodeo. I'm going to hit the rush seats first, so Claire can take some good pictures."

Claire smiled at the man, then leaned back as he bent toward her. What was he doing? He kissed her cheek. She felt her face grow hot.

"Now, don't you worry about Roy, here," Helen said. "He's just an old flirt. He did some team roping with Devin when our boy was starting out."

"Oh, that's nice." Claire tried to smile, then resorted to studying her food. Of course the talk would come around to Devin. This was probably the first of many conversations about him she'd have to endure today.

"Where is the boy?" Roy said, scanning the crowd in the tent.

"Oh, he's here somewhere," Helen said. "He left home hours ago. He had no interest in waiting around for me."

"Devin's here?" The question flew out of Claire's mouth before she could stop it. "I thought—"

Helen's eyes twinkled. Then Claire realized that she'd thought exactly what Helen had wanted her to. She froze and waited for Helen to speak.

"Devin said he couldn't bring me because he'd be coming over at seven. That schedule didn't work for me." She smiled at Roy. "You'd think that boy was still in the rodeo."

Claire's heart pounded. She glanced at the people seated at the neighboring tables. What if Devin saw her? Could she avoid him? For the whole day? Helen wasn't looking at her, but Claire was sure the woman appeared excessively satisfied.

"I'm heading over to the petting zoo." Roy cleared his throat, as though embarrassed he'd confessed that. "My granddaughter won't get off the pony, so I left all my girls over there to look after her while I grabbed a bite to eat. I'll maybe stop by the horses on my way through and see if I can't catch Devin."

Roy glanced at Claire, then turned back to Helen. "I ain't seen him out for a good long time." Roy shook his head. "Is he doing okay?"

"Things are coming around again," Helen said, smiling at Claire. Claire wished she could excuse herself without making a fuss.

"I tried to talk to him, but he wasn't having none of that," Roy said.

Helen squeezed Roy's hand. "I know."

Claire wished she wasn't so curious about their conversation. She should give them some privacy. How could she leave without being too obvious? Get more napkins? More cream for her coffee? Claire set her plastic fork at the edge of the paper plate and was about to make an excuse when Roy cleared his throat again.

"All right then," he said, "I'll see you young ladies a little later." Roy grabbed the tip of his cowboy hat and dipped his head before leaving.

Claire settled in her seat and picked at her now soggy pancakes. She could guess what had kept Devin from the rodeo. Devin had loved Livy. Despite Livy having said time and again she and Devin were miserable together, he had loved her. It was looking like Livy had just been melodramatic in her complaining. After all, her death had made Devin turn away from his friends and the rodeo. He'd kept Livy's studio exactly the way it'd been when she'd lived. His grief must have been overwhelming.

Or was that guilt? But guilt over what? At Livy's funeral, Claire was sure his intoxication pointed that way, but she may have been wrong. He could have simply been a man grieving over the loss of the love of his life.

Everyone deserved to love and be loved.

Now Devin was acting as if he was interested in her. That incident in the barn had kept her awake every night since it had happened. But what if she was sick? Really, really sick. Cancer sick. Of course, he didn't love her the way he'd loved Livy, but if she let him get close to her, knowing that she was potentially ill, that wouldn't be fair. She couldn't hurt him that way. She couldn't have him sitting at her side, trying to atone for some sort of guilt or lingering grief from Livy's death.

Now she was thinking about her own demise. Yet again.

"Oh, now, don't look all glum," Helen said. "I didn't lie to you. So what if Devin is here? We'll have a wonderful day."

Claire nodded. Helen was right. It would be a wonderful day.

She was here and she'd make the best of it. She'd pushed Devin away the last time she'd seen him, so he wouldn't wander in her direction again. He would think what he liked when he saw her, but she didn't have a choice in that. Perhaps it was time to live by her grandmother's credo: this life she was living was not a dress rehearsal.

Claire had never been to a rodeo, and today it was time to grab life by the horns and live it fully.

CHAPTER 19

Much to Claire's surprise, rush seating was located immediately beside the events themselves. The bleachers were tucked at the center of the rodeo. The hottest part of the day was bearing down on them as they found a place to sit. The coolness in the air had been lost and the day promised to be a scorcher. Claire wiped perspiration from her brow and took stock of her surroundings.

Luckily, the sun was high in the sky now, minimizing the chance of glare in the photos. The bull- and bronco-riding arena was only ten feet in front of her, much closer than she had imagined, so she changed the lens on her camera and waited.

Thanks to the rodeo booklet and a few words from Helen, she figured she had a good handle on the rodeo events themselves. Bareback riding, bull riding, saddle bronco, steer wrestling, roping—who knew there were so many ways men could try to get themselves killed by farm animals?

Promptly at one o'clock, the event started with an anthem and a prayer. Then a man with a deep voice, who sounded like he'd been born to call rodeo events, announced the start of the bareback riding.

Claire leaned forward and turned on her camera. A cowboy was poised atop a horse in a chute beside the arena, then the gate was thrown wide, and man and beast careened into the open. The animal looked some pissed, charging around the pen, jumping and bucking. The cowboy had one arm flung back and the other holding a little leather handle as he was tossed up and down. As far as Claire could tell, he was doing his best to get whiplash. His hat flew off. Then, half a heart beat later, he somersaulted over the front of the horse.

Oh God, he was hurt. He had to be hurt after all that.

She rushed to her feet. Where were the medics? What could she do to help? She only knew rudimentary first aid. Then she realized everyone else was clapping and cheering.

Claire put her hand over her heart, willing it to slow. She watched a couple of other men settle the horse and get it out of the arena so the next competitor could do his thing. The cowboy was already standing. Grinning, he waved to the audience, and in return, the crowd and the announcer hollered their support.

They were insane. All of them.

Claire sat beside Helen. She held her camera, but she hadn't taken a single photo.

"That boy's getting better." Helen said. "He might turn pro like his dad." She sounded approving.

Good grief, the cowboy leaving the field was a kid, just eighteen or nineteen.

Then the next competitor and horse barreled into the arena. This cowboy was kicked in the ribs after he fell, Claire was sure of it. He winced when he stood, but he walked out. What were these men made of? It didn't seem they had the same type of flesh and bone she had.

"When Devin competed, did he participate in this event?"

"In the beginning, he tried all the events." Helen paused as she focused on the next competitor, who managed—somehow—to make his eight seconds. The crowd roared. "But he was best at bull riding."

Based on Claire's own imagination, combined with the description in her booklet, she could well see Devin competing in the event described as the most dangerous.

Stupid man.

But what would it be like to do that? To be down there with those wild animals doing perilous things? When had Claire ever done anything risky? Sure, her parents thought she was living dangerously by staying in Morning Lake by herself, but no one else in the world would agree with them. Certainly, the men and women here would think she was a sissy. Hell, *Claire* thought she was a sissy.

Midway through that first event, the rodeo started to make sense to Claire. All these men were living on that tight edge between life and death. They had mastered fear and were facing that which they had no control over, attempting to conquer it with finesse. It was awe-inspiring.

From that moment on, she experienced a thrilling blast of excitement when each competitor rushed into the field. How exhilarating would it be to compete? She could well imagine it would be like an addiction. How did Devin live without it?

She cringed when each cowboy fell, hooted for the ones who made their eight seconds, and clapped for everyone. She'd never felt quite as consumed as a spectator for any other kind of sport.

The afternoon progressed quickly and she continued to be captivated. By the time they'd gone through steer wrestling, boys' steer riding, team roping and the saddle bronc events, Claire was hooked. There were two more events, tie-down roping and ladies' barrel racing, before the bull riding. Devin no longer competed, but Claire knew she had to stay to see that event.

"Well, dear, I see our neighbor Julie over in the stands. I should probably go say hello." Helen stood.

Claire gathered her bag and started to pack up her camera. Helen touched Claire's shoulder to get her attention. "You stay here with the seats. I'll just be a minute."

Claire nodded and focused on the roping.

The barrel racing was starting when Claire realized Helen wasn't back yet. In fact, Helen was nowhere to be seen. Should she look for her? The place was packed. Helen knew where to find her if she stayed here, but if Claire left, they could easily miss one another. Shoot, she should have gone with Helen.

Claire put her camera in her bag, then asked to borrow her neighbor's binoculars. She scanned the crowd in the opposite stands, but Helen's bright shirt was MIA.

What should she do? She returned the binoculars and chewed on her bottom lip.

Helen must have found someone else to talk with when she was returning.

Where was she?

Then Claire saw Devin. Her heart leapt. Even with his black hat, white shirt and scowling face, he was a beautiful man.

He was staring at her. Claire clenched her bag like a shield.

CHAPTER 20

Devin stared at Claire and cursed. Why the hell was she here? No, he could figure that out well enough. His mother and her schemes were going to kill him. Tonight, the minute he got home, he'd be sitting down with his darling meddling mother and they'd have a long chat about how she was going to quit interfering.

Claire had cringed when she saw him, then she glanced away. Her reaction was exactly what he would have expected. She'd told him clearly enough he was an ass the last time they'd been together. He'd had his hand in her pants, and she'd told him to get lost. That was pretty damn clear.

When she looked at him a second time, he motioned for her to come down. He probably should go up there and explain things, but she was sitting in front of Hanna May, the busiest busybody on the circuit. That woman didn't miss many rodeos and she certainly never missed any gossip. His mother had probably planned that, too.

Claire took a deep breath, then nodded. When she stood, Devin had to drag his gaze away. She was wearing a snug T-shirt and jeans, displaying her tight little body. Making him think about things he really shouldn't...couldn't. He was not going to gawk at her breasts pressing against the thin material.

He wasn't.

Devin tapped his foot and turned to watch the barrel racing while Claire climbed down through the spectators. She was going to be as pissed as he was. Hell, the last time they'd spoken she'd essentially said she never wanted to see him again.

When Claire arrived at his side, he forced himself to look at her. He expected her to be tense but she had an easy smile on her face.

"I've never been to a rodeo before," she said. "It is wonderful. You should see the pictures I've taken."

Devin nodded and drummed his fingers against the railing. "My mother called."

Claire's eyebrow lifted.

"She's left the rodeo. She asked if I could take you home."

"You're joking, aren't you? She was—" Claire squinted toward the seats they'd shared.

"No joke." Devin rubbed his neck. "Listen, I'm sorry."

"Is she okay?"

Devin cleared his throat. "On the phone, she started off by saying she thought she might have gotten a bit of heatstroke, but—"

"We should find her, check on her. She shouldn't be driving. She should have come and got me." Claire started to press through the crowd beside the bleachers, then she stopped. "Are you coming? I don't know where you're parked."

"Stop for a minute." Without thinking, Devin put his hand on her arm to stay her. Her skin was warm from the sun and smooth as silk. He jerked his hand away. "Mom doesn't have heatstroke. The truth is she—I don't know how to say this—she's got this idea that you and I…" He glanced at the people beside them, but no one was paying much attention.

Claire stared at him.

"I'll talk with her," he said.

Claire fiddled with the strap on her camera bag, like she had in the barn the other day. No, he would not think about what had happened in the barn. He cleared his throat.

"You think she brought me here and then left so that you'd have to take me home?"

Devin shrugged. "That about sums it up."

"Are you blushing?"

"God, no," Devin said, adjusting the angle of his hat. "She doesn't know about…well, she doesn't know you'd prefer to stay away from me. I'll find someone else to take you home, okay? That way you don't have to worry about anything."

"You're going to ask someone else to take me home?" The way Claire's eyebrows came together, she looked a bit hurt. But damn it, she was the one who kept putting up roadblocks between them.

"If you want."

"No." Claire straightened her shoulders. "That is not what I want."

It was Devin's turn to raise his eyebrows.

"I want to watch the bull riding and any other event that is still to come. Then if you are ready, you can drive me home. Don't you dare pawn me off on someone else." She stared up at him, as if she was daring him to defy her.

"Bulls, hey?"

She lifted her chin. "Yes."

Devin tapped the front of his hat and nodded at her. She was taking this situation with more grace than he'd expected. "Yes, ma'am."

Claire nodded back at him.

He guided her to the fence where he'd watched most of the events. Old Jimmy had let him go pretty much anywhere he wanted. One flash of his championship buckle and most other people didn't question it either. That polished bit of metal was his backstage pass—at least it was at a rodeo this size.

Claire pulled out her camera again. They'd missed most of the barrel racing, but she had said she wanted to see the bulls and there would be plenty of that. Devin leaned against the fence, propping one foot on the lower rung. The last rider had rounded her final barrel and was charging to the finish.

"Do you miss it?" When she asked the question, she stared straight at the rider who was pulling her horse to a halt to see her time.

He didn't want to talk about his rodeo life. At the time, he'd loved it, but he hadn't seen the damage it'd done to his home and his marriage until it was too late. Besides, he didn't want to think about Livy today. He didn't answer.

Instead, he watched the crews in the arena preparing the ground for the bull riding. He pulled his pack of gum from his shirt pocket and offered Claire a piece. She shook her head. "They're taking the barrels off," he said.

He popped a piece of gum in his mouth.

It always struck him how different it was to be on this side of the rail. The crowd was waiting. He could feel the anticipation building. Claire was waiting, too, for him to answer her question. He could feel it in the silence between them.

"I'm too old. I've broken enough bones."

She looked at him then. He could see she was about to tell him he hadn't answered her question, and that was true enough. But he'd be damned if he was going to get all nostalgic.

"The first rider is in the chute," Devin said, as the announcer introduced the rider and the bull.

Claire held her camera up to her face and started clicking when man and beast burst into the open.

"That bull is a mean son of a bitch," Devin said. The bull reared and spun, putting his all into getting that rider off. "It's in his genes. His sire damn near broke my back. I was lucky to escape with bruises."

Claire's camera seemed to shake, but he wasn't sure why. So he adjusted his hat and watched young Hornby be thrown clear.

"He's still learning, but he's got good body position. It won't be long before he gets a check for this event. It might not be much of a check to start with, but it'll come."

85

Then the next rider was out.

"See, now, Jack there, he's got control. See the way he spurs?" The cowboy jumped off at his eight seconds. "He'll be proud of that score."

Claire continued to snap her pictures. Was she listening to him?

Devin chewed on his gum. It was nice talking to her about the event. He almost wished he'd been with her through the day to teach her about the rodeo and find out what she thought of it all. A good city girl from the east, she was probably horrified.

But she didn't seem horrified. If he wasn't mistaken, he'd say she was enjoying herself. Even if she was with him.

The next bull stormed out of the chute. This was going to be a good one. The bull kicked and twisted; its muscles clenched and rippled. The animal's power was an awesome thing to see.

The cowboy, one of the few guys Devin didn't recognize, was doing a fine job. He made his eight seconds and rolled from the bull, but he didn't roll quickly enough. Shit, the bull stomped on his leg. That was going to hurt like hell.

Where were Charlie and the others? Devin stepped up on the fence, waving his hat to get the bull's attention. Finally Charlie, the best rodeo clown there, caught the bull's attention. The animal snorted. Then 2,000 pounds of pissed-off bull charged the man.

Charlie ran and jumped into his barrel. Instead of ramming the barrel, the bull veered, changed directions and charged the fence. Straight for Claire.

Christ. What if the fence didn't hold? Claire wasn't reacting. She was oblivious, snapping her photos. If the bull continued on its path, she would be thrown back. If the fence broke…

The bull kept rushing toward them. Damn it, he wasn't going to stop.

Devin grabbed Claire by the waist. He spun with her, putting himself between her and the bull, with his back to the charge. The earth vibrated beneath his feet. He braced. The bull slammed into the fence. The fence panel clanged against its posts. Something creaked. Was it the fence? The posts? Would it hold? People screamed. When the bull crashed into it again, the heat of the beast's breath shot across Devin's neck.

He looked over his shoulder. The bull banged into the fence one last time, then turned and trotted off.

Claire started to tremble. He tightened his hold on her.

"I'm okay," she whispered.

"Of course you are, darlin', but let's hold up here for a minute." He needed to settle his own heart. Shit, he felt like he'd been thrown off that damn bull. How many times had he dealt with angry bulls? Most of those times would have been without a fence between them.

This little incident? It shouldn't have bothered him but, shit, this was different. Claire shouldn't be facing down a bull. She was so small. What if that bull had broken through? Devin had seen it done. He'd seen the fence break and the bull charge straight into the audience.

Damn it, he should have left her up in the stands with Hanna May.

Old Jimmy darted up to him. His gnomelike face was alight with excitement. He whacked Devin on the shoulder. "Well, wasn't that a hell of a thing? How's the little miss?"

Claire straightened and pushed away from Devin. "I think I need to sit down for a minute."

"Sure, sure," Old Jimmy said. "Let's find you a seat over here behind the bleachers. Don't you worry. Devin can carry your equipment."

Devin took the camera out of Claire's hands and picked up her bag.

He was shaking.

CHAPTER 21

Claire was certain her heart was trying to break free from her chest, but at least she was now sitting on a chair and not about to collapse at Devin's feet.

"Holy crap." Claire shook her head. "No, holy fuck!" Then she clapped her hand over her mouth and laughed. Devin's mouth dropped open. He was holding her camera like it was going to pee on him. "I never say fuck, but holy fuck."

Devin knelt beside her and wrapped his fingers around her hand, stroking it, as if to soothe her. "Are you feeling okay? Maybe… God, what do they always say on TV? Put your head between your legs and take some deep breaths?"

Claire laughed. "Here, give me my camera."

Devin passed it to her, then rested his hand on her knee.

The camera was still on. She reviewed the last several photos. She'd set her camera to the high-speed sports setting, where you take a gazillion photos in an instant. "These are—wow, would you look at that?" She turned the camera to Devin, showing him a photo of the bull scraping the ground as he stared straight into the lens. Devin ignored what she was showing him, so Claire examined the picture again. The cow looked ready for revenge. Her heart thumped violently just from the image. She clicked through the images quickly. "Look at that, would you? It's like one of those flip books. Yes, that's it—a flip book movie of the cow charging us."

"Bull," Devin corrected.

"Hmm?" She zoomed in on one of the photos.

"It was a bull." Devin touched her cheek. "Look at me."

She blinked and lowered her camera. When she glanced up, his beautiful dark eyes were soft with concern.

"What's wrong?" she asked.

"I'm sorry. I should never have brought you over here. You'd have been safer up in the stands. And I shouldn't have waved to get the bull's attention." Devin pursed his lips. He was pale. Was he worried about her? He didn't need to be.

"I'm okay." Claire grinned. "Wow, that was wild, wasn't it? Is that what it was like all those years on the rodeo for you? Is it? No, I guess it wouldn't be, would it? I can't imagine it. You actually sat on top of them." She laughed. "That was fantastic."

"No, it wasn't the same." His voice was soft; his tone was serious. "Not the same at all."

She turned her camera off and put the lens cap on it. Her mind was still reeling. She hoped the pictures would look as great on her laptop as they did on the camera.

"Okay, let's go," Devin said.

"What?" She paused in the act of putting her camera in her bag.

"I'll take you home."

Claire tucked her camera into the proper compartment. "No," she said.

Then she grabbed his face with both her hands and pulled him close. She kissed him hard and full. God, his mouth was wonderful against hers. Everything faded but the feel of his body pressed to hers. His arms circled her, drawing her closer. She could lose track of the whole world when kissing him. And this time, she would let it go.

Beside them, she heard Devin's old buddy shout, "Whoop!"

Right! They were still at the rodeo! Oops. When she pulled away, Devin blinked. "You are going to take me to the beer tent and buy me a good strong drink."

The confused look on his face cleared instantly. "I don't think—"

"Okay, then, don't think. I need to buy you a drink instead." Claire laughed and patted him on the cheek. "God, I haven't felt so alive in forever."

She slipped her bag over her shoulder and stood. Her legs were as sturdy as overcooked asparagus, but the sensation made her laugh again. She fit her hand in Devin's and pulled him to the beer tent.

They served more than beer, thankfully. Claire asked for two hard alcohol tickets, but before she could give the woman at the ticket table her money, Devin paid for them. Then they waited in line at the drink table. Devin was still pale. She ordered a scotch for herself and Devin ordered himself a rye.

She swirled the golden liquid in her plastic glass before raising it to him. "Cheers."

Plastic hit plastic. It made more of a soft tick than a clink, but the process was satisfying enough.

Claire swallowed hers in one gulp. She pounded the whole thing. Then Devin swallowed his drink, too.

She grinned at him. "Do you feel better now?" she teased.

The muscle in Devin's jaw bulged. Was he clenching his teeth? That whole bull thing had affected him more than she'd have thought it would. Wasn't he the rodeo guy?

"Let's grab some burgers," Claire suggested. "I'm starving."

CHAPTER 22

Devin was at a loss. Claire was acting carefree and happy. Probably the most relaxed he'd ever seen her. Meanwhile, he was all tied up in knots. He just wanted to take her home, make sure she was safe, then head home himself.

Didn't she know what she was doing to him? Each time she brushed against him his brain replayed their time in the barn like a slo-mo porn flick. He really had to get away from her. Get her home. Safe and unmolested.

But she wasn't interested in leaving. He could have insisted, he supposed, but that dimple was on full display just now and he didn't want to do anything to make it disappear.

"I'm starving," she declared. "Can you see where they serve the food?"

Devin surveyed the beer tent over the sea of cowboy hats. There had to be food here somewhere. Then he saw the telltale plume of smoke curling through the air in the far corner. "Follow me."

Claire slid her hand in his again. She smiled up at him. "Lead away."

His heart thudded. He could almost envision a future with her.

No, he'd tried that future thing with Livy. It didn't work.

But damn, the whole thing just seemed so natural. So perfectly natural.

Instead of pulling his hand away, he squeezed hers. She leaned forward, as if she was going to grab him for another kiss.

Devin turned from her and led them through the crowd. Maybe if he got her a burger, she'd agree to leave. The next band was setting up on the makeshift stage, so the dance floor was nearly empty and the noise from the crowd filled the air. People shouted and laughed, starting to get their rowdy on. Devin pulled her across the floor in front of the maze of tables and chairs.

"Well, I'll be." A woman's voice pierced the din. "If it isn't Devin Trent."

Devin paused. Shit, it was Roy's daughter, Penny. When Roy had tracked him down earlier to do his whole AA confession thing, he'd said he'd come with family. If she was there, Roy was probably in the area, too. The last thing he needed was to see Roy again. Especially after what his old partner had told him earlier.

Penny sashayed up. Yep—sashayed—that was the only word to describe the way she moved. She was all glamour and tight jeans. She had always been a bit of a looker, she'd even been a princess at the Calgary Stampede ages ago, and the last few years had certainly been kind to her.

Claire pulled away. His palm tingled with the loss.

"Hello, Penny," he said as he bent to kiss her on the cheek, but she swiveled at the last minute, and his lips met hers.

He tried to pull back, but she had circled her arms around his neck.

Penny giggled and pressed her curves against him. "Ah, come on now, you need to give me a proper greeting," she whispered in his ear. "We're better friends than that, aren't we?"

He cleared his throat. With all that rubbing and mewling, she was like a cat in heat.

Then there was a light tap on his shoulder.

"Devin? I'll meet you over by the grill." The joy in Claire's voice was gone.

"Claire, wait." Devin pulled Penny's arms off him and stepped away.

Penny batted her long eyelashes and bit her bottom lip. He knew she was doing that because a lifetime ago he'd told her that would bring him to his knees. Today, it didn't do squat for him. "Claire, meet Penny."

Keeping one elegantly manicured mitt on Devin's arm, Penny turned to Claire. She boldly eyed Claire up and down. Her gaze lingered on Claire's blue sneakers. "I think you met my daddy Roy earlier. He said he'd seen someone with Helen. A friend of the family, yes?" Penny's emphasis on *of the family* wasn't lost on him, and, judging by the slight flare of Claire's nostrils, it wasn't lost on her either.

"I figured we'd run into some of Devin's *old* friends," Claire said. "How nice to meet you." Her tone was at odds with her words.

This was bad.

Penny cackled as she caressed Devin's arm. "Oh, we're a little more than friends, aren't we, sugar?"

Claire's eyes flashed with what he could only imagine was anger. He tried to step back from his past, but she followed him.

"Penny's dad and I." Devin cleared his throat again. "We used to rope. I, um—she was like a sister."

The way Claire's eyebrows rose further and further up her forehead told Devin she wasn't buying a word of it.

"Of course." Claire's tone was sweeter than his mom's fudge. She was pissed.

"How is Sadie?" Devin said. He had to do something, anything to steer the conversation in a new direction, and asking about Penny's daughter was the easiest. "The last time I saw her—shit, I think she'd just turned two. Or was it three?"

"She asks about you." Penny took her hand off him to pull out her cell phone. "She's growing faster than old Danny's beard." Her smile appeared genuine now.

Some of the tension ebbed from Devin's shoulders. At least it did until he saw Claire. He needed to finish up here, or there'd be hell to pay.

He let Penny show him a few photos of her daughter, then he nodded. "Sadie is beautiful. She's the very image of you at that age. But, listen, we were—"

Damn, Claire was gone. Devin scanned the crowd. She was too damn short. She could get lost in the throng and he'd never see her. His temples throbbed. Then the band started.

Penny shook her head. "Not a friend of the family?"

"Not exactly," Devin said. "It was good to see you."

She gave him a peck on the cheek. "If you change your mind…"

In that moment, they both seemed to understand that he wasn't going to change his mind. She didn't finish her sentence.

Devin pushed through the mob and headed to the grill in the corner. Claire wasn't there. Where would she be? The food area was set up so one table faced inside the tent, but the grill and the cooks were outside.

Devin exited the tent. Finally, there she was, waiting beside the grill. He let out a long, slow breath as he came up to her.

"Hungry?" he asked, gesturing to the two buns she held.

Claire smiled. At least he thought she did. The motion barely turned her lips. "I thought you'd be hungry for one, too."

"Thank you."

The burgers sizzled, the guy flipping meat was sweating, and black smoke filled the air. Claire didn't say anything. What could he say to tease her happiness out again?

When they'd fixed their burgers, Claire turned to enter the beer tent.

"Let's stay out here for a minute," he said.

She shrugged and followed him to an empty picnic table. The music and noise from the beer tent's patrons reverberated through the air. The sun was getting lower in the sky, but it was warm. This time of year, it'd be light and warm for hours yet.

"You slept with her, didn't you?" Her question wasn't a surprise, but she didn't look at him when she asked it. "It is none of my business, but—"

He'd just taken a bite of his burger. He chewed and tried to figure out how to answer her. Truth was usually the best option. "It was a long time ago."

"Is Sadie yours?"

"God, no." He wiped his mouth on the paper napkin. "Do you think I'd let years go by without seeing her if she was mine? What kind of man do you think I am?" He shook his head, but could see she wasn't quite finished yet. "What else do you want to know?"

Claire nodded. Her face was bright red now, like she wasn't entirely comfortable with her questions either, but couldn't stop herself from asking them. "Did you cheat on Livy?"

"Jesus." Devin looked over to where the sun was slithering behind a big poplar tree, taking cover. If only he could.

"I guess I know the answer to that." She tore off a piece of the bun and rolled it between her fingers. "It's all over your face."

"I don't have to justify anything to you." He'd given up on excuses years ago. There was no way to put a glossy finish on his behavior and make it okay. He'd cheated. He was a rotten son of a bitch. He'd messed up royally with Livy—and as his dad always used to say, a donkey couldn't deny it'd always be an ass.

"No," Claire said, "you don't."

They finished their burgers in silence.

CHAPTER 23

Claire was itching to jump out of the truck. Thank God they were finally back at Morning Lake. The drive from Bannister was only an hour, but it'd felt like forever. Devin was still brooding. She was still brooding. Together, they were a bloody gothic novel.

Why couldn't she stop thinking about that horrid, over-painted tramp mauling Devin? All the things Livy used to say about Devin had seeped over Claire's mind like a clogged, overflowing toilet. *He'd abandoned Livy, cheating with every barrel rider in the west, right when she had needed him the most.*

But Claire knew Devin. He wasn't like that, was he? Sure, he'd allowed himself to be groped and he'd admitted to cheating, but he wasn't the abandoning kind. She knew he wasn't. So why had she torn into him?

Because she was an idiot.

When Devin turned down Claire's street, the sun was floating ever closer toward the horizon and the sky was red. Her driveway and the street in front of her place were packed with cars. Oh, for crying out loud, Jay was having another party. Why tonight? Shouldn't his parents be here? It was the weekend, wasn't it? Of course, Bob and Anne must be here entertaining. *Please let it be Bob and Anne's party.*

Devin parked his truck at the first spot he could, which was two doors down from her place.

"Thank you for driving me. Don't be too mad at your mom." Claire cleared her throat. "Listen, I'm so—"

Devin pulled the keys out of the ignition and got out of the truck. Fine, he didn't want her apology. Wait, what was he doing? He circled the front of the cab and yanked open her door. "I'll walk you to your place."

"You don't have to," Claire said, regretting that she hadn't just hopped out when he'd parked. However, as much as the drive home had been awkward, she was reluctant to go and face Jay and his mob of teenagers.

He waited. She climbed out of the truck, and then they walked to the apartment. Rap music filled the street, getting louder with each step that brought them closer to her home. It was obvious Jay's parents were not having this party—they seemed excessively conservative—which meant Bob and Anne were AWOL again and the teenager was entertaining.

"Did you know about this?" Devin asked.

Claire shook her head. God, what would they break this time?

This party was bigger than the last one and noisier, too. The neighbors would probably call the police. Damn, she'd worked hard at getting to know her neighbors since Grandma died. Just when she was finally feeling part of the community—well, except for when that one old man, three doors down, referred to her as *the girl from out east*—Jay had to go jeopardize her acceptance here.

Would her neighbors start distancing themselves again because of her summer renters? Claire couldn't give up the extra income. That was the only way she could afford to keep the house and pay her bills. At times like these, she felt a twinge of regret. She could make enough money if she went back to engineering. But at what cost? She'd be miserable.

As they walked beside one car, Claire saw two people kissing in the back seat. Devin slammed his fist on the roof of the car, and the heads sprang apart.

Claire hurried to the garage. She needed to figure out how to deal with this, and Devin's presence was not going to make this easier. She couldn't think with him close. The sooner she was in her apartment, the sooner Devin would leave.

He followed her up the steps.

She fumbled with the keys. When the door opened, she set her camera bag inside before turning to him. "Thanks. Um…you can leave now."

Devin crossed his arms. "What are you going to do about this?"

"About what? The party?" She rubbed her forehead. "I'll talk to Jay."

Devin nodded. He didn't leave.

"This isn't your concern, Devin. You can go."

"If it's all the same to you, I'll stick around in case you need help."

Claire shrugged. "Suit yourself." She turned on the light in her apartment and motioned for him to enter.

"You're not going to talk to the kid now?"

She took off her glasses and cleaned them. "It is a kids' party. They'll be fine."

"You laugh off being charged by a bull, but you are scared to talk to a few teenagers?"

"No, that's not it." She put her glasses back on. "I don't want to embarrass—"

"To hell with that," Devin said. He spun on his heel and headed for the stairs.

"No, wait. I'll go have a quiet word with him now," Claire said. "He'll have been drinking, so I don't see how this is going to help, but if it'll make you happy—"

"I'm not happy about any of this."

Claire cringed. No, of course he wouldn't be happy. She wasn't either. "Stay here."

He was about to argue with her, she could tell, but the look in her eye must have convinced him.

Claire was dismayed to see the number of teenagers in her back yard— there had to be nearly a hundred people. Some kids were running naked— yep, naked—into the dark lake. She'd never had the guts to do that.

There were a lot of things she hadn't had the guts to do.

At the fire pit, flames were shooting up six feet high and some girl was throwing on another log. At that rate, their eyebrows would be singed off by the end of the night.

Claire stopped a couple heading to the driveway—probably leaving for some make out time in one of the other cars. "Where is Jay?"

"Who's that?" the girl slurred.

"The boy who's staying here." Claire clenched her teeth. They didn't even know who Jay was. Why the hell were they here? Oh, right—no parents, a fire pit and the lake.

"Oh," the boy said. "I saw him go to the house with Melody."

Her tenants deserved their privacy. Under other circumstances, Claire would have knocked before entering, but tonight the door was wide open.

"Jay? You in here?"

No answer. Claire walked into the kitchen. Opened bags of chips and spilled drinks coated the counter tops.

"Where are you?" she called out again. The music wasn't as loud inside, so he should be able to hear her. "Jay?"

Claire circled through the dining room. Where was he? Then she pushed open the door to her grandfather's den. In a blink she saw the whole thing—the knocked over bottle of vodka at Jay's feet, the pretty blonde lying across the desk with her shirt gaping open, her long tresses flowing past the edge of the desk, and Jay leaning over her, tracing one of her grandfather's glass paperweights over the girl's flat, bared stomach.

Claire squealed, darted out of the room and slammed the door shut.

She was *so* not prepared to deal with this.

With burning cheeks, she rushed out through the yard and up the stairs to her apartment. It wasn't until she was at the door she remembered Devin was in there.

She should go down again and stop them. She should have stopped them before, but she'd been too surprised. As a landlord, was she supposed to monitor her renters' sex lives? What if they were teenagers?

This was *not* part of the lease agreement.

The door swung open.

"What is it? I heard your footsteps on the stairs. What happened?"

Claire charged into the apartment, pushing Devin aside.

"Did you talk to him? They didn't turn the music down."

"I...I saw Jay. Listen, it's okay. Why...why don't you go home?"

Devin narrowed his eyes. "You didn't talk to him, did you?"

"It's okay. I'll call the cops." She probably should have done that from the start. "Yes, I'll call the cops."

"Give me five minutes," Devin said. "Where is he?"

Claire stared at him. "In the den."

Devin snapped his head in a quick nod, and then disappeared out the door. It was stupid to let him do this. She should be able to deal with this on her own, but, God, it was a relief to have someone else do it.

CHAPTER 24

"Melody Catherine Carr." Devin's voice boomed through the book-lined room. "Dress yourself and leave before I call your parents."

The girl grabbed her shirt closed and scrambled off the desk. "Uncle Dev?"

He wasn't actually Melody's uncle, but he'd known the Carrs his whole life. Shit, he'd known Melody her whole life. Since her grandparents sold their farm, her mare had been one of his boarders. He saw the girl damn near every week, and now every time he saw her he'd remember this moment.

"You better believe I'll be following you to your car to make sure you leave," Devin said. His voice was steady and calm, making Melody's eyes widen with alarm.

"Yes, sir," she said. She was still trying to button her shirt.

The boy stepped up to Devin, his face twisted in a sneer. It was hard to believe this was the same kid who had helped him muck out stalls. "What do you think you're doing?"

"She is only fifteen. Fifteen last month, right?"

Jay spun and looked at the girl. Melody's cheeks were bright red.

"You'd better hope her daddy doesn't find out about this, and I hope for your sake she is still a virgin."

"Uncle Devin!" Melody's cry of embarrassment was enough to assure him.

"Fifteen? But she said—"

"I don't care what she said." He pointed at the kid. "You are going to get rid of those people outside. You have five minutes. If they are here when I leave this house, I'll get rid of them. You don't want that. Understood?"

The boy put his hands on his hips. "I don't have to do anything you say."

"And then you are going to put this house to rights." Devin stared at the kid, who didn't do anything but stare back. Then Jay clenched his hands.

"You should think again before taking a swing at me. You wouldn't enjoy how that'd end."

"Listen to him, Jay." Melody stepped up to them. Her shirt was buttoned incorrectly. "Uncle Devin, you won't hurt him, will you?"

"Melody, you take those glass things into the kitchen and wash them." Devin pointed to the door. "Make sure you don't break them. Then you're going to put them back where you found them." He paused. "While you're gone, he and I are going to have a little discussion."

Melody didn't want to leave—he could see it in the way she pursed her lips—but she finally nodded. When she left the room, Devin closed the door. "Listen, kid, I don't know what you're thinking but you should probably know I'm going to have my way in this."

Jay's face was so red it was starting to turn a purplish color.

"You aren't my dad."

"No, I'm not. Should we call him and see what he has to say about this?"

The kid lost some of his defiance. "You can't come in here and tell me what to do."

Devin cocked his head to the side. "Is this your house?"

"It is for the summer." His chin notched up a fraction of an inch. "In fact, you are trespassing and I'm going to call the cops."

"Nice try, kid. Try again." Devin leaned against the wall.

The teenager folded his arms over his chest. "Why are you here, anyway?"

"Get these kids out of here," Devin said. "Your party is done."

"But it isn't even eleven yet." Jay's attitude had crossed from angry to pouting. This argument was nearly finished.

Devin raised his eyebrows.

"Fine." Jay picked up a bottle of vodka from the floor and took a swig. "Someone said one of the neighbors had threatened to phone the cops anyway."

Great, that'd be just great if the cops showed up. Devin reached over and grabbed the bottle from the kid's hand. "And you kept partying?"

Jay shrugged and wiped his mouth with the back of his hand.

A knock on the door interrupted Devin's reprimand. "Come in."

Devin straightened as Melody entered. She scanned Jay up and down, as if to make sure he was okay. Then Jay stormed out.

Carefully, Melody arranged the paperweights on a glass shelf behind the desk. Devin waited. When she turned to him, she didn't meet his gaze.

"How are you getting home? Do you have a ride?"

Melody nodded. "We have a DD." He'd known her long enough to see she was telling him the truth. "Nothing happened. I mean, we didn't...it didn't, you know, go that far."

Devin decided to take pity on her. "You should fix your shirt. You've missed a button or two."

She hugged her arms across her body. "Are you going to say anything to my dad?"

"Nope."

She smiled up at him then. "Thanks so—"

"But you are."

She started to protest, then her shoulders slumped and she nodded. "Listen, I told everyone to leave. I'm not sure about the summer folk, but the townies are leaving now."

"Thanks." Devin nodded. "I'll walk you to your car."

On the way through the kitchen, Devin dumped the remaining vodka down the stainless steel sink.

Melody had told the truth. By the time they walked out of the house, the music had been turned off, the fire was doused, and kids were scurrying from the yard like cats fleeing a burning barn.

There were four girls waiting for Melody at her car.

"So, Melody, did you and that hot guy get it on before—" The girl froze when she saw Devin.

God, it was Roger Cressman's kid. Devin remembered the day she was born. Roger had given him a cigar. He really didn't want to think about all these kids having sex. Did their parents suspect the shit they did?

The girls jumped in the car and were gone in less than a heartbeat. Devin stood in the driveway and looked up and down the street with his arms folded over his chest until the cars and trucks had sped away. Then he waited another minute.

Satisfied things were reasonably under control, Devin returned to the back yard. Claire still hadn't made an appearance, but he knew she was up in her apartment. Waiting. But he wasn't sure he could do that just yet. He needed to get control of his wayward impulses first.

Jay was sitting at the dark fire pit by himself. Devin almost felt sorry for the kid. It probably wasn't easy being stuck in a strange small town for the summer. To top it off, the kid didn't know anyone in Morning Lake. His parents probably didn't even realize how cruel they'd been.

Devin sat in a chair next to Jay. There was a cooler beside him. Devin opened it. A six-pack of beer and a couple of pops were tucked in some ice. Devin gave Jay a cola and he pulled out a beer for himself.

The last of the kids shouted goodbye to Jay and then they were alone.

They cracked open their drinks and stared out to the lake, where a lone kayaker cut through the calm water. Devin didn't think a kayaker, especially a solitary one, should be out on the lake this time of night, but that, at least, wasn't his problem. A few minutes after the kayaker drifted from view, Jay cleared his throat.

"I'll clean it up," Jay said.

"I know." Devin propped his feet on the fire ring.

"The gallery is boring," Jay said, as if to fill the quiet. "Uncle Peter...he and I don't get along."

Maybe the kid just needed to talk to someone. Devin took a drink from his beer. God, it was the cheap shit. It tasted musky, but he took another drink anyway.

Jay leaned back and studied the stars. "I like your horses."

Devin nodded. "Me, too."

Jay slurped at the rim of his pop can. "I guess I messed up, hey?"

Devin shrugged. "You're a kid."

"She never said she was fifteen." Jay fidgeted with the tab on his can. "I thought she was older."

Devin figured it was better not to comment on that. Jesus, little Melody had been all laid out there for Jay's pleasure. The kid was lucky she had her pants fastened and her bra in place.

Devin finished his beer in one last gulp. That shit was vile. He crushed his can and glanced up. The light was on in the windows above the garage. He should probably tell Claire what was going on, then he needed to get the hell away from here.

Jay extended his hand. "I'll take your empty."

"Thanks, kid." Devin stood and tossed the can to Jay. Jay plucked it out of the air.

When Devin walked through the opening in the hedge, he heard a rustling.

"Is it safe to come back?" a boy whispered.

"Get the hell out of here. The party isn't coming back here." Devin's voice boomed through the silent night.

"Shit, it's Mr. Trent." The boy cursed, then he and another kid ran to the street.

He was getting a hell of a reputation with the local teenagers. Devin rolled his shoulders and watched to make sure the kids weren't deking around the side yard.

He waited for a minute. Silence.

Would they return? What if they trashed the place because he'd shut down their party? Teenagers were sometimes stupid like that. He knew—he could still remember all the dumb-ass shit he'd done.

Damn it. This was going to be a long, long night.

CHAPTER 25

Devin knocked on Claire's door. When she called for him to come in, he took a deep, steadying breath before entering.

Claire was curled up on a small sofa with a book in her lap. In an instant, he knew something had changed. He'd lived as long as he had by paying attention to his instincts. It'd saved him from the unpredictable turn of a bull more times than he could count, but what was it trying to tell him about Claire?

He studied her. He didn't believe for a minute that she'd been up here reading peacefully since he'd left her, but damn, it was nice to see her. Even his self-preservation instincts couldn't argue with that.

What was it about her? Her grace? Her dimple? Her laughter? Her independence? He couldn't put a finger on it, but she soothed his soul. He sensed that if they'd met at another time, before all the hell that comes from living and hurting had cut through their lives, he could have been happy with her. He figured he could be with her all day and feel peace in his soul for every second of that time. People who found that kind of peace and love in their lives were damn lucky bastards.

He really needed to tie up those kinds of thoughts—tie them up and throw them away. After all, she hadn't even deigned to try polite conversation since they left the rodeo. He had to remember that.

"The kids are gone." Devin didn't dare step beyond the threshold. "For now."

"For now?"

"I think some of them may try to sneak back." He glanced over his shoulder at the driveway. Nothing moved in the murky shadows. "I just sent a couple of the little beggars on their way again."

"Oh," Claire said as she placed her book on a tiny white side table. There was no mistaking the furrow of worry in her forehead, and he wished he'd kept his mouth shut.

"I don't want to get in your way, but I thought I'd stick around a while and make sure they don't return. I'll—"

As Devin stepped forward, he glanced around the apartment for the first time. Jesus, was that her bed? He froze. This place had no interior walls and it was probably smaller than his travel trailer. How had he not noticed that earlier? He'd been so focused on Claire at the party he'd missed the fact that he'd been essentially hanging out in her bedroom. "I'll wait out in my truck for a bit." He cleared his throat. "Then I won't be in your way."

Claire threaded her fingers through the silky tassel of her shiny throw pillow. "You don't have to. Stick around, I mean. You've already stopped the party, so I'm sure it'll be okay. If anyone comes back, I'll call the police."

"If they retaliate because I—"

Her eyes widened. Shit, now he really had her concerned.

"I don't mean *retaliate* exactly."

"You really are one of the good guys, aren't you?" She licked her lips. Damn, why did that little action always send his blood galloping? "You'd wait out in your truck, wouldn't you? Even if I tried to send you home, you'd stay."

Devin crossed his arms. He wasn't going to let himself hope for much with Claire's good guy assessment of him. Besides, it wasn't true. "I'm not a stray that you shoo back to its owners."

Her tension seemed to ease and she managed a smile. Her dimple flashed, then disappeared again. "Come inside and close the door. You're letting in the moths."

"That's a bad idea."

Claire stood. In about three steps, she'd crossed to her sorry excuse for a kitchen and was pulling out glasses from her one bank of cupboards. Jesus, his beer fridge was bigger than the one in her kitchen. "What would you like? Coffee? Wine? I don't have any beer."

Devin swallowed. He prayed she was joking, and that his tension wasn't that obvious. He hooked his thumb toward the door. "I think I should head 'er."

She was at his side in two steps and he was too stunned to move. "Relax, okay?" She placed her petite hand on his cheek. She didn't move it—she just rested it there. "Thank you for being here."

He pushed his head into her touch just a fraction. He couldn't stop it. Her pink lips opened slightly. Neither of them moved for eight seconds at least. He should have been jumping clear by now. Then she pulled her hand back—small mercy that it was—and she swung the door shut behind him. "And if you are going to play at being the hero, I might as well make you comfortable."

He remained frozen in place, until she brushed against his arm. Then he jerked away. "I'm the same SOB you couldn't stand to talk to the whole ride from Bannister."

Claire sighed and turned to the kitchen. "Devin, just come in and sit down, okay? This has been a long day for both of us."

She'd made it clear time and again that she didn't want him, and that was a good thing. He could stay and chat for a bit, just until he felt comfortable that the kids had settled at a new party. Devin patted his pockets for gum and came up empty-handed.

"I'll have some water," he said. Other than the bed, there was only one soft piece of furniture in the place. It was a diminutive pink sofa, the size his mother called a love seat. He grabbed an armless wooden chair from the modest kitchen table and swung it around. He straddled the chair, with its back against his chest.

He drummed his fingers on the slats while he watched her pour water for him and a glass of red for her.

After she'd given him his glass, she returned to the sofa. She settled into the soft cushions, curling her bare feet up beside her. He could imagine her sitting there on a rainy night, cozy with her wine and her book.

"What were you reading?" Devin was desperate to think about some neutral topic. That seemed safe.

Claire glanced at the worn hardcover book on the table. "*Pride and Prejudice*. I read it every year."

"Oh." He wanted to find out if she read it ritually because she was lonely. He figured his mother was, and that was why she structured her life around her soaps. But maybe he didn't want to know if Claire was lonely. He might want to do something about that.

Claire should have a life filled with laughter and beauty, with someone who was worthy of being with her. Devin took a quick sip from the water, then set it down on the table behind him. "My being here is keeping you awake." He started to rise. "I'll—"

"Stay where you are." Claire's voice held more authority than he'd heard in a long time. He settled back down on the hard chair. She'd used that same tone that day in the gallery, the first time he'd met her.

Things had changed a lot since then. When had he started to care about her so much? God, he'd loved being with her at the rodeo, well, right up to that end part with Penny. Nothing had gone right after that.

But before...

He nodded slightly.

She watched him for a heartbeat or two, then her cheeks flushed. What was she thinking? Was she thinking about him? In her tiny little home with that big bed right over there? He could have her there in about three seconds, six if he stopped to kick off his boots.

He was *not* going to think about that. Devin cleared his throat.

Claire cast her gaze around her apartment. Had he mistaken it, or had she paused when she saw her bed? "I didn't think I'd like to live in such a small place."

Okay—that was *not* what he'd hoped she might say.

"When I lived in Toronto," she continued, "the rent was astronomical. You see, I always thought I required a big space. I spent most of my paycheck every month just to stay in my two-bedroom apartment. I didn't care about the view. No, for me, it was all about the square footage."

Devin watched her as she spoke. The way she waved her hand through the air was elegant. Her gestures, the turn of her wrist and the long, slender curl of her fingers mesmerized him.

"But," she continued, "I think I like this apartment, the economy of it all. It holds what I need, nothing more. Moving in here made me realize there were lots of things in my life that were clutter." Claire looked at him. "I was engaged to be married once. Did you know that?"

Married? Devin didn't answer her question; he was too busy trying to ignore the sudden tightness in his chest. Why was she telling him this? Her conversation was drifting all over hell's half acre, but there had to be a reason for it.

"He didn't quite leave me at the altar, but it was *this* close." She held her finger and thumb up so they were almost touching. "He told me after the rehearsal dinner. Family had flown in from all over the continent. I had that damn dress, heaps of decorations, and the stupid cake topper. Nobody will buy that stuff and you can't give it away because it's tainted with bad luck. At least that's what I thought at the time." She shifted in her seat and played with the hem of her T-shirt. "With so much money invested, it didn't feel right to throw it out, so I kept it in a box. A big box. Heck, I even paid a moving company to haul it all the way from Ontario. But guess what? There wasn't room for it in here." Claire gestured to the walls. "This place is all about essentials, and that box was not essential, so I got rid of it."

"I'm sor—"

"No," Claire interrupted him. "If you are going to say you're sorry, don't. My life is better without him or that stuff."

She took a sip of her wine, then swirled the red liquid in the glass. The alcohol left lines streaking down the sides of her goblet. Livy probably would have made some reference to the bouquet or the *legs* of the wine—as if anyone cared about that. But Livy wasn't here. Instead, Claire was telling him some bizarre story about moving. "Do you know why I'm telling you this?"

He shook his head slowly. He had no idea why she was confiding in him, but he did know he'd love to track down the idiot who had broken her heart and give the guy a hurt all his own. Sure, Claire was talking as if it didn't matter, but it did. Maybe she'd been able to move past the pain in a way he'd never managed to do himself, but there was no doubt she'd been hurt, badly.

"I shouldn't have asked you about Penny." Claire shook her head. "Or Livy, for that matter." Her gaze held his. The intensity of her attention warmed his body—in spite of her topic of discussion. "It is yours. Your clutter, if you will. I have, or rather I *had* my own clutter to deal with. You have yours."

She shrugged. "Now, I'm not saying those things don't matter, because they do, but they aren't essential to me. To us."

"You shouldn't use the word 'us' when talking about you and me." Devin said. There is no 'us.'" He grabbed his water and took another drink.

She tilted her head slightly, exposing a long stretch of her beautiful neck. She pulled her forefinger down the length, right along a line he wished he could kiss.

He shifted in his chair.

No. No kissing.

If he were with any other woman, he'd think she was trying to seduce him.

"I'm going to turn on this table light, okay?" Claire motioned to the lamp beside her. "I want to turn off the ceiling light. My eyes are getting tired, and the fluorescent light overhead is too much."

Who cared about the light? Hadn't she heard what he'd said? One of them had to stay sensible about this. It was usually Claire who stopped things, so it was nice to be the levelheaded one.

He really needed to leave this apartment.

Devin glanced out the window to the yard instead of watching her adjust the lighting. He had to because the more he watched her move, the more he wanted to touch her. And that wasn't going to happen, so he forced himself to watch for wayward partiers.

Moonlight cast hues of navy blue over the landscape. He couldn't see any returning teenagers yet, but he spied Jay bending by a flowerbed and it appeared as if he was holding a big garbage bag. The kid was actually cleaning up. Good for him.

The later it got, the more secure Devin was that the partiers had relocated. But what if they did come back? He would kick himself for exposing Claire to drunken, rowdy teenagers.

Who was he kidding? He couldn't make himself leave because of Claire. He wanted to be here with her. It was foolish, but it was the truth.

Then he dared to look at her again.

The small white table lamp cast a warm glow over the room. The whitewashed wooden walls and stark, utilitarian apartment felt cozy now, intimate. Claire's skin, bathed in the soft light, was golden and gorgeous.

She was always beautiful, but in this room, in this moment, she was something extraordinary, and he was the same worthless SOB he'd always been.

"That's better, don't you think?" She smiled. "But you still seem stressed."

Devin rolled his shoulders and two of his vertebrae cracked. "I'm good."

"I think you'd feel better if you sat on something more comfortable." She patted the sofa beside her.

"I said I'm good." God, if he got any closer to her, he'd probably do something stupid like try to kiss her.

CHAPTER 26

Claire wasn't sure when she'd decided to seduce Devin, but she'd be damned if she'd give up without a good solid try. She had been dropping hints like bowling balls, and it seemed he was oblivious to all of them. Considering his reputation, that was surprising.

What if he wasn't interested any longer? She studied him. No, she was sure he was interested. The way he drew his fingers over the side of his glass had her imagining his hands on her skin. She'd read somewhere that if a guy started to play with his glass it was an indication of his interest—it had something to do with circular objects and his subconscious wanting to play with breasts. Devin's hands slipped and glided over the smooth surface, rolling the glass back and forth. If the theory was correct, he was definitely interested, though he was trying desperately to deny it.

Heat licked over her skin. God, now she was thinking about his hands on her breasts. Her body tingled with awareness.

How to move him from interested to action? Claire bit her bottom lip while she considered her options.

His eyes widened a fraction, he stared at her mouth for a moment, and then he looked away from her quickly. He spent the next minute studying the throw rug at his feet as if examining the coarse weave was the most important thing in the world.

"Are you okay?" she asked.

Devin blinked. "Oh, sure."

This was going to take a more direct approach. Who would have guessed? A second later, Claire was at his side. She took the glass from him and set it on the table.

"What are you doing?"

"You're tense," she said. She circled him until she stood at his back. He was turning to see what she was up to when she picked off his cowboy hat.

"Hey! What are you doing?" He craned around as she set the hat on the table, too. "Nobody handles my hat but me."

When Claire touched him, his body went rigid. At least he'd stopped complaining about his hat. She gently nudged his face forward. "I'm just going to massage your shoulders."

His muscles tensed again, and he was ready to bolt. "No."

Ignoring his veto, Claire put her hands on his shoulders. Man alive, he had good shoulders. Probably all those steers he'd wrestled and rope he'd thrown, and then there was the bull riding. Claire traced the muscles of his shoulders through his shirt. Her hand appeared so small on that solid, bulging—what was that called again? A deltoid?—wonderful, yummy deltoid.

"Claire, don't."

She leaned against his solid, muscular back. She could melt into him.

"I want you," she whispered in his ear. Thank God he was facing the other direction, because as soon as the words were out she expected he'd run from her in disgust, and she was too scared to see the expression on his face when he did. No, she had come this far and wasn't going to give up now. Her pulse thrummed. "I'm sorry about earlier. I'm sorry about everything. I guess I was..." Was she really going to say it? "Jealous."

Devin was very still. "Whatever Penny and I had, it ended a long time ago."

Claire rested her head against his shoulder. He smelled so good—spicy, masculine and entirely delectable. She turned her face and brushed the tip of her nose along his neck. She wanted to taste him, but he was still too tense. He would pull away if she did that too soon, she just knew it.

"But Claire, it's true," Devin said slowly. "I cheated. I'm not a good man."

She felt the urge to refute him, but instead she listened to Devin's breathing, sensing that she needed to let him talk. She turned her head away from the skin that was enticingly exposed above his collar, and just hugged him.

"You don't want me. I could give you all kinds of excuses for what I did—hell, Roy gave me another one today—but none of that matters. Claire, I saw it in your eyes today. My cheating disgusts you. Remember that. If I'd been a better man, Livy would be alive."

"She died of cancer, Devin. You had nothing to do with that."

"But I did." He shook his head. "She blamed me, Claire. Livy blamed me for everything, and she was right to. She didn't tell me until it was too late. Did she tell you that? For months, she had struggled alone and I didn't have a clue. I was out at the rodeo in Strathmore when she finally called and told me. Why didn't she tell me when I'd been home earlier that week? Hell, why hadn't she told me when she was first diagnosed? I quit the rodeo when I heard. I quit Penny. I quit everything."

Had he ever talked to anyone about this? Claire didn't dare move or say anything in case he stopped. She knew in her heart that he needed this.

"Jesus, I'd known Penny nearly all my life, but we'd only been together before I dated Livy. So it was easy—too damn easy—to think about being back with her, before I found out about the…about Livy. I'd been talking to a divorce lawyer that morning. I was planning to leave Livy, marry Penny and be a daddy to that little girl of hers. Sure, I never slept with Penny while I was married to Livy, but I wanted to. Penny didn't even know what I'd been thinking, but I wanted what she promised—to be wanted, and to be a dad. In my heart, I'd already turned away from the woman I'd sworn to be faithful to. Damn it, don't you see? I'd wanted to be with a different woman. I'd *planned* to be with her that very night."

He took a deep breath. "Livy had never wished for kids. She never told me that, not until after she was sick. How does a man not know his wife despises children? That's the word she used—*despise.*"

His shoulders slumped. His voice was barely audible. "How can a man be oblivious to his wife's cancer until after it's spread and clogged up all her lymph nodes? Shouldn't I have seen it?" He bent down, his head resting on the back of the chair. "Ah, hell, why am I telling you all this?"

Claire ached at the hurt in his voice. She hugged him, wishing she could reach inside him and wipe away all his hurt and scars. "I'm sorry, Devin, so sorry for all the pain you've endured."

He stiffened again. "I deserved it, can't you see? Reap what you sow and all that." He sat up and pulled at her hands, removing them from his chest. He stood and spun around to look at her, then stepped back, away from her. "And you deserve more, a better man than I could ever be. You know that as well as I do."

Claire took a steadying breath. "I don't know about what I deserve or don't deserve, but I know what I think and what I feel. And no one, not even you, can tell me any differently."

"No, Claire." Devin shook his head. "You're wrong, trust me."

Desperation choked his voice—she ignored it. "Do you want to be with me, Devin?"

"Don't ask me a question you already have the answer to." His eyes pleaded with her to stop, and she ignored that, too.

She grabbed the bottom of her T-shirt, and in one motion, she'd cast it aside.

Devin stumbled back. "Don't." He pushed his hand through his hair.

"Look at me, Devin. You said the other day that you wanted to see me." Claire reached behind and undid the clasp on her bra, then she let the straps slide down her arms. The bra dropped to the floor with a whisper.

Excitement warred with self-consciousness. Her nipples tightened in the cool air, but her skin was warmed by her boldness. If he turned her away, she'd probably be mortified tomorrow. Tonight, though, Claire couldn't think of anything else she'd rather do than show Devin just how much she wanted to be with him.

"Sweet Jesus." Devin sucked in sharply when Claire pulled her fingers over her bared skin, tracing a slow path from her stomach to her breast. She'd never been so brash before.

And what did Devin do? He took yet another step back, until he was trapped against the kitchen counter.

"Say you still want me," she whispered as she stepped toward him. "Or say that you don't."

She approached him until she was almost touching him, until she was close enough to see the heat and desire in his eyes. This was as far as she was going to go. If he didn't act now, she'd let him leave.

Then his restraint finally cracked, and he grabbed her arms. Her pulse jumped, then raced in anticipation.

"Are you sure?" His words sounded like a plea.

"Absolutely."

His mouth came down fiercely on hers, hard with passion, hot with need. He crushed her against his chest. His hands, calloused and rough, glided over her back. Heat rippled through her.

She needed him and today, there would be no stopping. She would have Devin with her in bed, with her completely.

She pulled his shirt from his jeans, eager to have him unclothed. She wanted to rip the cloth from his body, but she'd probably shocked him enough for one night. Hell, she'd probably shocked herself enough for one night. So she undid the buttons, groping her way from one to the next until his shirt fell open. When she shoved it off his body, he groaned.

He moved his hands to the front of her jeans, ripped open her button and zipper, then forced the denim over her hips. When the pants slid to the floor, he scooped her up and carried her to the bed.

He laid her gently on the silky comforter. "You are so beautiful. Claire, I don't—"

Before he could say he didn't deserve her again, she grabbed his belt, stopping his words mid-sentence. The big shiny buckle slid easily from the notch, exposing the button beneath. A second later, Claire shoved his jeans and boxers to the floor. Devin wavered on his feet. God, she loved making this cowboy weak for her.

There he was. Beautiful. And wanting her. She ached to feel his body against hers.

She reached for him, but before she could touch him, he climbed up beside her and pushed her into the pillows. His eyes were dark with desire.

"Please," Claire said. "I want you—"

"Not yet," Devin whispered. "I've had a lot of time to think about what happened last time, and all the things I wish I'd—"

Claire reached down. This time he didn't evade her and she touched his flesh. She stroked and squeezed his hard length until a low growl vibrated from Devin's throat.

"Vixen." He grabbed her hand, then held both her wrists together, trapping them above her head in one of his hands. "You got me in your bed, and now it's my turn to have some fun."

He nudged his muscular thigh between her legs, until he pressed against her. Claire's breath came short and fast, but she kept her gaze locked on his as she opened herself to him. His black hair swept over his forehead when he pushed against her again.

She whispered his name. He smiled.

"You said you want me, Claire. Can you guess what I want? I want you to tremble when you call my name." He rubbed his face against her neck. His words were hot against her skin. "I want you to be wet and throbbing for me." His fingers traced circles around her nipple with agonizing slowness. Then his touch slid lower, over her belly. He skimmed the top of her panties.

She was still wearing her panties? Those had to go. Claire shifted under his hand, willing him to move the thin material, to rip it off.

But he didn't. His fingers followed the edge where material met skin, down between her legs, softer than a murmur. Claire opened her legs wider when he cupped her. "I want to taste you when you come against my mouth."

Claire moaned when he pushed against the material, pressed his fingers inside her a little. He rubbed and stroked her, using the friction of her panties against her.

"You want that, too, don't you?" His voice was deeper, heavy with desire. He wasn't as controlled as he'd have her believe. She writhed against him. If only she could touch him, then he'd quit teasing.

He lowered his mouth to her breast. His lips were warm when he drew her nipple into his mouth to suck it. Hard. His hand remained nestled between her thighs, and he moved his fingers in rhythm with his mouth. When he pressed his fingers deeper into her, Claire arched against him.

As he moved to flick her other nipple with his tongue, he nudged her panties aside. Then he slipped under. Her breath caught. Finally, skin met skin. His groan vibrated against her skin as he delved into her soft, wet folds.

He rose up on his elbow and watched her. He let go of her wrists then, but she couldn't move. He stroked her until she was trembling, begging for more.

"Come," he whispered in her ear. "Come for me, beautiful." He took her earlobe into his mouth. The sound of his panting breath filled her. She was so close…

When he moved away, she whimpered.

"I'm still here, beautiful." He moved into a slightly different position, then she felt his hands on her again. Devin pressed kisses along her throat as his hand slid between her legs again. This time, he slipped under her panties and plunged his fingers into her.

She reared up to meet his thrust and grabbed his shoulders, clinging to him as his hand pumped into her, faster. Urgency flashed over her. Then she shattered, crying out before she fell limp onto the mattress.

He kneaded her gently, extending the rippling bliss surging through her. He kissed her lips tenderly, then lifted himself so he could watch her.

She should have felt embarrassed. She'd never allowed any other man to watch her. She'd never wanted anyone else to see the power they might have over her in this moment, but with Devin, it wasn't about control or power. He wished to bring her pleasure.

So she let him. She didn't try to distract him from what he was doing to her. When she trembled with each lingering caress between her legs, she didn't suppress it. She probably wouldn't have been able to, even if she'd tried.

Devin kissed her cheek, her temple, her forehead. The throbbing of her orgasm was starting to fade, though he was nurturing it, trying to fan the flame. He didn't think she'd do that again, did he? She was a one-orgasm kind of girl, and even that was pushing it.

But when he crawled down her body, leaving a trail of kisses in his wake, she couldn't stop him or form the words to tell him he was wasting his time. She felt him nudge her panties down, but she didn't have the energy to raise her hips to help him. The fabric skimmed over her skin, down her legs, then off.

He cast them aside.

Then he touched her feet with his hands and her ankle with his mouth. Tingling sensations rushed over her. His tongue left a warm damp trail along her skin that cooled as he moved up her body. He caressed the sensitive flesh behind her knees, before he lifted them, bending her legs.

Her skin quivered with each new touch and kiss. Her body was coming alive again. He inserted his hands between her thighs, opening her wider to him. He left kisses, hot and wet, along the sensitive skin of her inner thigh.

He slipped his hands under her, grabbing her, kneading her flesh. Then he placed his mouth against her. This was no tentative taste, no faltering exploration. No, he used his lips and his teeth on her until she craved more, and need grew in her again.

He drove his thumb into the core of her. When Claire pressed her fingers into his hair, he paused. She saw him, with his dark hair nestled between her white legs, and nearly exploded again. The sensation of meeting his gaze while his thumb teased her in small circular rhythms was one of the most erotic things she'd ever experienced.

No!

What was she doing? Oh God, how could she have forgotten? She tried to squirm away from him. He held her tight.

She wasn't right down there. She was sick. Ill. She didn't want him so close to— Claire pushed him off and tried to slide out of his reach.

"Claire, let me please you."

"No." Tears welled in her eyes. How could you want something and fear it all at the same time? She didn't want to think about being sick. He wanted so much to please her, and now she'd ruined it. Again. "Please."

"But you liked it. What happened?" Devin rocked back on his heels. "Did I hurt you? You look scared to death. Shit. What did I do?" He scrambled off the bed. "I just tried to— Damn it, tell me what I did!"

"Everything you did was wonderful. Honestly." She was trembling, but she wasn't sure if it was from her near orgasm or from her panic. Why couldn't she forget about cancer for one night? "I think I…" What could she say to make this better? "Come back to me." Claire reached for him. "Please."

"Something is wrong. What did I do?"

"Devin, I'm so sorry." Unshed tears blurred her vision. "Please come back."

He shook his head. His whole body was shaking. "I want you, Claire, but I will not force myself on you. You said stop."

"I didn't say stop." Claire crawled toward him. Why couldn't she forget for one night? She had to make this right. She grabbed his hand and pushed it between her legs. His breath caught. "Can you feel how much I want you?"

"I don't want to hurt you. Ever."

"You won't." Tears streamed down her cheeks. Why was she crying? She didn't want to cry. "Just don't…don't do *that*, okay?"

Devin wiped her tears from her cheeks. He drew away from her grasp, where she was trying to entice him to caress her again; instead, he pulled her into an embrace. His arms were strong and warm. She rested against his chest, and she could hear his heart thunder beneath her ear. "Tell me what happened a minute ago."

"It's nothing."

Devin sighed, but he continued to hold her. He stroked her back and her hair, not erotically, as he had done a moment ago, but tenderly.

Though some of the tension in her body eased, tears formed in her eyes again. "Why are you so good to me?"

His comforting caress paused for a moment before resuming. "What happened?"

"I panicked," she said. At least it was a partial truth. "I…I'm sorry. It was stupid."

Devin tensed. "Did I scare you?"

She pulled from his embrace, and stared up into his face. "It wasn't anything to do with you. It was…" She swallowed. "You were perfect. I just got overwhelmed, I think." She glanced away from him. "I'll understand if you want to leave."

"Are you sure that's it? Are you sure I didn't hurt you?"

She nodded. "I'm sure."

"Do you want me to leave?"

Claire choked down a garbled laugh. She'd worked so hard to get him into her bed tonight, and he still wasn't sure. At least she could be truthful about that. "That's the last thing I want you to do."

Devin leaned closer to her. "I want to hold you, Claire. It doesn't have to be anything more than that."

"Make love to me, Devin. Make me forget about the rest of the world." She'd never called it making love before, but the phrase glided off her tongue. It felt right to make love with Devin instead of have sex. "Make love with me."

Devin buried his face in her hair. "You scared me."

"I'm sorry," Claire said. She guided him onto the bed.

He stretched out beside her and kissed her softly. His lips were oh, so gentle, as if he was scared to lose control, scared he was going to break her. His touch was light as a feather over her skin. The urgency that had existed a moment ago continued to simmer between them, but he seemed to be trying to suppress it.

He pulled her against him. She could almost believe, as he enveloped her in his strength, that he could ward off anything, protect her from anything. If only she'd let him. However, she knew he was holding back, as if he was trying to shield her from the full depth of his desire.

It was clear he was waiting for her to set the tone and pace of what was going to happen next. She pushed him to the mattress. He didn't resist. Instead, he watched silently as she explored his body, teasing awake the sexual beast he was trying to hide from her. She kissed, stroked and caressed him, and all the while he struggled for control, but he didn't stop her. When, at last, a groan tore through his body, ripping through his self-restraint, Claire stretched out beside him again.

"Please come inside me," Claire said between kisses. "I need you."

Devin mumbled against her mouth—it sounded like "You're killing me"—then he rolled away from her.

"Wait. Where are you going?" Claire reached for him.

"I'm getting a condom." He took her hand and slipped her forefinger into his mouth. He dragged her finger out of his mouth in a lingering pull, while his tongue teased its length. Her body tightened and quivered. She had no idea her finger had such erotic potential. "I'm not leaving you."

Claire sank back onto the bed. He bent to the floor and pulled a square packet from his jeans.

"Do you always carry those in your pocket?"

He tore the packet open and grinned at her. He pushed the condom from its foil and handed it to her. "No."

"You're asking me to put it on you?" Claire gaped at the slippery latex on her palm.

"I bought them a week ago. Let's just say I was full of wishful thinking."

"About me?" She eyed him.

"You've been the only one, in more years than I can count right now."

"Oh," she said. Her stomach fluttered at his words. "I haven't put a condom on anything since the banana in Sex Ed class."

Devin laughed. "Well then, let's get you educated, because I'm hoping this won't be the last one."

"No, I hope this isn't the last one either." It wasn't exactly a declaration of love, but Claire felt giddy nonetheless. She fumbled with the condom, remembering the process more clearly than she thought she would.

Who would have guessed it was akin to riding a bike?

CHAPTER 27

Devin couldn't help it. When Claire placed the latex against his skin, he pushed himself against her palm. His body craved her and his control was crumbling. She smiled like she understood, and his body responded by surging forward again.

After the condom was in place, Claire stretched on the mattress and extended her arms to him. This was what he had dreamed of for weeks, but if she said one word of worry, one whimper of panic, he would stop and get the hell out of there. He wanted to know why she'd cried out. He couldn't handle the thought of hurting her. He should stop and convince her to tell him what was going on.

His chest tightened. God, she was literally taking his breath away.

He wanted to tell her he loved her. It was stupid. He could not love her already—they had only known each other for a short time—so he bit his tongue until he tasted blood.

She deserved so much more than what he could offer, but she wanted him. He didn't understand why, but she did. He trembled and covered her soft warmth with his body. He was a hulk next to her. He braced. What if his weight crushed her?

God, he hadn't worried so much since he was a virgin.

She should be on top. Before he could shift, Claire draped her legs around him and yanked him closer, pulling him off balance. She laughed and nuzzled his neck. She didn't seem to mind his weight; in fact, she was wriggling beneath him, trying to position their bodies closer. But he wanted to see her. He wanted to watch her when their bodies joined. He lifted his head.

"Devin, you're bleeding." Claire brushed her finger against his mouth.

"You're beautiful," he whispered. Then he kissed her fingers where they lingered against his lips.

She blushed and drew her hand away. His body ached for hers, begging to slide deep into her. He nudged against her slick heat and her mouth opened in a small "O". Her eyes were bright in her flushed face—her tears were long gone. Her lips were red and swollen from his kisses.

When she met his gaze, her hands stilled in their exploration of his back. When he moved his hips, her eyes fluttered closed and her fingers dug into his shoulders. He pushed into her slowly, until her tight warmth enveloped him and her breath came in fleeting gasps. The orgasm he had given her was fading, but she still throbbed in random sweet vibrations against him.

She whispered his name, and he had never heard anything so sweet. He could almost pretend she was about to say she loved him.

Then, with her graceful body stretched around him, his restraint splintered. Soft, beautiful moans broke from her lips each time he thrust into her. Her hands grabbed his hips, her legs clamped around his as she urged him to go faster.

A rumbling groan ripped out of him as he rocked into her. Then she cried out as she crashed into another orgasm. Her body shuddered around him, squeezing him. Then he lost himself in her, flying over that hot edge of need into pure white joy.

His body, hot and slippery with sweat, quaked as he released himself deep inside of her. He collapsed.

When his muscles could work again, he pushed up on his elbows and tried to memorize how she looked at this moment. He wanted this every day. What would it be like to make love to her every day until she was carrying his child? Again, the words "I love you" teased his tongue.

Instead, he kissed her. Trying to let her understand, without words, what he didn't dare say. What he didn't deserve to say aloud.

CHAPTER 28

"What a wonderful way to wake up." Claire stretched. She could almost purr in the early morning sunlight splashing over the bed. Her body was trembling, but perfectly sated.

Devin lay behind her, with one arm snug against her stomach and the other beneath her head. He traced his lips along her neck.

"We could do that again." His voice was husky. Was it from want or was this how he sounded every morning?

Her still-throbbing body tingled anew at his suggestion.

"Don't you have to—" Her words ended on a gasp when Devin cupped her breast and flicked his thumb over her taut nipple. He had remained inside her, and she could feel him stirring again, getting harder with new desire.

His mouth was against her shoulder. Claire wiggled closer to him, and was rewarded when his body stiffened. His muffled groan shuddered against her skin. His hand slipped down her body.

Claire shifted, letting his fingers slide between her legs. He caressed her sensitive flesh until she shook with want.

He was full and rigid inside her again, and he started to rock. This was not the hot, demanding need they'd succumbed to when they'd first woken in each other's arms. No, this was intimate and loving.

Her body quivered and she could do nothing but feel him. He encircled her, his arms and hands in front and his hard body pressed along her back. His spicy, masculine scent mixed with the smell of their sex. The taste of his kisses was on her tongue.

With each tender stroke of his body, he exposed and cherished her. He made her vulnerable and safe at the same time.

Tears slipped down her cheeks onto his arm.

Devin pulled her closer, cradling her in his arms. He whispered in her ear, soothing, beautiful words that burrowed deep into her soul. When he

120

neared his crest, he repeated her name like an ancient, magical chant. His breath was its own caress over her skin. Then it caught on a strangled gasp, and he held her tight, carrying her with him into a trembling climax.

He cradled her in his arms while she slowly floated back to reality. Her heart ached with the love she felt. When she stirred, he eased away from her. He kissed her neck. She rolled toward him, to face him. His gaze was tender, loving, and for a moment, there was a flicker of sadness, too. He brushed the tears from her face. He didn't ask if he had hurt her. In that one look, he seemed to realize their loving had overwhelmed her.

She needed to get up—get away—before she opened her mouth and all her feelings fell out.

She tried to muster a smile. "You take the shower first. I'll make coffee."

She leaned over, gave him a peck on the cheek, then jumped away before he could pull her into another embrace. She grabbed the terry cloth housecoat she kept on a hook beside the bed and bolted away from Devin's reach.

He didn't speak, though he might have sighed. She kept her back to him to give him some privacy, but her studio apartment wasn't designed to offer solitude for more than one person. When she turned to pull the coffee from the cupboard, she glimpsed him sitting up. Her legs nearly gave out on her at the sight of his big, muscular body in her bed.

She spun around to face the counter again. She braced herself, lest her body slip to the floor and start crawling toward him. How could she want him again? So intensely?

When she heard the shower running, she allowed the panic to sweep over her for a moment—he would be out in a flash, so she didn't have more than a minute for this self-indulgence. No, she didn't love him. She couldn't. They had only known each other for a month.

No, no, no.

Claire measured out the coffee, but somewhere between the tin and the filter, most of the coffee grounds scattered over the counter. *Stop shaking.* She tossed in another spoonful. Pouring the water had much the same result.

She turned on the coffee maker, then paused to reprimand herself.

Get a grip.

She cranked on the cold water in the sink. When the stream was good and cold, she scooped a big handful and splashed her face.

The shower stopped. Shit. Claire turned off the water, then grabbed a cloth from the counter and dried her face. A moment later, Devin stepped out of the bathroom with a small purple hand towel wrapped around his narrow hips.

She tossed the dishcloth she was holding to the counter. Devin smiled at her. How did he look so calm?

"All yours," he said.

Claire nodded and moved past him, but before she could shut herself in the bathroom, he grabbed her around the waist. He pulled her tight against his damp chest, then he grinned as he leaned down to her.

"Good morning." His words were muffled against her mouth. She closed her eyes and clung to him. He smelled like her lavender shampoo. His kisses tasted like her toothpaste. It was disorienting, because what was under her hands was pure cowboy. When he pulled from her, she blinked.

"The cups are in the cupboard above the sink," Claire mumbled, then she fled to the bathroom.

The small room was humid and steamy. Devin had just been naked in here. Her imagination was alive, giving her a vivid image of his body filling the space. She shook as she cast aside her housecoat.

Claire climbed into the shower stall and turned the water to cold.

CHAPTER 29

Devin sat in a lawn chair beside the fire pit and drank his coffee. The sun was burning off an early morning mist from the lake. Mother Nature was gearing up to hit them with another hot day.

He hadn't hung around upstairs, waiting for Claire to come out of the bathroom. He figured she would need a bit of privacy. Besides, if he waited up there, there was no guarantee they'd leave that apartment until tomorrow. He couldn't get enough of her, as evidenced by that mistake this morning.

But he didn't always think clearly where Claire was concerned—particularly when her temptingly bare body was pressed against his. He should have removed himself from her and changed the condom before making love to her that second time.

He hadn't.

What kind of risk had he imposed on her? Had he subconsciously been trying to get her pregnant? That was a sobering thought.

The coffee did little to wash down the sudden bitterness in his mouth.

Devin didn't need to study a clock to know he would be late getting home. At this point, his mother knew he had not come home—and at his age, it shouldn't matter if he stayed out all night—but he was realistic enough to predict that his mother would already be surfing the internet for wedding invitations. Christ, how was he going to curb her matchmaking?

He would have to proceed straight to the barn as soon as he got home, just for his peace of mind.

"Devin?" Claire called from her door.

"I'm down here." He finished his coffee with one last swallow and rose to meet her.

She entered the yard and glanced around. "No damage? No mess?"

"I think Jay was busy last night."

Her eyes lit with appreciation. "What did you say to him to make this happen?"

Devin shrugged, then he raised his empty coffee mug. "I'll run this cup up."

He walked over to the steep stairs leading to her apartment, and Claire trailed behind him.

"Don't worry about it. I've already locked up. I'm going to be late. Why don't you leave it on the step, okay? I'll take it up when I get home tonight."

Devin stopped, but when he didn't move to place the mug where she had indicated, she yanked it from his grasp and set it down with a thump on the bottom step. "There."

He raised his eyebrows when he looked at the cup, but didn't say anything. She was obviously flustered. He fought the urge to grin as he followed her to the road—he liked that she wasn't as composed around him as she would wish. "Where is your car?"

She bit her lip. "I'm walking to work. It'll take about twenty minutes, so I need to—"

"It's Sunday," he said.

"The gallery is open." She glanced at her watch. "I'm in by myself this morning, so I have to get moving."

"I'll drive you."

She opened her mouth as if to argue, but then she nodded and followed him to his truck. It was parked in front of Mrs. Stapleton's place. The older woman was already out in the garden, with pruning shears in her hand and a big straw hat, complete with pink plastic flowers.

"Devin Trent? Is that you? Whatever are you... Oh, hello, Claire." Mrs. Stapleton waved at them. "Is that your truck, Devin? When I woke up in the night, I looked out and was wondering who could be parked in front of my place."

If his mother hadn't figured out what had happened last night, she would learn all the details about forty seconds after they jumped in his truck. There was no stopping the news from spreading now, so Devin just smiled. "You're as pretty as a daisy this morning."

"Oh, now, get on with you." Mrs. Stapleton, sporting a smile as wide as Morning Lake, adjusted the angle of her hat before returning to her deadheading.

A minute later, as Devin guided the truck down the street, Claire groaned and put her head in her hands. "What a disaster," she murmured.

"So, you never said—where is your car?"

"At the shop."

The way she spoke piqued his interest. "Routine maintenance?"

"Not exactly."

"Oh?" he asked when she didn't elaborate.

The air conditioning was off, but Claire adjusted the vent in the dashboard in front of her anyway. "Actually it might be done today."

"You took it to the place in town here?"

Claire nodded. Devin reached across the cab and opened the glove compartment. She stilled and watched his hand. He extracted one of the packs of gum and slapped the cubby closed. She didn't blink until he'd pulled his hand back to his side of the truck. He wasn't sure what she'd thought he was going to do, but he still liked that she was so aware of him.

"That's way on the outskirts. Here, why don't I drive you there now? You can pick up your car and then you will have it. Max will be there by now. I know you have to get to work, but I think you have time."

She bit her lip. Then she nodded. "Okay," she said. "Not having a car is driving me crazy."

A few minutes later, Devin followed Claire into the autobody shop. Max, the proprietor and top mechanic, was already under a car. His boots, the only part of him that was visible, were tapping against one another in time to the heavy-metal music that blared from the radio on the workbench.

Devin kicked one of the mechanic's large feet. "Hey, Max? Come out here for a minute."

Max rolled out from under the car. When he stood, he pulled his gray-streaked hair from his collar. It was long, and appeared to be tied back with a length of old packing tape.

"Heya, Devin, what can I do you for?" Max wiped his hand on a dirty rag hanging from his belt, and gave them a toothy grin.

"You finished with Claire's car?"

"Sure, sure." He crossed over and turned the radio to a mere roar instead of a blast. Then he smiled at them and shrugged, as if apologizing for the music. "That gets me going better in the morning than any cup of Joe."

"Were you able to fix it?" Claire asked.

Max looked offended. "Yes, ma'am."

"Can I pick it up now?"

Max nodded. "Yep, it's out back. Here, we'll settle up and then I'll take you around and open the gate."

"Oh, good," Claire said.

Max thumbed through the smudged and crinkled papers on his counter. "Now, I thought you'd call after I talked to Peter earlier this week. He explained it all to you, correct?"

Claire blinked at Max. Devin clenched his teeth. The idea of Max talking to Peter about Claire's car irritated Devin beyond all reason.

"Ah." Max tapped the counter. "Well, he said he'd talk to you, said to go ahead with the repair."

Claire tilted her head. "That's why I brought it here, to have it fixed. I don't understand what Peter has to do with any of this."

"Well, you see, the work came in a bit higher than we'd thought." Max scratched his temple with his thumb.

Her face paled. "Higher?"

"Now, you said you wanted it fixed. And I tried to call you. I called you at work—that was the number you'd left. That's where I talked to Peter. He said you were out. When I explained about the extent of the damage, he said he'd tell you, but to go ahead. So that's what we did."

Claire had the same look in her eye as that bull did at the rodeo, right before it charged the fence. Max glanced at Devin, as if seeking an ally, but hearing that Peter thought he could make decisions about Claire's property was enough to make Devin want to slam into things, too.

Max cleared his throat. "And it wasn't drivable the way it was. Not safe-like. I needed a decision. You see, I'm on my holiday for the next few weeks, so if I hadn't fixed it, you wouldn't have had a car." Max nodded to Devin. "Yep, the wife is making me take her to Europe. Of all the damn places in the world she'd want to go, why there?"

She didn't move. Devin wasn't sure she blinked.

"So we fixed it up for you. I talked it over with Peter, and since we couldn't get a hold of you, Peter and I agreed it'd be for the best. He said if there was a problem, you'd call. Now, Devin'll tell you that my price is fair. I'm not trying to swindle you because you're a woman or some such thing. I know what those documentary shows on TV say about mechanics, but that isn't the way I work."

Claire swallowed. "Mr…"

"Call me Max, ma'am." He gave her a toothy grin.

"Max, with all this preamble, you're making me nervous. How much do I owe you?"

He tallied the bill, then pushed it toward her.

Claire's jaw dropped when she saw the figure. "So much? But the quote…"

Max shook his head. "I see this is a bit of a surprise. So how about you pay me on a plan, something like?"

She was gripping the counter. Her knuckles were white. "But…but…"

"Max, why don't you grab the keys while I talk to Claire?"

Max nodded and wandered to the back of his shop.

"That's robbery," Claire whispered. "He quoted me half that much."

"It seems to me he made a mistake or he found more damage when he took the car apart. Now, I can tell it is a bit of a shock, but I, for one, am happy you are driving in a safe car instead of one that he just fixed to match the quote." He didn't want to think that Peter had Claire's best interests at heart, too. He would not share Claire the way he'd had to share Livy.

"So much?" Claire pulled her wallet out of her bag.

"Listen, why don't I put it on my farm account for now?"

"No," Claire said instantly. "Absolutely not."

"It's the farm account. Trust me, there is room on there. I've got everything paid up." *Finally*. But Claire didn't need to know he'd just made it into the black two months ago. "It wouldn't be any problem."

She thumbed through the credit cards in her wallet, as if doing a mental tally of how much the balance was on each. Red shot through her pale cheeks. "I don't have enough, and my insurance doesn't cover this."

Devin shrugged. "So we'll put it on my account, and we'll sort it out later."

She blinked. Tears were in her eyes. "I can't do that. It is so wrong…"

"Now, there's no need for that." Devin brushed her cheek. He wanted to gather her close.

"I should call my parents for a loan. God, they'll—"

"Just let me help you."

She stared at him for a crazy amount of time—she wasn't going to say no, was she?—then she swallowed and nodded. "But I don't want to be a burden."

"Honey, you are a beautiful, independent woman. It would be an honor for me to help you. Would you let me do that?"

More tears swelled and her lips trembled.

He couldn't resist. He pulled her into his arms and she pressed her face into his shoulder. He rubbed her back gently.

When she pulled away, she nodded. "Thank you, Devin. I don't know what I would have done."

Max had his back to them and was whistling loudly to the latest song on the radio. Devin knocked on the counter, and Max turned. Devin waved him over. Max set the keys on the counter while Devin told him to charge it to his account.

Max didn't even blink. "Done," he said a moment later. "That was some crash-up that you had. You're lucky it wasn't more serious. I suppose the insurance might have been ready to write it off if it was a little bit more."

A punch in the gut would have been easier to handle. "Accident?"

Claire pursed her lips.

"Oh, sure." Max nodded. "But it's good as new now."

Devin followed Max and Claire around to the fenced area of Max's lot, where he kept his clients' cars.

Max opened the gate, waved them through, then returned to his shop, leaving them to fetch the car.

Devin grabbed Claire and forced her to look at him. "Why didn't you tell me you were in an accident? Jesus, when did it happen? Within the last week or so? Is that why you were riding your bike into the city? Shit."

Devin pulled his hand over his face. "Is that why you were going to the hospital? You were hurt. Oh God, and then... Last night, were you sore? Did I—"

Claire put her hand over his mouth. "Devin, shhh."

His heart was ready to rip through his ribs.

When she lowered her hand from his face, she slid it along his shoulder to his arm. "I wasn't in an accident."

"But—"

Claire squeezed. "Yes, my car was in an accident, but not me. Did you see any injuries on me?" She raised her arms as if to display that she was fine. "No, you didn't, because there are none."

"I don't understand."

"Someone else took my car for a drive. They wrecked it, then they parked it back in my driveway." Claire shrugged. "I wasn't aware it'd happened until I was about to go to the hos—the city that day."

"Someone?"

"I don't know who it was."

"Jay?"

Claire glanced away. "I don't know."

"Son of a bitch. Did you report it to the police?"

"I had to fill out a report before the mechanic could work on it, but there isn't much anyone can do, is there?"

Devin wasn't too sure about that.

CHAPTER 30

The morning sun warmed Devin's back as he pounded on the door to the Underwood house. He didn't stop knocking until Jay arrived at the entry.

"What do you want?" Jay rubbed his bloodshot eyes. Creases crisscrossed his cheek, telltale signs his face had been plastered against his pillow a few seconds ago.

"You and I need to have another talk," Devin said.

"Now?" Jay yawned. "I cleaned up, didn't I?"

"Did you wreck Claire's car?"

Jay winced. That was evidence enough for Devin.

"Well, then you and I have a problem."

"Hey, I didn't—" Jay backed away, holding his hands up.

"Too late, kid, your face gave you away." Devin followed him inside.

Jay froze.

"Jesus, kid, I'm not going to hit you," Devin muttered. He pushed by Jay and went to the kitchen. It was a hell of a lot cleaner than it had been last night. "You've been busy."

Jay stumbled into the room after him. "Yeah, well, some old guy told me I had to."

"You got some lip on you." Devin suppressed a smirk as he sat down at the kitchen table.

"And quit calling me a kid, okay?" He opened a couple of cupboard doors, then closed them without even seeming to glimpse at the contents inside.

"Be straight with me, why did you crash the car?"

Jay pulled a carton of milk from the fridge and smelled the contents. He grimaced and returned the milk to the wire shelf.

"Jay, sit down."

"Fine." He slammed the fridge door, making the little jars inside clang against one another. Then he flung himself into the kitchen chair across from where Devin sat.

"Talk to me, kid."

"I didn't start off with the idea of messing with the car—"

Devin pulled out his pack of gum, slipped a piece free from the sealed wrap, and popped it into his mouth.

"Hey, can I have one?"

"Sure." He sent the pack skating over the surface of the table toward Jay. Jay helped himself and slid the package back to Devin. Then Devin waited.

"So, ah," Jay said between crunching the gum. "I didn't mean to wreck it."

"Did you tell Claire? Or your parents?"

Jay squirmed.

"I didn't think so," Devin said, leaning back in his chair.

"What are you going to do?" Jay traced the edge of the table with his forefinger. He didn't look at Devin.

"I paid the mechanic today."

Relief flashed over Jay's face, and he glanced at Devin.

"I'm not done yet," Devin said. "There was a lot of damage. It was expensive."

"Oh." The relief on Jay's face faded. He chewed, then noisily swallowed. "Why are you here?"

"I figure you owe me for the repairs."

Jay puffed up his cheeks, before letting out a long slow breath. "Uncle Peter doesn't really pay me. He says it's because we're family."

Devin stroked his chin. "We have a problem then, don't we?"

Jay's gaze darted from one side of the room to the other, as if he was trying to figure out how to extract himself from this predicament. Devin let him sweat it.

After a few minutes, Jay met Devin's gaze. "What can I do?"

"Last night you said you weren't happy at the gallery."

"Yeah." Jay shrugged. "So?"

Devin nodded. "Well, how about you work for me for the rest of the summer? We'll put your wages toward the debt you owe."

Jay's eyes grew wide. "Really?"

"Do you have a different solution?"

"Nah, it's just that I didn't think you'd...you know..." Jay picked at his fingernails. "That you'd want me after all I've done."

"Do we have a deal?" Devin stood and held out his hand.

Jay stared. Then he rose and they shook. His grip was firm, stronger than Devin would have expected. "Thank you," Jay said.

"Don't thank me yet, kid. You're going to have to work. This is the end of your vacation."

Jay tilted his jaw, a look of determination on his face. "I can do it. You watch. You won't be sorry."

"You'd better hope not." Devin patted Jay on the shoulder. "Now get dressed. You're starting in fifteen minutes."

CHAPTER 31

Claire huddled deeper under her fleece blanket and tried not to spill her tea. She hadn't taken a sip of it yet—she just cradled the cup, letting the warmth seep into her frozen fingers. It was wrong even to *think* about starting her furnace during the height of summer, but desperation was beginning to set in. Why were her toes taking so long to warm?

What a day! Thank God she hadn't needed to stay at the wedding to take candid photos at the dance. If she'd had to stand any longer in her wet socks and shoes, she'd be dipping her toes in her tea instead of drinking it. It may not be polite to say the day had been a disaster, but she was one of the hired help so she could be as objective as she wanted to be, couldn't she?

And, well, the wedding had been a disaster. It hadn't just rained—oh no, flash floods swept through downtown, the church roof leaked, and the stretch limo stalled in the middle of a gigantic puddle. The groomsmen had to carry the bride and her bridesmaids to the church, which could have been a fun photo-op if the bride hadn't been scowling and cursing through the whole endeavor. Instead, it only meant the groomsmen were soaked up to their knees. How long was it going to take to check each picture and fix them so the groomsmen's pants appeared crisp and pressed? The bride had shrieked when she'd seen them, but what had she expected?

Claire held her cup against her cheek and sighed.

Why did some brides go nuts on their wedding day? Had she been like that? True, she'd skipped the actual wedding day, but she'd had all of the rest of the planning and stress, then topped it all off by having a runaway groom. Being left so publicly had been painful and humiliating, and those emotions had overshadowed and tainted any other memory for so long that she couldn't recall if she'd been similar to today's bride. Had she been so consumed by the wedding that she'd forgotten about the marriage? Claire shifted, suddenly restless.

No, she couldn't have been like today's bride. That poor girl was unlike any bride she had ever seen. No matter how many times the mother had tried to convince the bride that rain on a wedding day was good luck, the girl wasn't buying it. In the end, the father of the bride slipped Claire a couple of extra hundreds, hoping more computer time would make at least one photo suitable to send out with the family's Christmas cards.

And wasn't that quite the challenge? The bride's eyes and nose were swollen and red from her weeping, and she'd spent most of the day scowling. How was Claire going to fix that—not to mention the fright in the groom's eyes?

Tonight, she simply wanted to get warm and dry. She'd try to adjust the pics tomorrow, after she put her check in the bank. A shiver swept over her, leaving goose bumps in its wake. Claire tucked the blanket closer around her legs. She should probably draw a hot bath, but the idea of being wet again was a huge deterrent.

Yes, that check was exactly what she needed. Most of it was earmarked for her property taxes, but at least a fraction could go toward the huge debt she owed Devin.

Devin. Claire groaned as the thought of him sent another shiver over her body, but this one was a very different kind of shiver. He'd been on her mind more than once during the day. Once she'd wondered how he'd look waiting at the end of a flower-and-ribbon bedecked church aisle.

Which was perfectly ridiculous.

Claire straightened and took the first sip of her tea, but she couldn't shake the *perfectly ridiculous* idea as easily as she should have. She hadn't seen him in a week—not that she'd been counting the days—but she changed the sheets on her bed every Saturday morning. They'd talked on the phone a couple of times, but she'd been so busy with the preparations for the wedding and then there was the fundraiser, the book and so many other things. She hadn't had any time to see him. Not that he'd been waiting at her door—he had a life, too. Still, she hadn't realized how much time had passed since he'd spent the night until she stripped the bed that morning. A week ago, she'd changed the linens before Helen picked her up for the rodeo. Today was Saturday again.

How pathetic was it that she'd been reluctant to change the bedding when she'd realized the timing? Devin's scent had lingered in that fine weave, enveloping her each night, teasing salacious dreams from her mind while she slept. She'd almost left the sheets for another week, but common sense—and cleanliness—had prevailed and the linens were changed.

Why hadn't he been waiting on her doorstep? Had he thought she was brushing him off? With so much time having passed since they'd been together, she hoped it wouldn't be awkward when they finally did manage to get together again.

Or was he done with her? Or had he been as jolted by their intimacy as she'd been?

Think about something else.

Claire wiggled her toes in her slippers. Feeling was starting to come back to them for the first time in hours. She should have paid more attention to the forecast before going to take photos of drenched, grumpy wedding attendants for the afternoon. How had Devin spent his Saturday?

Stop asking those questions.

Claire had asked herself the same thing every couple of hours every day since she'd last seen Devin at Max's autobody shop. She should call him, but the thought of his voice sent shivers down her skin, and heat flashing through her blood.

Quit it.

There had to be something in this apartment to consume her thoughts. Her gaze landed on the window over her bed. The rain had stopped for the moment, but the weatherman that morning had warned it'd probably continue to pour through the night. The sun set about nine this time of year, but with the clouds choking out the sky and the sunlight, darkness had closed over the neighborhood earlier than normal.

She'd probably be toasty warm if Devin were here. She could hop in her car and go for a visit.

And see his sweet smiling mom in his living room.

She really liked Helen, and she didn't think the older woman would have any qualms about Claire spending more time with Devin—especially given her matchmaking endeavors at the rodeo last weekend—but it would be awkward. Claire wanted to spend a bit more time alone with Devin before they had an attentive audience.

She heard a vehicle's engine. She wouldn't normally have heard it at this time of night on a Saturday, but wet weather had chased the community indoors so the street was quiet.

Wait—was someone idling in the driveway? Then a door slammed. Someone was here. Please let it be Jay's parents. They really shouldn't abandon their teenager. She'd talk to them first thing tomorrow morning. Claire pulled the blanket close and walked to the window facing the driveway.

She arrived in time to see a truck—was it Devin's?—reverse out of the driveway. The puddles glimmered under the yellowy headlights. Jay waved to the truck, then walked to the house. So, not his parents. But it couldn't be Devin, could it? She must have been mistaken about whose truck she'd seen. It was a farming town—a lot of people had pickup trucks.

Obviously Jay was making friends, quiet ones finally. He had stopped coming around the art gallery, and she had to admit that she rather missed him. That had surprised her. Peter, though, had seemed relieved when he'd advised her Jay had called to say he'd be hanging with new friends for a couple of weeks. That first day she'd come home expecting to see swarms of drunken teenagers in the yard, but the place had been empty, as it had been every day since.

Meanwhile, at the gallery, it was strange to be alone with Peter. It had never been uncomfortable before, but over the last few weeks, Peter was taking a more obvious interest in her. She'd suspected for a few months that he might be attracted to her, but it'd never been a problem. Things were changing now, and Claire wasn't sure why. Once, when she was sitting at the desk in the office, he'd come up behind her. She could have sworn that he'd brushed his fingers over her hair, but when she'd swung the desk chair around, he'd already stepped away.

Had she imagined his touch that time? It was possible, but she hadn't imagined all the other occurrences. He'd touch her on her arm or on the small of her back as he passed her. The frequency was growing, and the pressure was increasing, too—from mere brushes to near caresses. If they were in a small area like the office, she could perhaps dismiss the touching as accidental, but the gallery, where most of the wayward touching occurred, had nothing but space. She'd tried to talk to him about it twice, but customers had interrupted them both times.

God, she hated having to deal with shit like this, but it was also complicated because of how desperately she needed this job. With her car repairs, her upcoming taxes and her need to eat, her bank account was accumulating cobwebs, not cash. What was she going to do? Small towns were notorious for their lack of job opportunities, which was why so many people her age moved to the city.

Claire swished the curtain closed and returned to her sofa.

It was obvious she needed a new job, because even if she did talk to Peter and he quit all contact, it'd continue to be awkward between them. She'd leave things as is until the gala. Then she'd have to make a change.

CHAPTER 32

Devin white-knuckled his steering wheel and forced himself to drive away. Jesus, it was as if Claire had a magnet attached to her—one strong enough to be owned by a Bond super-villain—and it was pulling at him. It was taking more effort each day to drive away from the Underwood place, away from Claire. He met Jay at the curb every morning and dropped him off every night. Usually he didn't know if Claire was home or not.

Tonight, though, the light had been on in her apartment over the garage. He recognized the warm glow. It belonged to the little lamp she'd turned on when he'd stayed the night. He knew how her skin appeared under that light—beautiful, golden. Jesus, the memory alone had him hot and hard.

Before the window had slipped from his view, he'd seen her shadow. He'd had to call up every ounce of self-discipline to make it down that block. Each inch that he moved farther away from her ripped at his soul.

But he couldn't go back.

He hadn't seen her for a week. She'd kept blowing him off, saying she was too busy with the wedding and work. It was possible that she was too busy. Or, maybe she'd finally come to understand how miserable he would make her. God, he wanted her to be happy. He was falling in love with her—no, that was a lie. He loved her already.

That sounded cheesy, like some damn chick flick his mom watched on TV, but it was true. She muddled his mind and made him believe anything was possible.

But that world of possibility was a lie—one of life's many lessons.

He didn't deserve love. He'd tried explaining that, but she kept dismissing his words that night. That night, her lust and loneliness had overcome her common sense. She would come to see his love had made Livy unhappy—desperately unhappy—until all she had wanted to do was die instead of live with him.

He wouldn't wish that misery on anyone—especially not Claire. He'd protect her, even from himself.

The vast darkness of the night enveloped him as Devin kept his truck heading for home, the town lights fading in his rearview mirror.

CHAPTER 33

Even with all doors open to let in the midday heat, Devin figured the double garage was about five degrees cooler than the sizzling air outside, making it a welcome change from the flat open pasture where he'd just been. Jay was bent over the scarred and grease-stained workbench that sat against the back wall, and Devin crossed straight to him. The remnants of Claire's patio chair were strewn across the length of the wooden surface, and each piece was in varying degrees of being stripped of paint.

"How is it coming along?" Devin patted Jay on the shoulder.

"It isn't so bad." Jay shrugged, as he continued to scrape at the wood in front of him. "I think there are about six layers of paint. Most are green or white, so it's hard to tell for sure. One layer was purple."

"A slow process?"

"The chemical stripper only takes a couple of layers off at a time." Jay wiped the sweat from his brow with the back of his glove-covered hand, then he returned to his task.

"Okay, kid, why don't you finish that piece you're doing, then we'll go check the fences."

Jay frowned. "But, the chair—"

"Nah, you've been in here long enough today," Devin interrupted. "Besides, it is high time we got you up to a gallop."

Jay had been working without complaint on Claire's chair and the other chores Devin delegated to him. So Devin set aside half an hour every day to teach Jay how to ride a horse, which wasn't the most natural thing for either of them. Devin couldn't remember ever having been taught to ride, but he figured his parents had taken the time at some point. If only he could remember some kind of lesson, it'd be helpful as hell, because he had no idea where to begin. So far, teaching Jay to ride a horse was a bit like trying to teach someone to walk. Devin had no idea what to say or how to give directions—riding was just something he did. At least the kid smiled when he was on a horse, and Devin was pretty sure that didn't happen a whole lot.

Devin wanted to check the fences, anyway. Usually he'd have taken the ATV out, but the kid needed the practice riding.

Jay stopped scraping. "Really?"

"Really. Come to the barn when you're ready."

Ten minutes later, Jay was at Devin's side. "I'm done. I cleaned up the scraper and everything."

Devin nodded. "Okay, let's go. Why don't you put the saddle on by yourself?"

"Me?" Jay's eyebrows shot up.

"What's the matter?"

Jay shook his head. "Nothing."

Devin turned to retrieve his own saddle and gear, so the kid wouldn't see him smiling.

A few minutes later, Devin checked what Jay had done.

"Looks good, kid." He scratched the horse behind its ear. "Let's head out."

Jay was grinning as he climbed on the horse the way Devin had taught him.

They'd be able to check most of the fence from the ditch around the perimeter of the property, so Devin led Jay toward the road. They were at the end of the driveway when an older style minivan turned in to the farm.

Devin waved at the driver, Cathy, Melody's mother. In the passenger seat, Melody stared at Jay with her mouth gaping. When Melody saw Devin, she snapped her mouth closed. The van slowed, then stopped beside him. Cathy rolled down the car window.

"Hey, I'm glad I caught you," Cathy said. "I didn't see your mom at the Bannister rodeo. Is she doing okay?"

"She was there for a while. She's fine," Devin said. They hadn't talked much that week, but his mother hadn't seemed to care, nor had she paid much attention to his reprimand when he'd come home from Claire's the last weekend. No, she just kept biting the inside of her cheek to hide her grin. After all, it was damn obvious he hadn't come home that night, and thanks to Claire's neighbor, his mom had been informed of where he'd stayed.

God, his blood still stirred at the memory of that night.

Devin cleared his throat and tried to focus again. "Are you and Melody out for a ride?"

Cathy glanced at her watch. "I have to run to town for an appointment, but Melody's been going stir crazy. She's been grounded for a week, and I think we're both about ready to ship her off somewhere."

"*Mom.*" Melody groaned from the passenger seat.

Devin chose not to say anything on that point. Beside him, he could sense Jay's anxiety. Beneath him, his horse, Jackson, was motionless but for a few twitches of his ears, showing he wasn't immune to the tension between the teenagers.

"Hey, Dev, could Melody join you? I realize she's old enough to ride by herself, but she's on restricted privileges. Chris doesn't know I've brought her out here. But like I said, my sanity is more important." Cathy turned to her daughter. "Besides, you know what you did wrong, don't you?"

Melody looked ready to melt into her seat. "Mom, never mind, I've changed my mind. I don't want to—"

"Don't be silly," Cathy said. "I didn't drive all the way out here for you to change your mind. If you come with me, you'll pout and mope all afternoon while I do errands."

Devin patted Jackson's strong neck. "Melody, you can ride out with us if you want, but I may put you to work."

"Perfect," Cathy said.

"Perfect," Melody mumbled, her tone suggesting it was anything but. She hopped out of the van. "I'll go get Nola."

Devin nodded. This would be interesting. He wondered what Melody had told her parents. It was obviously enough to get her grounded, but Cathy hadn't spared a glance in Jay's direction.

Devin considered Jay and Melody. They were both trying to ignore one another, but Jay's face, from his neckline to his ears, was bright red, so Devin knew the kid wasn't immune to the situation either.

Should he say something? No, he'd probably done enough to the teenagers. He expected they'd figured out he wouldn't tolerate any hormonal experimentation. He didn't need to bring it up again.

Over the course of the afternoon, they fixed four sections of broken wire. Jay and Melody both knew how to handle a wire stretcher now. He'd have to go out again and pound in some new posts before winter, but the fences would hold for today.

The kids spoke to Devin, but they didn't speak to each other. They barely glanced at one another. They both worked as if they were doing penance.

Is that what he and Claire were doing, too?

CHAPTER 34

Three days after the horrible rainy Saturday, Claire decided she'd done all she could to salvage the wedding photos. She printed some of the best, then burned a DVD of all the photos. They could do what they liked with them.

The couple was on their honeymoon in Banff, but the parents had seemed pleased when Claire dropped the package at their summer cottage. The mother of the bride had oohed and aahed, murmuring repeatedly that she'd known the wedding had been beautiful. The dad had slipped Claire another hundred.

When Claire drove away from her final wedding obligation, she felt liberated. She rolled down her window and let her hand cut through the breeze as she drove. The sun was bright, the fields were turning golden and the sky was cloud-free. It was a great day to be alive.

She'd been so busy with the wedding, the rodeo and thoughts of Devin that she hadn't had the time to worry about her health. Her next procedure was a month away, but for a few days she'd felt almost normal again.

Normal.

Devin did that to her. He made her feel cherished and healthy. Her parents had certainly never done that—particularly after she *ran away to Alberta*, as her mother liked to phrase it. Wouldn't they ever understand that she wasn't returning to Ontario? She didn't want to be an engineer. She'd paid off her student loans, so there was no obligation left to make her live a lifestyle that'd made her miserable.

Her parents coddled her, reminding her with every phone call that being left by her fiancé had been a good thing. It had been years since that horrible event. Couldn't they move on?

Couldn't they accept that *she'd* moved on?

No, that was unfair to them. They loved her, wanted the best for her. They just didn't understand her decision. Claire tapped her fingers on the steering wheel. If she was honest, she probably *had* run away to Alberta. At the time, she'd convinced herself she was visiting her grandmother, then she hadn't left. It was fate, she told herself a few months later when her grandmother had been diagnosed with an aggressive form of lung cancer.

When she'd moved into the studio apartment a few months ago, it was the first time she'd actually opened those horrid wedding-filled boxes. Truth be told, she probably hadn't been ready before that.

Claire's fingers stilled. Devin hadn't so much as blinked at her story. But then again, he probably understood the pain better than her parents had. They didn't really understand why her life wasn't as perfect as their own. It wasn't their fault. It was just who they were.

Devin, on the other hand, he understood. He looked at her and he saw everything that she was and he didn't tell her that she was lacking. He thought she was beautiful, even with her faults. He accepted her as she was and didn't try to change her. He didn't even seem like he wanted to change her.

Oh, God—I love him.

She'd been trying to deny it for more than a week, but it was there—right there in her soul—and it wouldn't be ignored.

She didn't need to be a genius to conclude that his feelings for her had him spooked, but that was okay. She was a little spooked herself.

Maybe it wasn't really love. It could be something else. Lust? Loneliness? A need for comfort?

But didn't they need to know? And they wouldn't figure this out if they kept avoiding one another.

No. To take that chance now before her abnormal cell situation was resolved would be selfish, wouldn't it? What if her procedure was unsuccessful? What if she did have cancer?

If she did have cancer, wouldn't it be wonderful to have one more memory of his embrace that she could cling to during those moments of pain?

No, she couldn't think like that. Devin had been through too much.

And it *was* selfish.

Yes, he made her forget about her uncertain health. Yes, he made her forget about her money problems. And God, she wanted to forget, but it wasn't right. Claire shut off the car.

She was at Devin's place.

How did that happen?

CHAPTER 35

Claire's cheeks burned as if she had a blistering sunburn when she knocked on the front door. She was going to leave the farmyard, but she really did need to start paying Devin the money she owed. She could do this.

"Claire, honey, how are you?" Helen clapped her hands when she saw Claire on the front porch.

Could this be more uncomfortable? Helen had schemed to throw Devin in her path, and it'd worked. Devin's mother *knew* what they'd done. Sure, they weren't virginal teenagers—her parents knew she'd had sex, and Devin had been married, for pity's sake—but facing his sweet mother was awkward enough to make Claire wish she could duck and hide.

"Is Devin here?" She wished she could dunk her face in a bucket of ice, it felt so hot.

"Come in, Claire." Helen opened the door wider to let her pass.

"Thank you," she said. "Is he here? I really need to—"

"He's out in the field today." Helen led her into the kitchen.

"Oh." Claire said the word before she snapped down on her disappointment. She sat, and before she knew it, Helen had a plate of oatmeal cookies and a full pitcher of iced tea on the table. "Thank you, but I really can't stay."

Helen grinned. "I thought you might say that, but you can't blame an old woman for trying to wheedle out some news."

If she dropped and crawled under the table now, would this conversation end?

"Devin's out with the swathing machine at the old Miller place."

Claire blinked. "The Miller place?" She wasn't quite sure what a swathing machine was either, but she figured that was less important.

"Sure, honey, just head north from the drive for three miles. Then turn left. Go another five miles and the Miller place is on the right."

Claire memorized the directions.

Then Helen sent her out the door with a snack for Devin in her hand.

A few minutes later, Claire parked her car behind Devin's truck, even though he was nowhere in sight.

She got out of her car. Around her, farms and fields stretched for miles. The mountains, no longer capped in white, lined the horizon to the west. Then she saw a huge green tractor cresting the top of a hill. Her breath caught. He was coming.

The tractor circled the field, mowing down the next line of the grasses. Narrow lines of cut grass followed behind. It was all so tidy, geometric and charming in its own way.

Claire leaned against Devin's truck. If he saw her, great and if he didn't, she'd tuck the money under his truck's windshield wiper blade. The machine rumbled to a stop.

Claire's heartbeat tumbled. The air seemed oddly quiet now.

Devin opened the tractor door. The creak of the hinges shot across the quiet field. He scratched his head and stared at her, as if he didn't know what to do about her, then he climbed down and strolled across the shorn grasses toward her.

He pulled his dusty baseball cap off and knocked it against his leg. Then he put it on again.

When he got close, he nodded at her. Stubble darkened his jaw. His eyes narrowed. *Sexy, sexy, sexy.*

She could swoon—and wouldn't that be embarrassing?

"I'm sorry to pull you away from your work," Claire's words rushed out. She held the money out to him. "But here is the first installment of the money I owe you. Oh, and a treat from your mother."

Devin ignored her offerings. "Didn't Jay tell you?"

Claire stepped forward and jiggled the bills in front of him, urging him to grab them. "Here, take it."

"Jay's working off the cost of the repairs."

Claire curled the money in her fist. "What do you mean?"

She asked the question just as all the pieces fit together in her head, starting with Jay's sudden disappearance from the art gallery. God, it *had* been Devin's truck in her driveway that rainy night. He had been at the house and he hadn't come up to see her.

"I thought he'd tell you," Devin said.

"You should have told me."

He patted his shirt pockets, a scowl spread over his face. He bent down and pulled a blade of grass from the clump at his feet. As he started to chew on the end, he looked away to the horizon. "Yeah, I suppose I should have."

She waited for an explanation of his arrangement with Jay, but he kept his gaze pinned on the distant mountains. She counted to ten, then another ten. *Oh, this was ridiculous.* Claire turned and stumbled to her car. She yanked open the door and hurled the hundreds inside. The bills fluttered to the seat. She almost climbed into the car and sped away from him.

Instead, she slammed the door, then charged up to him and poked her finger against his wide chest. She'd expected him to be hot and sweaty, but his shirt was surprisingly cool under her touch, and he smelled of soap and *man.*

"So you've been avoiding me?" Claire asked. Now that she was touching him, her anger was dissipating and her body was becoming preoccupied with other, more wanton thoughts.

When he didn't answer, she pulled the grass out of his mouth and tossed it to the ground. He opened his mouth as if to speak, but then he shook his head.

"Do you remember what you said to me that day in the barn?"

Devin clenched his jaw.

"You asked me if I longed to see you…if I couldn't stay away…Well, guess what? I do long to see you, and I've had a hell of a time staying away." She flattened her hand on his chest. Now she could feel the heat of his body seeping through the material. "What do you say to that?"

Devin closed his eyes. He covered her hand with his. He leaned over and rested his forehead against hers. "I don't know what to say to that."

"This doesn't have to be difficult," Claire whispered. "It can be whatever we want it to be."

He kissed her forehead. She felt his heart thumping wildly under her touch. "You humble me." Then he wrapped his hand around hers, and they stood in silence at the side of the field.

CHAPTER 36

As he held Claire—*his* Claire—in his arms, Devin peered at the endless blue above them. A hawk soared high through the air, reveling in that great expanse. With a few flaps of its long wings, it rose higher. With Claire standing next to him in that field, he knew what that hawk experienced. He knew the cresting greatness. Everything else in this world was minuscule and unimportant at that height. It was the flight that mattered—and Devin knew he could only fly with Claire.

Claire shivered. He wrapped his arms around her. Her hand rested over his heart, as if she could mend it and make it whole with just her touch.

She tipped her face to his. The tenderness in her eyes made his resolve crumble. Devin bent and brushed his mouth over hers.

She broke the kiss after only a moment and leaned away from him. Her gaze trapped his. "Devin, I need to tell you something." Claire swallowed like she was rallying to say something important. "Since I met you, I've been…oh, I don't know how to say this. You see, I need to tell you something big because I think I l—"

"Shhh, no words."

She shook her head and started to speak again, so he traced a finger over her pink lips to silence her. She'd almost said she loved him, he was sure of it, but he couldn't let her say that. It was too binding. Too much. She needed to be able to step away from him. He should stop.

But that wasn't going to happen today. Today she was here with him. And he was that hawk.

Devin glanced at the vehicles. He couldn't make love to her beside the road where any passing truck could see them. The tractor was an option, with air-conditioning even, but it'd be damn uncomfortable, as would her tiny car and his bucket-seated truck.

"Stay here," he said. Then he went to his truck and pulled the seat forward. Sure enough, the quilt his mother had insisted he put in the truck last winter was still there. He shook it out. Then he went to the tall grasses between the three old grain bins at the edge of the field. He glanced toward the road—they'd be hidden from view. He walked on a patch, trampling a spot for them, and then he flicked the blanket, sending it billowing through the air, before it finally settled over the uneven ground.

When he looked at Claire, she had her hand over her heart. Was hers beating as fast as his?

She waded through the swaying grass and joined him. His soul broke free and climbed higher. Today he and she would be one. Today he'd let himself believe, one last time.

With her, he'd ascend, rise up from this damned life of his and grasp, if just for a few minutes, the joy he could only find in her arms.

CHAPTER 37

Claire walked to the edge of the blanket, kicked off her sandals and tossed down the paper bag she'd brought from Devin's mother. What did it say about her that being with Devin at the edge of a field was the most daring thing she'd ever done? Probably that she was horribly boring…and that she'd do anything to be with Devin.

Devin tossed his hat aside and knelt in the middle of the patchwork pattern. He presented his hand to her, beckoning her to him.

She trembled as she slipped her hand in his and he led her to the soft fabric. She wanted to tell him about her procedures and her worries as well as her love, but he'd shushed her a minute ago. And like a coward, she'd let him. But now that she knew the truth of what was in her heart, it was difficult to contain. She needed to show him if he wouldn't let her tell him.

Face to face, they let the heat of the sun warm their skin. Devin hadn't progressed from holding her hand. The tenderness between them as they gazed into one another's eyes was enough for a moment. Expectation was there, but there was no rush.

The distant caw of a bird, the vibrating buzz of the insects around them, and the faraway droning of a neighboring tractor serenaded them. Claire cradled Devin's jaw, needing to feel him. His whiskers scraped her palm when he pressed into her touch and lowered his eyelids. Licking her lips, Claire walked on her knees toward him until her body met his.

Devin's free arm circled her and hugged her closer. *This! This was what she wanted.* Their bodies were still clothed, but the heat of him exhilarated her. "Devin," she murmured.

He bent to her, brushing his lips to her temple. She opened her mouth, anticipating his kiss. Longing for it. Then he swept his lips over her cheek, finally arriving at her mouth. Claire melted into the soft, moist pressure of his tender kiss. What if he was expressing his love, too?

She smoothed her fingers down his neck. His pulse throbbed. She counted his heartbeats—one, two, three. Were hers in sync with his? It seemed as though they should be.

Devin raised his head. The corner of his mouth kicked up as he searched the line of small pearl buttons on her sundress until he found the top one. He twisted the fabric over the smooth finish of the button. Her breath hitched. With each inch of her flesh he exposed, his heart rate came faster under her fingertips.

With a leisurely pace, he undressed her. A nudge of the strip of fabric on her shoulders sent her dress billowing to her hips. A flick of his thumb had her bra unclasped and slipping to the blanket.

When her clothes were scattered around them, only then did he look away from her eyes and lean away from her touch. Sweet heat followed his gaze over her skin. "Claire, you are a gift."

She reached for him, but he evaded her.

"Let me," he said.

He removed his clothing with the same care as he'd taken with hers. Claire reclined on the blanket and watched, mesmerized, as he tugged his worn T-shirt free from his faded jeans. Then, with an achingly smooth but slow motion, he drew his shirt up, uncovering his tight abs, then his nipples. All the time he watched her. His intense, dark gaze was only hidden for a moment when he pulled the shirt over his head and cast it aside.

Anticipation bellowed through her blood—she wanted his touch, ached to feel his skin—but he stayed her with a tiny shake of his head.

He could be a striptease artist.

Seeing his chest exposed, with its smattering of dark hair leading to his belly button and lower, made Claire vibrate for more, but Devin kept his unhurried pace. When his hands moved to his belt buckle, Claire swallowed. So close. He'd be over her soon, holding her.

"Devin." Claire tried to plead with him to go faster.

Devin grinned. Reaching into his pocket, he drew out a handful of condoms and tossed them to the blanket beside her. There were at least five. She warmed at the promise resting beside her knee.

"Have your breasts ever been kissed by the sun?" The underlying tenor of his words sent shivers of sexual need over her. She shook her head. "Where is the sun kissing you, Claire? Show me."

Claire grabbed a long swaying piece of grass from beside their makeshift bed. She plucked it and twirled it in her fingers. The blade was rough and strong. She lifted it to her skin, skimming the tip of the grass across her shoulder, then outlined her collarbone with it. The leaf tickled, making her nipples harden. Devin's eyes darkened as she drew it lower, circling her breasts. On impulse, she dropped the grass. The blade slid down her belly to the ground.

She'd captivated him, and she didn't know what to do next. He'd put on a show for her—she should do something more. When Claire cupped her breasts, Devin sucked in his breath. Emboldened by the reaction, she pinched her nipples, then gasped, as arousal shot through her. Heat pooled between her legs. Claire crawled toward him. "Are you going to touch me already?"

Devin's hands were paused on his zipper. His erection was pushing against the crotch of his pants. *Soon.* His gaze was locked on where she was still touching herself. He liked this. Claire arched her back and swept both hands over her body again. She lifted the soft weight of her breasts up, as if offering her tight nipples to him. "Are you going to taste me?"

He grinned. "You look like an offering to a pagan god. Your eyes are the same color as the sky behind you. Did you know that?" He slipped the button on his jeans open. "And your body is delicious." He inched the zipper down. "I definitely plan on tasting."

When Claire stilled her hands, distracted by his words, he raised one eyebrow.

"Or were you just teasing?" His voice was deeper with his own rising excitement.

"Oh, no," Claire said. "I fully intend on carrying through with every promise." She'd meant her words to be light and flirty, but they carried a deeper meaning. She did have promises to keep with him. She'd promised herself she'd never hurt him.

"Claire?" Devin's hand was on her cheek then. She hadn't seen him close the distance between them.

"I want to hold you, Devin."

"Aw, Claire, I was just trying to slow myself down a little. When we touch—" he cleared his throat "—you undo all my self-control. Did you think—"

Claire pressed her lips to his, her breasts to his hard chest, her body to his. His skin was now warm from the sun.

In the distance, an engine rumbled. Was it getting closer? Some part of her brain registered it didn't sound like a car or truck, but then Devin was covering her body with his, and she forgot everything else. His thigh was between hers, and the coarse fabric of his jeans pressed at the junction of her legs. His scent curled around her, exciting her more.

He rubbed against her, and she dug in her heels, trying to push closer, but the hard earth beneath the slippery quilt offered no traction. Devin slid his hand under her, holding her tight against his leg. She rocked against him, wrapping her arms around his smooth shoulders. His belt buckle scraped across her belly.

Claire's eyes blurred.

"Devin, wait, my glasses."

She felt his mouth smile against her lips, and his pace quickened. Claire

150

wrenched her glasses from her face, and held the little plastic arms tight in her fist. Able to see again, she grabbed his dark hair with her free hand and forced him to meet her gaze. She didn't know why, but she needed to see what this was doing to him. Was he as moved as she was?

Intimacy wound around them. Devin brought his free hand around to cradle her head. He held her in place, surrounding her with his heat and his hardness. Her heart raced.

"I have too many clothes on," Devin whispered.

"Yes, you do," she agreed.

Devin rolled off, and shoved his pants to his knees. He flopped over and pulled his pant legs off one at a time. Anxious to see his boxers gone, too, Claire reached for him.

Shit. Her glasses dangled from her fingers—the temples were bent at an unnatural angle.

"Oh, no." She laughed. She had to set them down—somewhere she wouldn't roll on them. She crawled toward the edge of the blanket and tossed her glasses on her sandals. They slid to the dirt.

"Claire—" Devin's voice trembled. "No! Stay right there."

Claire wiggled her butt at him.

"Look at you," he whispered, as he came for her, "glistening in the sunlight. So beautiful, so—" He paused as he drifted his hand along her spine, trailed it over her, down her. He squeezed, exposing her to his view. "Are you ready for me?"

"Devin, what are you doing?" Claire rocked against him, trying to shift her position. Then his thumb skated along her crease, until he could test her moist heat. Claire trembled and clenched around his invasion.

He kissed the small of her back, while his thumb slipped easily into her. Then he switched to his fingers. They both groaned when he plunged in again. "So ready."

Claire's gasp was part sob. Words were impossible. She oscillated in time with his thrusting fingers, dropping her head to her hands. Her breasts swayed. A weak breeze floated over her like another caress.

God, she was out in a field with Devin with only the bees as witnesses and the grass as walls. She could scream, she could do anything at all, and only she and Devin would ever know. She'd always tried to stay so quiet. Even in the studio apartment with Devin, when no one could have heard, she'd still felt confined. But here, anything felt possible.

Claire whimpered, and spread her legs wider. Then words tumbled out. Naughty ones. Groans. Sobs. Devin's hand stroked her faster, urging her to do more.

"I need to be in you," Devin choked. "Stay…just…like…that…" His words were garbled between panting breaths.

She looked over her shoulder as Devin grabbed the condoms and tore open one of the square packages. His gaze was riveted on her body as he pushed the latex over his length. Claire tilted her hips, causing Devin to grunt. When she laughed at his response, he finally glanced at her face.

"I want to have you just like this. It would feel so good. So very—" Devin shook his head. "But I need to see your face. Your eyes." He stretched out on the blanket and crooked his finger, motioning her to join him.

Claire scrambled toward him, grinning. When he grabbed her by the waist, she laughed aloud. She swung her leg over and straddled him. When his hardness settled against her heat, her laughter tittered away on the breeze.

"I told you your eyes match the sky, didn't I?" Devin combed his fingers through her hair, tucking it behind her ear. Then he traced along her neck, down her arm until he could entwine his fingers with hers. A sudden urge to cling to him, to hold onto everything that was vibrating between them, rushed through her.

Instead, she squeezed his hand as she lowered onto him. The urge to tell him she loved him was overwhelming. Maybe he sensed it, because he sat up and kissed her, giving her lips something else to do.

He settled his hands on her hips. Claire lifted, then sank back down. She'd anticipated a frantic race when they'd finally joined, but this rhythm was intense in an entirely different way. The moment was deceptive in its quiet strength.

She felt cherished.

Their combined energies merged, until their delicate pace quickened. She clamped tight against him. When he moaned against her lips, it sent tingling vibrations coursing through her body and settling where they'd joined. She needed to move faster—her body craved it.

Devin must have felt it, too, because his grasp tightened on her. He leaned back on the quilt and gave her the freedom to ride him.

Claire cried out his name as she drove them to a building peak. A moment later, pleasure crashed through her in waves. She collapsed over him, and he thrust up into her one last time before his body followed hers. When his body jerked against hers, his low guttural growl broke across the quiet field.

CHAPTER 38

When the farmhouse door swung open, the familiar aromas of homemade split pea soup and sourdough bread greeted Devin. Jay stepped in behind him, but didn't catch the screen door before it slammed against the doorframe. Devin glanced at Jay, but didn't say anything.

"Sorry, I forgot."

Devin patted the kid on the back. After all, he couldn't blame him, the door's spring needed to be replaced. The Chinook winds had caught the door last winter and Devin hadn't gotten around to fixing it yet. They could do that this afternoon.

It was good to have the kid around to help: the barn was clean, the buildings were painted, and the grass was mown. The place hadn't looked so good in years—probably since his father had died. Devin and his dad had worked at those little never-ending chores together. Most of the work was done in silence, but it had been a companionable silence. Devin hadn't realized how much he had missed that until Jay started coming out to the farm.

That morning, Jay had removed the final bits of paint from Claire's chair and started to arrange the pieces for assembly. He would probably have the thing together by the end of the day. He had been disappointed to stop even now, but Helen had called them for dinner.

"It's a bit cooler today, so I put on a pot of soup," Helen said when he and Jay entered the kitchen. Without asking what they would like, she started to measure the soup into waiting bowls. As a kid, Devin had always wondered how she could serve like that and never leave a trail of drops on the counter.

"Wow, Mrs. T," Jay said. "Is that all homemade? Not from a can?" He rubbed his belly. "It smells sick in here."

The soup ladle clattered to the counter, and soup splattered across the laminate and up the side of the pot. Well, that was a first. Devin wanted to grin, but held his face straight when his mom spun around to Jay. She planted her hands on her round hips, and straightened to her full sixty-two inches. "I beg your pardon?"

Jay glanced at Devin for help, then Devin did grin. Having worked with Jay for a while now, he had almost figured out the kid's slang. "You two can sort out the generation gap on your own."

"Good," Jay corrected. "It smells good. No, great."

"Of course it does." Helen lifted her chin. "Nothing sick about it. Now, go wash up."

When Jay sped off to the washroom, Helen turned to Devin. She was smiling now. "I like that boy."

His mom had been great with Jay. She didn't say it, but Devin was sure she was starting to eye him as a surrogate grandchild. She was angry as a cornered badger about the kid having been abandoned at the lake for the summer. Jay had shrugged off her concerns, saying that his own mother had planned to stay more often but some emergencies had arisen at work. So Helen had stepped into the gap and taken it upon herself to care for the boy in any way she could. If she could figure out how to get Jay to move into the farmhouse, she'd do it.

"You work him too hard," Helen said. "The boy needs to take a break from working for a while. Take him out riding." Then she eyed Devin, pausing for effect. "Without having him fix something while he's out there."

Over the last few weeks, Devin had tried to explain to her that Jay had wanted to do more, work harder. And the kid did work hard. He wasn't scared of it like some kids.

Devin respected that.

But his mother could be right—just because the kid kept asking for more work didn't mean Devin should give it to him. It was the kid's summer holidays after all. Jay had put in enough hours that he was probably close to paying off the debt for Claire's car. They had never talked about an hourly wage, so it was hard to say.

They should talk about that. Devin got the sense that Jay would want to keep coming out here and working, regardless of the car. They would have to work out some kind of arrangement.

As they ate, Jay carried most of the conversation. The kid was getting more talkative with each meal they shared, and they had been sharing a lot. Devin's mom couldn't stand the thought of Jay eating alone. Jay said his parents put money in his account for groceries, and they expected Jay could handle it from there. Helen, of course, disagreed.

She pushed the plate of sliced bread so it sat directly in front of Jay, and he obliged by taking two more thick slabs.

"I think I can finish the chair today," Jay said between bites. "It shouldn't take more than an afternoon."

As she stirred the steaming soup in her bowl, Helen pursed her lips and silently urged Devin to intervene.

"Ah, Jay," Devin said. "Why don't you do that tomorrow?"

Jay looked up, surprised.

"Let's ride out to the south coulee this afternoon."

"Oh?" Jay mumbled, his mouth full of food.

"Jackson needs a good run."

Jay swallowed. "Okay."

Helen winked at Devin.

After lunch, Jay helped Helen with the dishes. On the way out, the kid asked if he could have a bowl of soup to take home with him for a late night snack. Helen beamed.

At the barn, Jay went out and got his horse without waiting for Devin to give him instructions. The kid was grabbing the equipment from a hook on the wall when Melody entered.

Jay dropped the bridle at the sight of the girl. Devin shook his head. He had done the same thing himself when Claire had surprised him at the barn. God, he and the kid had more in common than he would like to believe.

Melody offered Jay a whisper of a smile, which the kid completely missed because he was too busy scooping the bridle from the ground. A bright red blush stole over her cheeks. If he wasn't mistaken, she looked as if she was wearing more makeup than she normally did at the farm.

"Your mom here?" Devin said.

"Nah, she had an appointment in town."

Devin nodded. "We're heading out for a ride. Do you want to join us?"

Melody peeked at Jay, who had his head down. He was rubbing some speck of dust off the metal bit, but from Devin's angle, it was obvious that Jay was very aware of Melody's presence and was waiting to hear what she would say.

"I suppose," Melody mumbled, as she tucked a lock of hair behind her ear.

Who would have ever suspected that Devin would be chaperoning two hormonal teenagers?

A short while later, Devin dismounted Jackson so he could open the gate to the south pasture. The day was perfect for a ride—not too hot, not too cool. The sky was overcast and there was a bit of a breeze, but Devin didn't smell any rain in the air.

Just as he slid the wire loop off the gatepost, his cell phone buzzed, breaking the nearly tangible silence.

"Devin, you need to come back," his mom said. "That man is coming about the yearling. He is leaving town now."

"Now?" Devin groaned. As much as he wanted to sell the yearling, the prospect of a good hard ride was hard to surrender. "Okay, I'll be right there."

Devin studied the teens. Should he take them with him?

"Jay," he said, "jump down here. I need to talk to you a minute."

Jay glanced at Melody before obeying.

"I'm going to trust you and Melody to be together without supervision," Devin said loudly enough for Melody to hear. He looked Jay straight in the eye, and Jay didn't shirk the gaze.

The kid also didn't say anything, but color started wicking up his cheeks.

"You will be a gentleman," Devin said. This was not a request, and his tone said as much. When the kid didn't speak, Devin probed. "Do you understand what I'm talking about?"

Jay nodded. His cheeks were bright red now.

"You will not touch. You will not kiss. You will remain fully clothed."

"I know, gawd." Jay's gaze fell to his feet then. In truth, Devin was surprisingly confident Jay would treat Melody with respect, but that didn't mean it didn't hurt to remind him. Then Jay met Devin's eyes. "You can trust me."

"And be smart when you're riding. You're learning. Melody has been on a horse since she was a toddler. She is a better rider than you are. So don't be stupid. You can't do everything she can do. Okay?"

"Okay. Sheesh." Jay rubbed the back of his neck.

Devin was about to summon Melody for a similar chat, but she seemed to be ducking away from his gaze. By the pointed way she ignored him and the way she let the breeze blow her long blonde hair over her face, hiding it from him, he knew she had heard what he had said to Jay.

"I'm needed at the house, so it is all on you." Devin eyed Jay. "I'm trusting you, kid."

The kid squared his shoulders.

CHAPTER 39

The city man still had a store sticker on the ass of his jeans. What kind of man bought a pair of jeans just to go look at a mare? It was just one of the fake things about the man, whose name Devin had already forgotten.

"I'm not sure we can come to a deal," the man said, as he tapped his shiny black leather boot on the dirt and leaned against the fence. Devin was surprised the man deigned to touch the wood rail with his crisp white sleeve. In spite of his words, it was obvious the guy wanted the horse. No man like him drove this far to go away empty-handed. He was trying the kind of bargaining game they played on the reality shows his mother watched at night, and Devin hated games.

Devin adjusted his hat and watched the yearling frolic in the padlock. The man hadn't known the difference between a bay and a chestnut, for Pete's sake. To anyone with a crumb of knowledge about horses and two eyes in their head, the black points indicative of bays were dead obvious.

"Nope, I'm not sure we can," Devin said without looking at the man again. "Thanks for coming out. Do you need directions back to the city?"

"What? You aren't going to counter?"

The man had offered half the advertised price. At this point, Devin wasn't selling the yearling to this guy even if he suddenly offered the full amount, and he wasn't up for being manipulated in what should be an honest transaction.

Devin was about to explain that to him, when Melody came thundering over the field. She was bent forward, her long hair flew out behind her, and Nola's hooves beat the grassy earth.

The girl had a good seat. Devin watched for Jay to see how he was progressing, but the kid wasn't with her. Devin turned his attention back to Melody. There was something frantic about the way she urged Nola forward.

Shit. Something was wrong.

157

Devin left the city slicker standing at the fence and went to meet Melody at the gate.

"Hey, now," the man whined. "Don't walk away. We're just getting started."

Devin ignored him.

"Uncle Dev," Melody shouted. "Jay's hurt. You've got to—" Melody gasped for breath as she pulled her mare to a halt.

Shit.

Devin turned to the man. "Sorry. No deal." Then he swung to Melody, ignoring the sputtering noises from the indignant man behind him. "What happened?"

"He isn't moving. He didn't say anything when I talked to him. He's breathing, but—" Her words were punctuated with pants. Her cheeks were wet, and tears kept flowing. "Oh, God. It's horrible."

"We'll get him. It'll be okay. You need to tell me where he is."

"Down in the coulee by the big rock."

Devin knew where she was talking about—there was only one erratic in the south coulee. "Good, we can drive the truck in there."

Melody nodded.

"Jump down, Mel," Devin said. He extended his arms to Melody to help her. She trembled under his touch when he set her on the ground, so he squeezed her in a quick hug before straightening. "We're going to tie Nola to the fence, here, okay? Are you okay to return with me? Help me with Jay?"

New tears filled her eyes, cascading down her cheeks. "Y—yes."

"Good girl."

As the truck bounced over gopher holes and ruts, Devin glanced at Melody. She stared out the window and worried at the frayed cuff of her jean jacket. She hardly blinked. He shouldn't have brought her with him.

Damn it, the boy was supposed to be careful. What part of "be careful" led to not being able to move? He tried to quiz Melody on the details, but she wasn't making any sense. He should have left her at the house, but if Jay couldn't move, Devin would need help moving him.

As they descended into the coulee, Devin could see Jay's horse standing by the giant boulder. He couldn't see Jay. Jesus, had he been thrown on the rock? Fear as toxic as battery acid pooled in Devin's chest.

He had seen a lot of people thrown from animals—he was in the rodeo, for Christ's sake—but Jay barely knew how to ride let alone how to fall, not that you always had a choice.

Devin should have had them return when he couldn't accompany them. It was his fault that the kid was injured.

What if the kid was—No. He wouldn't think like that.

He parked as close as he could, then jumped out—leaving the truck running—and made for the big boulder. The diesel truck rumbled behind him, breaking whatever silence he feared he'd find on the other side of that rock.

A breeze caught the tall grasses, swaying them in a rhythmic motion that was in stark contrast to the stillness of Jay's body. He was pale, except for a darkening smudge on his cheek, but there was no blood. That had to be good. God, let it be good.

"Jay?" As Devin knelt, he watched the boy's chest to make sure it rose and fell. He reached for Jay's neck—the pulse was strong beneath Devin's touch. At least he figured it was strong because he found it immediately.

Jay's eyelids fluttered, exposing a sliver of his irises.

Devin let out the breath he had been holding. "Son of a bitch, kid, you scared me."

The boy's eyes rolled back.

"Come on," Devin said. "You gotta stay with me."

Jay moaned.

"Come on, kid. Open your eyes. What hurts?"

How long had it been since Devin had taken first aid? Too damn long. For an unresponsive, injured person, what did he need to do?

He started to check Jay's limbs. He skimmed over the boy's hands and forearms, but stopped when Jay groaned and rolled to one side. He cradled one arm with his other.

"It hurts," Jay mumbled.

"What hurts? Is it your back?"

"I landed on—" Jay tried to rise, but ended up rocking on his side instead.

"Don't move, okay?"

"My back is—" Jay's sentence was cut off with a curse as he tried to shift. Then he hit the ground and closed his eyes. Shit, had he passed out?

"Jay? Can you hear me? Talk to me."

The kid took a ragged breath, and his eyes opened a crack. Good, he was still awake. Perspiration glistened across the kid's forehead. "It...it isn't my back... Shoulder."

"Your shoulder is hurt?"

Jay bobbed his head.

Devin pulled out his Swiss army knife and ripped open Jay's sleeve. The thin cotton of his T-shirt parted like a curtain. Devin slid his fingers over Jay's shoulder. It felt mushy, like the bone was missing. Devin had felt the same thing before on his own body, and that knowledge calmed him like nothing else could. The boy would be okay.

"I think you dislocated your shoulder."

Jay's eyes bulged open.

"We need to get you to the hospital." Devin glanced to Melody, who was leaning against the rock, and motioned her closer. Her reluctance was evident from her lethargic pace.

Jay took a deep, ragged breath. "I can walk. I'm sure I can…"

Devin figured that the way Jay was moving his legs and arms had to mean his back was uninjured. The guys at the rodeo who had injured their spines didn't move so much. "Okay, let's get you sitting upright, and then we'll go from there."

Jay nodded.

With Melody on the uninjured side and Devin supporting the other, they managed to help Jay sit and then to stand. The kid wove on his feet like a drunk at closing time, but he was able to walk.

When they got Jay into the truck, Devin felt a hell of a lot better.

Melody was white. So was Jay.

"You did good, Mel." He hugged her quickly. "I'll drive you back, then we'll call your mom."

Melody agreed but started walking to Jay's horse.

"Where are you going?"

She didn't turn to him. "Someone has to take Verity home."

Devin had planned to take the horse's gear off and then leave her in the coulee for the afternoon. "You don't have to do that."

"Yes, I do." It was two tries before Melody was seated on Verity. "Go on, Uncle Dev, I'll be okay."

Devin gave in and hopped in the truck.

As he drove away, he watched Melody in the rearview mirror. She was bent over Verity's back, shaking. Shit. He didn't have time to talk her into coming with him. He had to get Jay to the hospital. Devin hit a gopher hole and the whole truck bounced. Jay cried out and huddled against the door.

Devin turned his attention to the drive in front of him. He couldn't avoid the bumps as he drove out of the coulee and over the fields, but he tried. Each time the truck jolted, Jay grunted in pain. The sound gouged a hole into Devin's soul.

He pulled out his cell phone and called his mother.

"What did you say to that man from the city?" she said before Devin could speak. "He tore out of here like a race car driver."

"Forget about the man," Devin said. "Jay's been injured."

He explained the situation, or what he knew of it, and asked his mom to call the art gallery and tell Peter to meet them at the hospital, and then to go and collect Mel.

CHAPTER 40

Devin had been to the hospital a lot lately.

Last time, when he had chauffeured Claire to her mysterious visit, he had waited in the parking lot. Today he wasn't so lucky.

At least the emergency room had not been part of his daily routine during the time when Livy had been trapped at the hospital. That said, it felt the same in here as it did in the oncology ward. It was a hospital.

Sweat trickled from his neck down his spine.

The room was packed, not surprising since a couple of ambulances screamed into the emergency loading zone as he and Jay had arrived. From the bit of conversation he had overheard, there had been some big accident on the highway.

Jay had been triaged and his injury had not made the cut, so he hadn't seen a doctor yet. The kid clutched his arm to his chest, moaned and shut his eyes.

Devin drummed his fingers on his knee. This was wrong. The kid needed to be examined. Devin went to the admitting desk for the third time.

"The kid's in pain." He hooked his thumb and pointed to Jay.

The young man behind the desk peered at Devin with a damned annoying condescension. "I understand, but—"

"He's dislocated his shoulder. Shouldn't he be—"

Behind him, Devin heard a woman call for Jay.

Devin went to the kid. "Come on, buddy. It's your turn."

When Jay tried to stand, he wobbled and pitched forward. Devin grabbed the kid before he toppled. A moment later, the nurse, an older and less aloof person than the admissions guy, was at their side with a wheelchair. She guided Jay into the seat with the ease of experience. Her competence alleviated some of Devin's concern, but when Devin went to follow Jay, the nurse turned to him.

"Are you family?"

By her tone, Devin knew what was coming, but he couldn't lie. "No, ma'am."

The nurse gestured to the waiting room. "I'll need you to stay out here."

Devin suppressed the growl rising in his throat and pivoted on his heel. He returned to his chair. Across the room, a baby was hollering. Babies should not have to be here. No one should have to be here.

Where the hell was Peter? Devin waited. He tried to eavesdrop on the staff behind the admissions desk, but no one mentioned Jay. At least he didn't hear the kid scream from the other room. Devin waited some more. Peter still wasn't there.

What were they doing with Jay? Was the kid okay in there?

With every minute he was penned there, the emergency room noises and smells crowded over him more, obliterating any relief he had felt when Jay had finally been admitted. A woman's voice droned over the intercom, but no one stopped to listen. No, everyone in the waiting room was too busy crying or whispering or moaning. How did people work here? A faint stench of vomit lingered under the more oppressive smell of antiseptic. The gag reflex sputtered at the back of his throat. He swallowed to force it to relax. Livy's last days had been in this building. Her last breath had been of this horrible air.

Livy had not wanted to stay here. She'd said she wanted to sit in her studio one last time. She'd begged him to take her home. He hadn't. The doctor had said she would be more comfortable in the hospital, but was that the best thing to have done? Why hadn't he taken her home?

Devin's leg quaked. He could not stop it.

Peter needed to get here. He'd always been lurking around when Livy was here, so why the hell wasn't he here now? He had sent Livy flowers, too. Nice flowers. Roses. Why was Devin remembering that now? A lot of people had sent flowers to Livy.

Devin had already chewed through five pieces of gum. That was all there was in the pack he had carried in his shirt. He needed more.

And he needed some fresh air.

He was pushing through the doors when Peter charged up the concrete sidewalk.

"Where the hell are you going?" Peter wagged his finger at Devin.

Devin almost grabbed that damn finger and wrenched it in half, but Claire was scurrying behind Peter and the sight of her made him pause.

"Jay has been admitted," Devin said. This was Jay's family—Peter needed to know what had happened.

"So you were running away? You no good—"

Devin's hand was in a fist. His muscles rippled as he grappled for control. Peter could go fuck himself, but Devin owed Jay some decorum.

162

Claire stepped between the men. "How is he?"

Her worry cut through Devin's rising anger. He stepped away from Peter and shoved his fist in his pocket. "He's in pain. He fell off a horse. I think his shoulder is dislocated."

"Oh, God." Claire put her hand over her mouth.

"Get out of my way." Peter shoved Devin aside and rushed into the hospital.

Devin was surprised when Claire stayed with him instead of following Peter. "Are you okay?" she asked.

"The kid is going to be fine." He hoped that would soothe her. It wasn't much, but he couldn't think—his muscles itched to take him away from here, and the stink of that waiting room filled his lungs. Devin glanced toward his truck. He was sure there was a pack of gum in the glove compartment. "You should get in there and make sure that idiot doesn't cause any problems for the staff."

"Devin? Are you leaving?"

"I'll be back," Devin said, then he left her standing on the sidewalk.

CHAPTER 41

As Claire stared at the second hand on the large round clock by the admissions desk, her glasses slid down her nose. Why had she come to the hospital? The nurses had allowed Peter in to see Jay, and Devin hadn't returned yet, so here she was, sitting by herself in another waiting room. This waiting room, however, was a lot different from the one she had been in before her colposcopy.

She pulled her glasses off and tried adjusting the arm again. It'd never be right. She flushed with the memory of what she'd been doing when the glasses had been bent. Maybe she should look into getting contact lenses.

People coughed, sneezed and held parts of their bodies. Claire crossed her arms, trying to touch as little as possible of the things around her. There was no way she would pick up one of the dog-eared magazines on the small plastic table beside her. Germs would be coating it like varnish. If only she could hold her breath, too.

She should have brought her camera—not to take pictures of the sick people—but perhaps she could have taken some generic hospital or medical photos. She needed to build a better stock photo portfolio. She'd had some success at selling the ones she had uploaded—four people had purchased her charging bull photo—but unless you were able to take that one pic that everyone wanted, you needed to have millions available to make a living at it. At least that was what the math was telling her.

Claire was still considering what she could have photographed when Peter marched through the swinging doors. His jaw was clenched. His gaze darted over the crowd in the waiting room until he saw her, then he made a beeline for her. Instead of acknowledging her, he plopped into the seat beside her.

"Where is Trent?"

Claire shrugged. She'd been wondering the same thing. "How is Jay?"

"He'll live," Peter said. He squinted at his watch. "They'll release him soon. Can you believe it? Then what am I supposed to do with him? I don't see why they can't keep him in here."

"They're releasing him? That's great." No one would want to stay in this place any longer than necessary. Her grandmother had never asked to leave after being admitted at the end, but Claire knew it'd bothered her. Hospitals served an important role, but nothing could match being home with familiar things around you. Besides, she doubted Peter would stay here with Jay, so at least the boy wouldn't be alone if he was staying at Peter's house. "So, was his injury not so bad then?"

"No, Trent was right. It was dislocated." Peter slapped the arm of his chair. "Wait 'til I get my hands on him."

"I'm sure Devin—"

"What? You're pals now?"

"I beg your pardon?" She was not about to go into the details of her life with Peter. "I'm sure Devin is as upset by all of this—"

Peter held up his hand to stop her from saying anything more. "Enough."

"Will Jay's mom be here soon?"

"No, she's at some meeting in Chicago this week."

"Oh? His dad?"

"Stepdad," Peter corrected her. "And, no, he's with her."

Claire hadn't realized that Bob was not Jay's dad, not that it mattered, but it might explain a few things about Jay's relationship with his parents.

Claire couldn't think of what else to say, so they sat in silence for a few minutes. When a tingling sensation floated over her skin, she knew that Devin had returned. She turned to him, unable to stop herself. He was leaning against a wall close to the exit, watching her. Her whole body relaxed at the sight of him. Thank God he'd come back. He was okay.

"There's Trent." Peter bolted out of his chair and headed straight for Devin.

He poked his finger into Devin's chest as Claire arrived. "You irresponsible, sorry excuse for a man."

"Peter," Claire said in hushed tones. "Stop that, we are in a hospital. These people have enough to worry about; they don't need the two of you carrying on like this."

Peter was flushed. Devin, on the other hand, appeared eerily calm. The only movement was the working of his jaw—he was probably chewing on a piece of gum.

"This is your fault," Peter continued, as if Claire had not said anything. "What was he doing out at your place anyway?"

Claire expected Devin to defend himself.

Instead, Devin nodded. "Yes, it is my fault."

No, he didn't just say that, did he? What was going on with him?

Peter's eyebrows shot up his forehead. "You admit it?"

"Don't be absurd," Claire said. "Jay fell off a horse. That isn't anyone's fault."

Devin didn't spare her a glance. Instead, he stayed focused on Peter. "I should have stayed with him."

"You left him alone? Jay doesn't know a thing about horses. He's never been on one in his life."

Devin opened his mouth as if ready to speak, but then he stopped himself.

"Oh, don't be ridiculous." Claire waved her hands through the air, as if to sweep away the stupidity. Peter was being obnoxious and Devin was just taking it. Why? Why didn't he stand up for himself? Well, if he wouldn't, she couldn't just stand here and listen to this garbage. "Jay isn't eight. He is nearly a grown man. Let him take some responsibility for this."

"Why was he out there?" Peter said. "You are reckless. I told him you were reckless. That's why he went out there to your place with Claire in the beginning. For protection. You can't be trusted. Everyone knows that."

Dark anger flashed through Devin's eyes. He glanced at Claire, then back at Peter. "Jay didn't tell you?"

"Tell me what?" Peter demanded.

"Uncle Peter? What is going on?" Jay's voice silenced the argument as they all turned to him. When the nurse stopped the wheelchair at their group, she asked Jay if this was his family. Jay nodded and she helped him stand.

God, the poor kid couldn't stand without help. Claire wanted to rush over and give him a big hug, but he hadn't acknowledged her. He was concentrating on the obvious tension between Peter and Devin. One side of Jay's face was starting to turn purple—he must have hit it when he fell—and his arm was wrapped in a sling. Deep dark circles, which may not have been so obvious except for the pallor of his cheeks, were stamped under his eyes.

Claire looked at Devin. He was white, whiter than Jay.

"Trent is—" Peter started.

"I was explaining to your uncle what happened," Devin interrupted.

Jay took a deep breath. "I'm sorry. I—"

"There is nothing for you to be sorry for," Peter said. "This is Trent's fault. He admitted it. Claire heard his confession and everything. You won't be going out to that place again. I'm sure your parents will press charges."

Claire gasped. "Really?"

"God, Mr. Trent, I'm sorry," Jay said. "I messed up again." He chewed on the inside of his cheek for a second. "Uncle Peter, you have it all wrong. Mr. Trent didn't do anything. It was my fault."

"Should we discuss this later?" Claire said. "Jay needs to rest."

Jay shook his head. "No, I have to say this first. I totally fucked up Ms. Best's car—"

When Devin crossed his arms, Jay stopped and glanced at him. Devin didn't move or say anything. The boy's cheeks flushed. Jay nodded, just a little, then he turned to Claire. "Sorry about my swearing, Ms. Best."

He cleared his throat, then turned back to his uncle to continue his story. "I totally effed up her car, so I've been working off the mechanic's bill. I didn't tell you, Uncle Peter, because you're weird about Mr. Trent. But I think you don't know him. He has been giving me riding lessons for a few weeks now, but today I didn't listen to him. I thought I could jump like Melody. It was stupid. *I* was stupid."

Confusion wrinkled Peter's forehead. "You've been lying to me? For weeks?"

"I have a debt—to both Mr. Trent and Ms. Best." Jay regarded his uncle. He was standing straight, despite his injury. No teenage slouching. "I plan to keep working at the farm until I'm all paid up." He glanced at Devin. Some of the confidence of his demeanor slipped. "Unless Mr. Trent doesn't want me out there anymore."

Claire's heart was pounding. Jay had grown so much in the last few weeks. How much of that was Devin's contribution? How much was due to his fall from the horse?

Devin nodded. "You're always welcome on the farm, as long as your family allows it, but I'm not sure I'd blame them if they don't want you out there. I was wrong to—"

"No," Jay spoke over Devin. "I'm sorry to interrupt you, Mr. Trent, but this one's all on me."

Devin pursed his lips. It was obvious to Claire that he didn't appreciate Jay shutting him out of the blame game. But why? Had being at the hospital shaken him that badly? Suddenly she was glad she hadn't told Devin about her cancer worries. There'd be time enough for that when—if—her tests came back positive.

"Let's take Jay home now," Claire said. She placed her hand in the crook of Jay's uninjured arm, and gave it a supportive squeeze before she steered him toward the door. "If you two want to join us, great. But if you want to take this outside and start throwing punches, Jay and I will see you in Morning Lake after you've finished and can pretend you're adults again."

CHAPTER 42

Devin pulled into Claire's driveway. Her window once again revealed the glowing warmth of that little lamp. Good, she was awake.

His guilt had gnawed at him all night long. He couldn't shake it. Sleep had skirted him, so he'd gotten up and finished his chores in the dark. When his restlessness remained after all that, he got in his truck to drive the edginess away. That's how he found himself sitting in front of Claire's before dawn had broken.

Jay had fessed up to the car accident. That was something, wasn't it?

But Devin couldn't shake that stupid guilt. His mind kept going in circles like that ride, the merry-go-round they used to have in the school playground—the one where if the boys got the thing going fast enough, the girls would throw up. Except this time, he was the one clinging to that metal handle, praying he wouldn't be tossed off the bloody thing and lose his lunch on his shoes.

One minute he knew Jay's accident was his fault—the riding lessons, working off the debt, not talking to the kid's parents, leaving the kids to ride alone, all of it. Then, in the next thought, he wasn't so sure. Jay liked the farm—he'd kept asking for more work and had taken responsibility for his actions. That was a hell of change in the kid. A good change.

Devin turned off his truck and leaned back in his seat.

Devin was responsible for his own life and faults, he knew that, but he also knew he was responsible for Livy's death, Jay's accident and a whole whack of other things. Wasn't he?

But unlike Livy, who'd placed blame on him with her dying breath, Jay hadn't let him take the blame, regardless of how neatly it had fit on his shoulders. The kid had seen it differently.

Truth be told, if he'd been in Jay's place, there was no way he'd let anyone else take responsibility either. In the end, Devin had had no control over what Jay did on that horse. So why was it so hard for Devin to let Jay do this?

Livy.

It always came back to Livy, even when he was sitting outside of Claire's house, staring at that light in her window.

Had he had any control over Livy? Had he dictated her actions relating to her cancer treatment? No. Had he encouraged her affairs? No. But that didn't mean he wasn't in some way responsible for her self-loathing and self-destruction.

After Livy had died, his mom had told him he was taking too much of the blame—that Livy and God were responsible for her fate. That day, he'd walked away while his mom was still speaking. The topic had never come up again.

It probably should have.

Devin rolled his shoulders, but the action did little to loosen the tightness.

The morning sky was streaked with red—never a good sign—but the sun was rising, so he should get on with it. He needed to see Claire.

There it was—he needed her.

A minute later, Claire opened her door for him. She smiled when she saw him, then leaned forward and brushed her lips over his. What would his life be like if she greeted him that way every morning as the sun was rising? Pretty damn good, that's what.

"Come in," Claire said. Behind her, the kettle was whistling on her stove.

Devin followed her to the small bank of cupboards. "How's the kid? Is he staying with Peter?"

Claire poured boiling water into a waiting mug. "Do you want some tea?"

"Nah, I'm good." Devin rolled his shoulders, and his joints cracked.

Claire dipped a tea bag a couple of times, then turned to him. The flowery scent of the tea filled the air around her. Now that he was in the apartment with her, under good lighting, he saw she appeared dead tired—as if she hadn't slept any more than he had.

"Jay is over at the house. When we arrived in Morning Lake, he said he was okay. He video-conferenced with his mom on his tablet, and told her he was fine. She believed him, so Peter did, too." Claire cleared her throat. "Then Peter left him here."

"He what?" Son of a bitch.

When Claire lifted her tea to her face, steam fogged the lenses of her glasses. She sighed, then pulled the cup away without taking a sip. "I stayed over there. It was bad. The painkillers started to wear off—oh, I don't know—about midnight or so. I gave him one of the pills the doctor had prescribed, but they didn't kick in immediately."

She carried her drink to the table by the window, then sat. She looked out at the house, as if she could see through the siding and walls and confirm Jay was still sleeping. "He didn't fall asleep again until about four."

"Did you call Peter?"

"No, there wasn't anything he could do."

Devin paced the length of her pint-sized kitchen. "You could have called me."

She set her cup on the table. "Are you okay?"

Devin didn't answer.

"It must have been hard being at the hospital," Claire said. "Do you want to talk about it?"

"I don't like hospitals." Devin shrugged. "A lot of people don't." He didn't want to talk about Livy's death. Not now. Not while his internal merry-go-round was still spinning.

Besides, Jay was the priority. What could he do for the kid? His mom would have a litter of kittens if she knew Jay was by himself. He glanced at the annual calendar that was stuck on Claire's fridge with two car-shaped magnets.

"How long will the kid be in Morning Lake? It'll be a few weeks before Jay's shoulder—" Devin stopped and examined the calendar, counting the weeks the kid's arm would need to heal. A big circle around a day in late July grabbed his eye. Under it, there was a note with a doctor's name and a time. Devin thought back. Shit. He'd picked her up from the side of the road in the rain that day.

He turned to her. She squirmed, but met his gaze.

"What's the matter?" Claire lifted her cup and started to tap it with her fingernail.

"That's what I'd like to find out." Devin pointed at the square on the calendar. "What's this?"

She looked away and kept silent. Was that any better than a lie? God, why the hell did she always avoid answering him? Why couldn't anyone tell the truth? He was getting damn tired of the lies. Livy'd never said when she was first diagnosed. Claire wouldn't keep something like that from him, would she? He studied her.

Suddenly he wasn't so sure. "Claire?"

"It was just a woman's thing."

Devin remembered the first day he'd seen her in the gallery. He'd suspected she had been making a woman's appointment. She'd seemed upset that day. Something about that appointment had her tied in knots. That could be the one marked on her calendar.

"Why won't you trust me?" He stalked across the room toward her, stopping short at her side, then dropped to his knees. Peter's words from the day before echoed in his ears: *Reckless. Irresponsible. Sorry excuse for a man.*

Can't be trusted. They were so much like Livy's constant accusations. Was that how Claire saw him, too? He had to know if she trusted him. He lifted her shaking hands from her teacup and cradled them in his own.

Claire closed her eyes for a moment, then met his stare head-on. "Okay, I should have told you. I had to go to the hospital that day to meet with a doctor...for a day procedure."

"A procedure?"

Claire nodded. A flush was creeping up her neck. "A woman's..." She swallowed. "A woman's thing. We'd only just met. It was awkward. I realize now that—"

"It's okay." Devin interrupted her. "I don't need to know the details now. You don't look like you're ready to talk about it, and I don't want to push you. But thank you." Relief flooded through him, and he hugged her, trapping her hands between them. "God, I was so scared you were going to say you'd been diagnosed with cancer."

She stiffened. "Devin?"

He hugged her tighter. "I just don't know what I would have done if that's what you'd said." His voice was shaking with an emotion he couldn't contain. He buried his head in her neck.

"I have not been diagnosed with cancer, but..." Claire hesitated. "I do have to go back again."

Devin loosened his embrace, and rocked back on his heels. Her face was bright with a flush. He knew she was still keeping something from him. He could wait. He brushed his fingers along her cheek. "I want to go with you, okay?"

Claire nodded slowly.

Devin smiled and pressed a chaste kiss on her forehead as he stood.

CHAPTER 43

Four hours had ticked by since Devin had departed from her house, and Claire still hadn't napped. Her eyes were blurry, her blood pushed through her veins like glue, but that wasn't going to stop her. So she was standing in the grocery store, contemplating the ingredients on a box of cereal and trying to pretend she was contented, like she had been before she'd gotten involved with Devin Trent. He'd made her life as stable as a stool with one missing leg, and now she couldn't even read the calorie count.

She put the box in her cart and continued down the aisle, trying to remember what else she needed to buy. Peanut butter. Right. She needed peanut butter for toast. And bread—did she have bread? She couldn't remember. Her hand shook when she reached for the small tub.

What was she going to do about Devin? He'd been like a caged animal at the hospital. Defeated and beaten. She never wanted to see him that way again. Sure, he'd been upset about Jay, but it was more than that. Livy had died there. He was obviously still upset about Livy's death. How could she have a relationship with someone who was in mourning?

Behind her, a cart's wheel squeaked. Claire jumped. Then she realized she was cradling the container of peanut butter. The woman beside her raised an eyebrow in question. Claire set the jar on the shelf and left for the next aisle.

She pushed her glasses up her nose and studied the teas. A soothing blend would help. Chamomile was good, or peppermint. The choices blurred in front of her. Why was she crying?

Claire looked at the fluorescent light overhead and blinked away the tears. After her vision cleared, she grabbed three random packages of tea and tossed them into the cart. She needed to finish shopping and return to Jay. How could Peter have left him? Everyone needed someone. Didn't he realize that? If Peter wasn't going to be there for his nephew, then Claire would be.

Jay would need to eat, too. She glanced at her groceries. She hadn't thought about feeding Jay. What did he eat?

She scooped up four random packets of potato chips. Wait. She should buy healthy food, shouldn't she? She shoved the bags back in place and headed for the fresh produce area.

She needed to stock up on leafy green vegetables anyway. An article on her homepage had said those would help prevent cancer. But what if it was too late? What if prevention wasn't an issue anymore?

God, she couldn't put Devin through another cancer ordeal. She remembered too well the horror of her grandmother's cancer and death. There was nothing to do but watch.

She choked down the panic that was so quick to rise in her chest. Devin had gotten so angry with her when he'd seen the appointment on her calendar. She'd tried to tell him about her tests, but he'd been so relieved when he'd thought it wasn't about cancer. What could she say then?

He was too raw about cancer, illness and things he couldn't control. If Claire was sick, he wouldn't have control over that either. Could he survive watching her die of cancer? True, she wasn't the love of his life like Livy, but they were—what was the word?—*involved.*

She hadn't lied to him. No doctor had actually said, "You have cancer." But what would he think when he walked her into the women's health area? She couldn't remember if the word "oncology" had been on any of the signs.

God, it'd be nice to have someone to talk to though. She hadn't told anyone. Her parents would have insisted she return to Toronto immediately. Peter obviously didn't care, even about his family, so he certainly wouldn't be there for one of his employees. Devin would be upset she hadn't told him the full truth. But what if Devin pulled away from her to save himself from the hurt? She'd be a basket case.

But of course he wouldn't abandon her. She knew that. He'd be at her side, making up for all he felt he should have done for Livy.

She'd already been so self-centered with Devin. There was no other way to look at it, was there? She'd gone to him that day in the field because she'd wanted to forget. God, he'd been trying to pull away from her, trying to preserve some distance between them, and she'd cut through it and taken what she'd wanted from him.

She was an awful, horrible, selfish bitch.

Her chest ached. There seemed to be a hollow gap where her heart should have been.

Claire ignored the pain and forced two heads of romaine into a thin plastic bag. She needed to concentrate on something else. The gala and the subsequent show needed her attention—that was something at least. She could at least be certain that the show was good and pure.

Beside her, someone banged into her cart with theirs. Hers spun, the wheels shrieking in protest.

"Oh, I'm sorry," Claire said. "I'm in your way." She pulled her cart closer to the side of the aisle, then realized it was Shirley. Claire smiled.

"When will you be advertising the gala? I got an invitation, but no one else seems to know about it."

Shirley was unusually abrupt, but Claire kept a smile on her face. "We sent the first flyers out on Friday. The posters have been around town for a month or more. Peter found an online printing company for the book, and the layout has been submitted. Those should arrive before—"

"That's it? That's all you're doing?" Shirley smacked her cart into Claire's again, sending the nose of Claire's cart precariously close to a pyramid of oranges.

"I'm not sure what else to do. I phoned some of the local radio stations, but no one—" Claire grabbed the cart in case Shirley charged her again.

"Is this even a fundraiser? You say it is, but how do I know you aren't just trying to use my Olivia's precious art to make your own money, because you're a mediocre photographer?"

A slap would have been less offensive, or surprising. Before Claire could muster any response, Shirley blazed on. "You've been too busy, haven't you? Too busy getting into bed with my son-in-law." Shirley's voice was a shrill screech.

Claire gaped. She glanced around the produce displays. The two other people in the area had their ears cocked toward her. God, this was going to be all over town before dusk. "Shirley, I think—" Her whispered words were cut short.

"Don't you hush me," Shirley shouted, and pushed her fingers through her salt and pepper hair. She trembled. Had she been drinking again? That was the only explanation, wasn't it? "I heard about you and him. If I'd guessed you'd try to seduce him away, I'd never have met you out there at their house, my little girl's home. The whole town is talking about your scan—" Shirley hiccupped, "scandalous affair. One of our old neighbors, Henry Winston, saw the two of you doing it in the field, out in the open, like rabbits. Patchwork quilts are made with love and innocence, and not meant to be used to play some kind of dirty Twister on them." Shirley shook her finger at Claire. "Shame on you."

Someone had seen them? If they could identify the patchwork quilt—no, that wasn't something she needed to think about it. The sunburn she'd suffered after that afternoon was just fading, but the heat sweeping her cheeks was worse. Her face could blister with the sudden shame she felt.

Was that the plane she'd heard? Devin had tried to shield her with his body. Had he known it was a neighbor up in the sky? Claire shuddered. Even if she'd known, she wouldn't have cared in that moment. What did that say about her?

Yes, she should pull back from Devin—but not because some near stranger told her to ditch him. Channeling the strength of Elizabeth Bennet facing Lady Catherine de Bourgh, Claire straightened. "This is none of your business, Shirley." She was proud that her voice only broke once. "My relationship with Devin is mine. It has nothing to do with you or anyone else." Claire squared her shoulders. "I think you should remember that the next time I see you."

"Well, I never!" Shirley shrieked.

"Is there a problem?" A kind-faced man in a store uniform interrupted them.

"Ah, no. No problem," Claire mumbled. With a new player in this horrible play, her bluster deflated.

"She's the problem." Shirley thrust her finger at Claire. "Trying to make Devin forget my Olivia. Shame on you. Well, it won't work. Won't work at all."

"Perhaps the two of you would prefer to continue this discussion outside?"

Claire stared at the man. As he crossed his arms over his chest, his kind face morphed into a stern air worthy of the scariest bouncer, fit for the roughest nightclub. He was tossing her out of the grocery store. She'd never been thrown out of anywhere in her life. "But—"

"We can put your items aside for you." He lifted his chin, so he was peering down his nose at them.

"No...um...that's okay. " Claire grabbed her purse and bolted for the exit. She glanced back at the bunched-up reusable cloth bags she'd tucked into the corner of her cart.

"Let go of me," Shirley screamed behind her.

Nope, Claire wasn't going back. It was time to buy new bags anyway.

"Ma'am," the man said to Shirley, "I think you would prefer to return later to do your shopping."

"No, I wouldn't."

"Yes, ma'am, I insist." The man's voice boomed with a finality and authority that had Shirley abandoning her cart and following Claire.

Claire raced for her car.

CHAPTER 44

Devin rarely returned to the house in the afternoon. He'd made a practice of staying outside while his mother watched her soap operas on TV. Today, though, he was drawn to it. Thankfully, she'd gone to town to check on Jay—armed with fresh buns and beef stew—so she wasn't there to follow him around wondering what he was doing.

When Livy had first died, before Helen had moved in, he would drink himself into a stupor to find some kind of escape. More often than not, he'd wake the next morning on the floor of Livy's studio. Other than that, he'd pretty much stayed away from the room until Claire had entered his life. Today was the first time he'd gone to the room stone-cold sober and alone.

He paused at the threshold. Claire had rearranged Livy's artwork. The piles were more systematic now, organized by size and shape, than when Livy had worked there. Her large workbench, which was just an oversized table, sat empty and clean for the first time since he'd set it up. Livy always had it covered with sketches, glass, finished pieces, unfinished pieces, you name it. He was never sure how she'd kept everything straight.

Why couldn't he remember the day he'd brought the table home? Why couldn't he remember the expression on Livy's face? She'd been happy then, hadn't she?

Devin edged into the room. Livy's presence used to be overwhelming, but he didn't feel it as much now. He inched toward one of the stacks of her work. He shifted through the top few. What was he going to do with this stuff?

And what would he do with this place if it was no longer Livy's studio?

Devin circled the room, poking at this and prodding at that. All this stuff was foreign to him. Livy had never wanted his opinion. She'd never shown him anything she'd created.

He'd kept everything all this time, thinking that at some point he'd understand, but understanding had never come. If he got rid of all this stuff, was he giving up?

Devin sat at the tiny desk. It was tidy, with a bunch of pens and pencils in a shallow cardboard box to the left. His mother had probably done that. Livy had never put anything in its proper place. Devin pulled at the desk drawer. It didn't budge. What?

He leaned over to examine the drawer. It wasn't stuck—it was locked. He brushed his finger over the brass.

Of course. Livy always wore a key on a chain around her neck. Did he still have it?

A minute later, Devin was in his bedroom. Their bedroom. He stopped and looked around, really seeing it for the first time in years. Livy was everywhere in here, too, from that stupid frilly lampshade to her clothes in the closet. He never used the closet, so he'd lived around it. But he shouldn't. Not anymore.

He yanked open the closet. Jesus, if anyone had peeked inside they'd never suspect she was gone. Her silk tops were wrapped in plastic from the drycleaner's, her purses hung on hooks on the closet wall, and her shoes were in a heap on the floor as if she'd just kicked them off. Some secondhand store would take this, wouldn't they? Livy'd had good taste, at least that's what she'd tell him all the time.

Devin grabbed as much as he could. He hauled his load downstairs and out to his truck. He tossed everything into the truck bed.

After four more trips, the closet was empty.

He sat on the bed and studied the gaping hole for a minute. Was it wrong to feel this was the right thing to do? But Livy's fancy clothes weren't why he was here.

He closed the closet on his way to the dresser.

Her jewelry box was sitting precisely in the middle of his chest of drawers on a dainty doily—exactly as she'd left it. Devin pried open the lid. He'd never investigated that ornate little box before, yet he'd seen it every day for years.

Earrings, necklaces and bracelets formed a jumble of chains and hoops. He didn't remember much of the stuff in there. He pushed the contents around until he discovered the key. He pulled it out, but the chain was tangled in with the rest.

Devin growled and scooped up the box. The surface of the dresser appeared odd to him now, barren with its limp lace that didn't belong anymore either. He wiped the top of the bureau with the bit of cloth, then crushed it in his fist.

Back in Livy's studio, he tossed the doily into a plastic garbage can by the desk. Livy's multiple wire cutters were arranged on a narrow shelf over the desk. He grabbed a pair and clipped the key free from the other jewelry, then pushed the jewelry box aside.

He shoved the key into the lock before he allowed himself to reconsider. The drawer opened. He yanked the drawer out and carried it to the workbench, where he dumped the contents.

Coins rolled off the table and clattered to the linoleum floor, a few heavier objects thudded to the surface, but most of the drawer was filled with paper. Was it wrong to do this? If Livy had wanted him to see this, the drawer wouldn't have been locked. This was her private space. But what if there were answers in here? He couldn't throw away that chance, could he?

Devin plucked a notebook from the rest of the mess. The sketches were rough and wild. He turned the notebook for a different angle, then glanced at the stacks of her completed stained glass work. This must have been where she developed her ideas. Devin traced the strong lines with his finger. The pencil marks smudged under his touch. Had she been happy drawing this?

He was no art critic, but happiness didn't appear to have anything to do with these sketches.

Devin paused. Why couldn't he remember doing anything with Livy? Why couldn't he remember spending time with her? Laughing with her? Making love with her? They'd done all those things. They had to have done; they had been married.

He set the book to the side and picked up another. The first image was not for Livy's stained glass. It was a sketch of a man. A naked man.

The book slid from his fingers. Maybe this was a bad idea.

Devin pushed the notebook to the back of the table and grabbed a large envelope instead. The corner was marked with the Morning Lake lawyer's office. Devin slid the paperwork out. Shit, it was divorce papers. He thumbed through the pages.

Livy'd signed with the "O" of "Olivia" as an oversized, scrolling loop and a flourish over the i's. Her name looked cheerful—she'd obviously been happy to be rid of him. Bright stickies with hand-drawn happy faces marked the blank places where his signature was required.

He studied the date beside her signature. What was going on in their lives then? He couldn't remember. But she'd executed it, and it'd been done before she'd been diagnosed. Before her prestigious gallery contract.

Why hadn't she given them to him?

Had she just stayed with him to finance her show? And then, before she knew it, it was too late and she was on her deathbed? He'd always thought she'd worked so hard for the show because she believed her art would save her from the cancer, but what if it was because she wanted his money and then she'd pushed it too long? She'd believed that show in Toronto would set her up for life.

God, had he made her so unhappy that she'd ignored her chance at treatment just for the chance of financial independence and freedom from him?

Devin slid the contract back into the envelope. What else was hiding in here? A folded stack of papers with a rubber band caught his attention next. He flipped through them and discovered they were prints of emails. What would be so important that she'd need to print it? He pulled one from the stack.

Ms. Patterson—why wasn't he surprised that she hadn't used her married name?—*Thank you for your interest in our gallery...*blah, blah, blah...*our jury has reviewed the photos you sent of your work...* blah, blah...*Most of your pieces do not meet the quality of work we require, so we will have to pass on your work at this time. Please consider us in the future.*

Devin thumbed through the rest of the stack. It appeared Livy had sent photos of her work every three months for years, until the gallery finally agreed to show a selection of her work. Why had she lied?

He shook his head. Why was he still asking himself that question? Livy lied. That was what she did.

The remaining items were a random assortment, including a polished rock, a pressed flower, and a lipstick kiss on the back of—well, wasn't that interesting?—Peter's business card. Devin studied the contents as a whole. Were these things all mementoes?

He glanced at the notebook with the image of the naked man.

Should he look? Could he make himself? Wasn't it better to know?

Devin flipped it open quickly, before he lost his nerve. The shape of the drawing showed it was a man, but it wasn't clear who the subject had been. Jesus, she'd drawn that in their bedroom. That was their headboard.

The images that followed were no better, but it was clear Livy had had more than one man in his home, and they'd been naked in every damn room. Christ, he sat on that chair when he watched TV, and he ate at that table for every meal.

He recognized a drawing of Roy. Given Roy's confession at the Bannister rodeo, it wasn't a surprise, but Devin didn't need to see the proof in his own home. Then there was a sketch of Peter. No, there were more of Peter. Devin slapped the book closed.

She must have been so damn proud of herself.

So why did she cry every time he left for the rodeo? Her life was one big orgy.

Had she manipulated everyone? Him. Her mother. Those men.

He wasn't going to understand anything here. There were no answers. Livy had taken them with her. Devin grabbed the sketchbook and the divorce papers. These didn't belong in his home.

The west wind was rising. That storm the morning had warned of was coming in fast. But this couldn't be put off.

A few curls of wind twirled around the east side of the barn, but it wasn't enough to stop Devin. He tossed the book and the contract to the bare dirt, then he dug out a lighter he'd grabbed on his way through the kitchen. It took a couple of tries, but the flame finally caught hold of the pages. The wind blew out the fire three times, but Devin relit the pages each time.

When the fire had consumed the paper, Devin stared at the smoldering ashes and the remains of coiled wire. Why had he done that? Destroying the evidence? No, that wasn't it. He wasn't going to be corny and say he needed a rebirth from the fire, like some damn mythical phoenix. No, it wasn't that either.

So what was it?

Cauterizing a festering wound? That seemed more likely.

Livy had been so unhappy. She hadn't loved him. Had she ever? Considering the few memories he could summon, he suspected she'd never been happy or in love. Not with him. Had she loved Peter? Or Roy? Had she found her happiness with another man?

God, why had she married him? Shirley always used to tease him about how her daughter had landed herself a rich rancher. Was that all he was to them? God, no wonder Livy was unhappy. He was nowhere close to rich, not when they'd married at any rate. Earlier, sure, his family had done okay for themselves, but around the time he first started dating Livy seriously, they'd had to cull their herd of cattle due to BSE. One stupid mad cow and their whole way of life was destroyed. He'd tried to protect Livy from all those worries and problems. That was probably another of his many mistakes.

That was why he'd gone to the rodeo so much, in the hope of a quick fix. It had been stupid to think he could win the big prize, but he'd been desperate. No big windfall had come. His dad died one year after losing the herd. Devin had always figured it was from a broken heart after watching his beloved farm slip further and further into the bank's clutches. Things turned around eventually, but it'd taken a long time. Devin was only sliding into the black now.

Would she have married him if she'd known they were so close to losing it all? In those days, Livy, or perhaps the idea of her, had kept Devin motivated. And she had stayed with him and been miserable. She hadn't divorced him. Instead, she'd blamed Devin for her lukewarm artistic success. Blamed him for her cancer. Blamed him for her death. Did she hate him that much? He wasn't everything she'd imagined him to be, so she tried to take some kind of revenge out on him. Make him regret his loving her.

Because he had, in his own way, loved her.

Considering it now, that love was probably the foolish emotions of youth. They never should have married when they did—but he had loved her. He'd tried to give her everything, but it'd never been enough. When he'd finally realized his marriage was over, he strayed, maybe not with his body, but definitely with his heart. *Cheated.* Then Livy told him she was dying.

Devin stared at the remnants of Livy's sketchbook. The earth was stained with black soot. Could he risk losing his chance at happiness, too?

It was time to move on. It was time to sell Livy's artwork. It was time to make space in his life for Claire. He could see now that Claire's fibs were different from Livy's. The way Claire blushed when she tried to avoid his questions, the tone in her voice, or when she looked at him, touched him, said his name when he made love to her—the truth in those moments told him she loved him, no matter how much she tried to deny it.

Claire was a horrible liar, so why did she keep trying to lie? Was she trying to protect him or herself? Why hadn't he seen that before?

When he was satisfied there was nothing more to burn, Devin threw of bucket of water over the charred remains of Livy's deceit.

CHAPTER 45

The gloomy clouds overhead made the early evening seem later than it was, which fit Claire's out-of-whack internal clock exactly. Jay was settled in front of the TV with a bowl of popcorn, and seemed happy enough to be left alone, so she'd seized the opportunity to nap. When she closed the door to the house, lightning caught her eye. She paused for a moment and watched the streaks of light dance over Morning Lake's distant shore. She couldn't hear the thunder yet, so the storm was still a long way off. The air was getting heavy and moist, though, so no doubt rain would come soon.

But even the fiercest storm wouldn't keep her awake tonight. Claire yawned. She spared one last glance at the lightning, then crossed the yard. She passed through the opening in the hedge and stopped.

"Oh, my God." Claire stared at her parents. No, it couldn't be. She blinked, but the vision didn't go away. Her father, tall and wide as ever, was unloading luggage from the trunk of a rental car and her mother, as coordinated as a catalogue model, was standing back, directing things. "What are you doing here?"

They looked at Claire.

Her mother laughed, and opened her arms to Claire. "Is that any way to greet us? We've been dying to see you. You never come home anymore. So, we decided to take our holiday and come to Morning Lake."

Claire hugged her mother, then slipped free. Her dad shut the trunk.

"You should have called."

"Then it wouldn't have been a surprise, would it?" Her dad tapped her on the nose the same way he had since she was a little girl. "No hug for your old man?"

Claire stepped into his embrace and wished she knew an easy way to resolve this problem.

"So, let's haul these bags in, and we'll grab a pop and go sit by the lake." Her dad patted her on the back. "We're just in time to watch the storm come in over the water."

There was only one thing to say to that. "You can't."

Her mom hoisted her purse higher on her shoulder. "Don't worry if the house is a bit of a mess, love."

"No." Claire clenched her hands together. "That's not it. Listen, I didn't tell you. I didn't realize you'd come."

"Tell us what?" her mother prompted.

"I have summer renters."

Her mom pursed her lips and glanced at the apartment over the garage. "I never liked it when your grandmother rented the studio. You never know about people."

"Did you get credentials? References?" her dad said.

"Yes," Claire said. "I got references."

"Well, Claire-bear." Her dad shrugged. "I wish you'd told us about this, but if you checked the references—"

"The thing is," Claire interrupted, "they didn't rent the studio. They are in the house."

"What?" Her parents spoke in unison.

"I'm staying in the studio."

"But where are we going to stay?" Her mother glanced around as if searching for another place that might accommodate them.

"Why on earth? You need money, don't you?" Her dad tsked.

Claire bit her lip.

"You're broke?" Her mother's disapproval was clear. "You need to quit playing at this photography hobby and come home. I've heard that your cousin Charlotte's company has an ad out. They're looking for an engineer."

"Charlotte works for a mechanical engineering firm. That isn't what I do. Besides, I—" Claire stopped talking when she heard another vehicle pull into the driveway behind her parents' rental. It was Devin. Claire groaned. *Not now.*

Thunder rumbled through the air as Devin climbed out of his truck.

"Just a minute," Claire said to her parents, and she went to talk to him.

"Where are you going, young lady? We are having a discussion here." Her mother's voice trilled through the air.

Good God, she was thirty and her mother was calling her *young lady?*

Devin looked great—just seeing him made her chest clench. He seemed a lot more peaceful than he had that morning. Claire glanced up and down the street. Were their neighbors watching? God, someone was going to call Shirley.

"This is a bad time," Claire said.

"I shouldn't have pressed you this morning," he said. "I'm sorry."

"I can't talk," she said. "I don't think it is good for you to be here."

"We need to talk." He reached for her hand, but she pulled it away. "You said you cared about me. Well, I care about you, too. I'm sorry if I hurt you."

Claire glanced over her shoulder at her parents.

"Company?" he asked.

Claire clenched her hand. "Can we—"

"Who are you?" Claire's dad had marched over. "Are you renting the house?"

Devin tilted his head. "Pardon me?"

Her dad pointed at the house. "Are you staying here?"

"No, sir." Devin turned to Claire. "What's going on?"

"These are my parents."

Claire's mother swept over to them. "Claire, who is this man?"

Claire made introductions. They eyed him up and down.

"Are you dating my daughter?" Her dad crossed his arms over his chest.

"Yes," Devin said.

"Dad!" Claire said.

Her mother looked squarely at Devin, dismissing Claire's reprimand. "Then perhaps you need to tell her that she needs to start living up to her responsibilities. Did you encourage her to rent out our house?" Then her mother turned her attention on Claire. "Is this man the reason you are staying here?"

If only the storm brewing overhead could break now.

Devin smiled then. *Good God, what was he thinking?*

"Devin," Claire said. "Please..." Please what? She didn't know what she was asking.

Devin winked at her. "Mr. and Mrs. Best," he said. "It has been a pleasure." He nodded to them, but instead of getting in his truck, he went to the house. Probably to check on Jay. Her parents stared at Devin.

"Is he a real cowboy?" her father asked.

CHAPTER 46

Devin stood in the studio's doorway. Where should they start? His mom stood beside him with her hands on her hips. She hadn't asked him if he was sure about this decision. In fact, she hadn't offered any comment on his decision to remove Livy's things. She was just there with him.

He had sent Jay to the garage to finish sorting through the pieces of Claire's chair. This afternoon they could assemble it. Well, Jay could point to the pieces and Devin would nail them in place. The kid had a knack for figuring out the puzzle, but his arm was still trapped in a sling.

"We need to sort the art work." Devin considered the task. "We can't do that in here. There isn't enough space."

"It should be dry enough outside. We'll have to bring them in tonight, though." Helen nodded. "Good thing we didn't get that rain like they did in town."

Over the next few hours, Helen and Devin cleared Livy's studio. They arranged the pieces by size, laying them flat on the grass, which was already yellowing—just as it did every August.

What was he going to do with this artwork? He couldn't very well arrive at the secondhand store with stacks of this stuff like he had with Livy's clothing. That sales woman had been ecstatic with his load yesterday, but he doubted she'd be very thrilled with a truck full of stained glass. Besides, if he did that, Shirley would kill him.

"That man called yesterday about the yearling," Helen said, as she lowered two pieces to the grass.

Devin pushed a large piece over a few inches, to keep a path clear. "What did you tell him?"

"That you weren't interested."

Devin nodded. "That about sums it up."

They both knew the money from the yearling would help, but it wouldn't solve all their financial challenges. His mom would be the last one who'd want the yearling sold to the wrong person for relatively small gain, and they didn't need the money *that* badly. If his mother had seen that man's stickered ass and listened to him talk, she would have tossed him off the farm faster than Devin had. Besides, there would be other opportunities—he just didn't know what those were yet.

He'd hoped he'd have some business come his way after the Bannister rodeo. He'd been trying his damnedest to network. God, the word "network" alone made him shudder. He wasn't a businessman. He should have realized he couldn't do it, but at least he'd tried. Not that it'd done much good, since all anyone had wanted to talk about was his old life.

By late morning, the studio was empty of stained glass. The sun was blistering when they finished and the air was stagnant. The back yard was coated in colored glass, but it didn't look pretty—it looked treacherous.

Perspiration slid down Devin's back. He wanted everything out, including the tables and the desk, but his mom was sweating as much as he was. He should have insisted she take a break earlier.

"I'm going to check on Jay," Devin said. "Why don't you go rest for a bit? Get out of this heat."

Helen plucked a tissue from her sleeve and dabbed at her brow. "I'll mix us some lemonade and bring it out to the garage."

"It's okay, Mom. Put up your feet," Devin said. "Jay and I'll come in."

When his mom nodded, Devin rounded the side of the house and went to the garage.

Jay had the chair laid out like a skeleton over the oil-stained concrete floor. He looked up when Devin entered.

"There are only four broken pieces," Jay said. "I've traced them on some newspaper."

"Good idea," Devin said. "I've got some spare wood out in the shed; we should be able to find something suitable out there. Do you want to take a break now or cut the wood first?"

Of course Jay said he wanted to keep working. Over the next half hour, they found some wood and cut the pieces. When they set the new pieces into Jay's pattern on the floor, the kid looked pretty damn pleased with himself.

"That's perfect," Jay said. "If I had to do that at home, it would have taken days to get the wood, borrow a saw, figure out how to use it and all that. You've got everything here."

"You've done a good job, kid,"

Jay blushed. "When it's painted, you won't see the difference."

"Well, paint's something I don't have. We can buy some tonight when we go into town. What color do you want?"

Jay sniffed. "Do you smell—"

"Smoke." Devin rushed out of the garage. The acrid smell of burning wood filled the air. "What is on fire?"

Then he saw it. A black spiral rose over the house.

"Oh, God—Mom!" Devin ran and Jay was on his heels. A flash of orange—it could only be George—rushed by them, going in the opposite direction.

"Mom!" Devin crashed through the front door. He covered his mouth and nose with his shirt as he stumbled to the kitchen. She wasn't there. The air was thicker as he moved deeper inside. He ducked as low as he could. Smoke burned his eyes, but he could see she wasn't in the living room. The smoke was thicker upstairs, but what if she'd gone to lie down in her bedroom?

Damn it, where was she? Devin groped his way from room to room, but he couldn't find her. He returned to the living room. He couldn't stay in here much longer. He needed air. But he couldn't leave. Not without her. Where was she?

He tried calling for her again.

Then one of the windows broke beside him. A rock flew through the room, narrowly missing his shoulder.

"Devin, I'm outside." His mom's voice was clear and strong. Devin's heart eased, then he staggered blindly to the exit.

Outside he collapsed to the hard, dusty ground. Jay and his mom rushed to his side.

"Call..." His words broke on a croak.

"The fire truck is on its way. Jay called on his cell phone," Helen said. "Jay, you go get Devin some water from the office in the barn."

As Jay peeled off, Devin struggled to sit. "We need to—" But his words were stopped by an eruption of coughing.

Helen pushed Devin to the ground. "Breathe, son. Just breathe for a bit."

His nostrils were filled with the smell of his home burning, but Devin heeded the gentle pressure of his mom's touch on his shoulder, pinning him to the ground, and stared at the clear blue sky above. From this angle, he couldn't see the sooty streak rising toward the heavens. But it was there. He knew it.

Jesus, the house was gone. His home was burning and he was helpless to stop it. His mom and Jay couldn't run buckets from the well with him. Hell, he wasn't sure he could move without wheezing. "The horses, they'll be scared."

"Do you promise to stay put? I'll go let the horses into the pasture." Helen patted his cheek when he nodded. Tears streamed down her cheeks, a testament to her unspoken heartbreak over having lost her home—the home she'd built with his father and fought for years to keep. They sat for a moment, allowing the futility of the situation to encompass them.

"It is only a thing, Devin." Her voice was barely audible over the crackling of the fire. "Only a thing." Then she pursed her lips and stood.

Jay ran to them, panting and wincing, with an armful of water bottles. His shoulder was probably killing him, jostled around like that. The kid dropped the bottles to the ground beside Devin. Then Jay grabbed one, reefed it open and thrust it toward Devin. Jesus, the kid was frightened out of his wits.

"Thanks. Hey, kid, I'll be okay," Devin said, pleased that he got his words out without a cough. He forced himself to sit and gulped down the water. "You go help Mom with the horses."

Jay nodded fast and sharp, then he followed Helen back to the barn.

Devin finished the water, then he pushed from the ground. He could see flames shooting over the rooftop. He grabbed another bottle of water and circled to the back of the house.

The bit of grass where they'd placed Livy's artwork was ablaze. Thank God there wasn't a wisp of a breeze, nothing to carry the sparks out to the surrounding fields and the other buildings. Flames licked the siding, causing the paint to sizzle and blister, but the fire hadn't progressed as far as he'd originally suspected. It'd just crept over the studio, but—was he seeing things correctly?—the rest might be saved.

Devin emptied the water bottle over his head as he ran to the well. His chest burned, but he be damned if he'd let it stop him. Thank God they'd switched out the pump for a tap a few years ago, but where the hell had his mom stashed the hoses? Shit, he was going to have to do this the hard way. He filled the five-gallon bucket that hung beside the well.

He'd made two runs by the time his mom and Jay had found the garden hoses and connected them to the spout. His buckets and the little one-inch wide arc of water from the hose did nothing to abate the fiery onslaught. Mom was pacing, trying to think of what else they could do when three neighbors, John Quinn, Old Henry and Ryan Jenkins, pulled in to the yard, followed immediately by Wayne Jenkins in his water truck. They hollered a quick greeting, then got to work spraying the house.

About ten minutes later, the Morning Lake fire truck careened into the yard followed closely by the ambulance. The volunteer fire crew jumped to immediate action. Devin stopped long enough to talk to the fire chief, an old friend of his dad's, and inform him of the few details he knew. Devin's words were broken by fits of coughing and wheezing.

The chief motioned for the paramedic to join them. The tall freckled woman tried to steer him from the fire, but Devin refused to budge until he'd finished saying his piece. Then she guided him away with surprising authority.

A moment later, Devin was being assessed for smoke inhalation while Helen and Jay worked beside the crews to try to save their home. Every time Devin tried to rise and join the fighting, the paramedic stopped him.

"Sit," she commanded as if he were a dog.

Then the chief sent Helen and Jay to the paramedic, too. *About damn time.* Jesus, his mom wasn't strong enough to fight fires, but the paramedic wasn't concerned with Helen or Jay's breathing.

Devin escaped when the paramedic had her back to him and finally rejoined the fire fighters. Wayne came over and clamped his hand on Devin's shoulder. His neighbor's thinning, gray-streaked hair was wet with sweat.

"Thanks, Wayne," Devin said. "You can't imagine my relief when I saw you pull in."

"Good thing we saw the smoke when we did. We were going into town for parts." When Wayne shook his head, little droplets of perspiration flew from his comb-over. "Ryan, that damn boy of mine, hadn't filled the truck this morning when he finished his rounds, or we would have been here sooner. He's still mooning over that catalogue model he was dating back in the city."

Devin's laugh came out more like a wheezing, whistling noise.

Wayne shook his head. "That model told him she wasn't livin' out at Morning Lake, but he doesn't believe her. The kid'll figure it out eventually. 'Til then, I guess he'll be a little stupid. Wish I could've gotten here sooner, though." Wayne looked at Devin's house again and scratched his head. John Quinn joined them then.

"Doesn't look good, does it?" Devin contemplated his home. Black smoke billowed overhead, thick as ever.

"You are lucky, so lucky, no one was hurt," Quinn said. Devin knew the other man was thinking about his own family, who'd died in an accident a few years back. Quinn squeezed Devin's shoulder. "Sorry about the house, Dev, but all this can be replaced."

Devin tried to speak, but a cough obliterated his words. When his hacking eased off, Wayne patted his shoulder.

"You need to get that examined," Wayne said. "That paramedic can only do so much out here. Surprised she hasn't hauled you off. You sound like shit."

"She's been trying."

"You go take care of yourself, buddy," Quinn said. "We've got this under control. There isn't much more to do now. I'll go check on your animals."

"Nah, I—"

"What are you doing?" Helen interrupted. She looked madder than a cat with its tail caught in a door. She wiped her brow, leaving behind a streak of soot.

Devin gestured to the fire. He didn't dare speak, because he knew he'd start to cough.

She pursed her lips. Devin opened his mouth to argue, but shut it when his mother put her hands on her hips. Wayne laughed at her obvious irritation, while Quinn dipped his head before turning to head for the barn.

"Go on," his older neighbor urged.

Helen turned to Wayne, and started talking about Devin as if he wasn't standing beside them. "His father was stubborn, too," his mom said. "And stupid."

The neighbor shrugged, and started to ease away. "Don't you worry, Devin," Wayne said. "We got it."

Helen took Devin's arm and dragged him to the ambulance.

"I need to take him to the hospital," the paramedic said when Helen presented him at the ambulance. "We should have gone right away, but you've got a wickedly stubborn son, Mrs. Trent."

Helen studied Devin for a minute. Tears welled in her eyes, but then she looked away and mopped at her brow again. She cleared her throat. "Is it that serious? He wasn't inside that long. I thought he just needed—" She waved to the equipment in the ambulance.

The paramedic didn't bother to look at Devin. They were treating him as if he was a child, for Christ's sake. "There are lots of chemicals released in a house fire. It's best if the doctors can check him."

Helen nodded, then tapped Devin on the arm. "You need to do that, Devin. If the house is gone—" When her voice cracked, Devin's chest tightened. This time his pain wasn't related to the smoke-inhalation. She swallowed, then continued. "We need to be healthy to build everything up again."

Devin let out a sigh of defeat. Futility welled inside him and he struggled against what he wanted to do and what he knew he had to do. His yard was littered with people and hoses.

And he was going to the damn hospital again.

CHAPTER 47

Of all the times for her parents to arrive at Morning Lake, this had to be the worst. Jay was still having problems with his arm, she'd left a haunting half-truth sitting between her and Devin, and the show was the next night.

She had to find a way to tell Devin the truth before it came out some other way. She'd thought of nothing but how to explain things to him since she'd let him walk out of her apartment believing cancer wasn't an issue. Maybe Shirley was correct. Maybe she had lost focus of what was important with the gala. Before Devin, the fundraiser had always been the most important thing. But Devin was more important than any of that, wasn't he? When had things changed?

"This is where I work," Claire announced as she held the gallery's namesake red door open for her parents.

They assessed the business in one sweeping glance. From the slight sneer on her father's face and the tilt of her mother's head, it was obvious they found it lacking.

"Claire, there you are," Peter rushed out of the office and headed straight for her. He kissed her cheek before she could pull away. This was just another incidence of his escalating touchiness.

Her father cleared his throat.

Thankfully, the phone rang immediately after Claire made the introductions and Peter disappeared into the office.

"It's for you, Claire," Peter called.

When Claire realized it was the doctor's office on the line, she shooed Peter out of the office and shut the door.

"There has been a cancellation," the nurse explained. "You can have your LEEP procedure tomorrow morning, if you want."

"Tomorrow?" Claire sat in the chair. If she went tomorrow, she'd find out the results that much sooner. She glanced at the calendar on the desk. The checklist for the show tomorrow evening indicated all the big things were in place already. There'd be a bit of clean up and setting up, but most of the day she'd just be restless waiting for the event in the evening.

"You can keep your original appointment, if you prefer."

"I'll take the one tomorrow," Claire said. "What time do I need to arrive?"

A few minutes later, Claire's fingers trembled as she dialed Devin's number. He'd said he wanted to be there for her next exam, and she'd promised she'd let him. But it was so soon. She hadn't figured out how to explain things yet.

The phone rang. She lost track of how many times the ringtone sang in her ear. Why wasn't he answering?

When her parents peeked into the office, Claire hung up. She'd have to call him later.

CHAPTER 48

After hours of oxygen tubes, X-rays and breathing tests, Devin was released. Tears welled in his mom's eyes when the doctor said his smoke inhalation was only slight and that he could leave. His mom had worried her tissue to bits. Was that the same one she'd had this morning when they were hauling Livy's art out of the studio?

They walked across the hospital parking lot together in silence. When they arrived at his mom's truck, she gave him the keys. Apparently, if the doctor thought Devin was fit to go home, then his mother figured he was well enough to drive. Still, he couldn't remember the last time he'd driven her truck. The day must have worn her out—physically and emotionally.

"I talked to Meg after I dropped Jay at the Underwood place. We can stay with her tonight." His mom's voice was reedy.

"It'll be okay, Mom. I promise." Between the damage assessment and dealing with insurance, there was too much to do—he couldn't give in to worry, but his mom didn't have to be strong for him. Devin wrapped his arms around her. When had she gotten so small? She sniffled, then patted him on the back to break the embrace. He continued to hold her.

"Of course it will be," his mom said. She patted him again. This time he loosened his hold.

They drove to Morning Lake in near silence. The weight of the unknown stifled any conversation. His mom had followed the ambulance, so she hadn't seen what happened in the end.

Was it all gone?

Devin stopped in front of his aunt's bungalow, but kept the truck running.

"I'm not going to stay here tonight," Devin said. "Thank Aunt Meg for me, but—"

Helen patted Devin on the knee. She smiled weakly. "It's okay, honey. She'll understand. But come here if you need to."

What he needed was entirely different from the lumpy sofa bed in his aunt's basement. He needed to see Claire, but first, he needed to go home.

The twilight sky was clear when Devin arrived at the farm. There was no smoke spiraling overhead now.

He sat in his truck for a few minutes and stared. The building was standing. In fact, from this position, the farm appeared as it always had, except mud had replaced the grass in the front yard.

The fire truck and its crews had gone, but Devin wasn't alone. Another pickup truck was parked in the driveway. Devin exited his truck and took a deep breath. The scent of the fire lingered.

He needed to see what had happened.

He walked to the back. The studio was destroyed. Stripped of its roof and walls, the two-by-four frame was a blackened skeleton, but the rest? No, he shouldn't hope that it was livable. He needed to be realistic. Devin stepped closer. The remnants of Livy's artwork, which had been reduced to broken or melted glass, crunched beneath his feet.

"Hold up," a man called to Devin. Devin hadn't seen him in the gathering shadows of early evening until he stood from where he'd been crouched.

Devin stopped and greeted the man, who introduced himself as John Webster, the fire inspector.

"I can't let you inside until we have a chance to check it for damage," John said.

Devin looked at the house and nodded. "I figured as much. I have to admit, I'm surprised there is anything left."

"We'll have to do a proper investigation, but I thought I'd stay and see if I could get a start on figuring out what happened. Now that you are here, I can ask you a few of my questions."

Devin answered John's questions, most of which were focused on what was stored in the back yard. John nodded when Devin described Livy's work. Finally, Devin asked his own question.

"What happened?"

John clicked his tongue and glanced over the site. "This is only preliminary, so keep that in mind, but I'd say the fire started outside, over there by that shrub. I couldn't figure it out until you mentioned that glass. I'll bet you that glass started it, same as kids and their magnifying glasses. That sun was pretty intense today, and grass is dry this time of year, a kind of tinder."

Devin shook his head. He was finally making inroads into getting his life back on track by trying to clear out Livy's possessions, and it had nearly destroyed him. Unbelievable.

When John left, promising to return first thing in the morning, Devin drove to Claire's. He should have called first, but the need to see her consumed him.

Her car was missing from the driveway, her windows were dark, but Devin knocked anyway. Silence greeted him. Then he tried the main house, but no one was there either.

Had she gone to see her parents? Were they staying in Morning Lake or the city? He had no idea.

Devin drove by the gallery, hoping she was working late, but it, too, was empty. Her car was nowhere in sight.

Circling back to her house, Devin considered waiting for her, but talked himself out of it. Tonight probably wasn't the best time to talk. He was wrung out from the day he'd had.

His little travel trailer would have to be his home for the night. Devin grimaced. He hadn't slept in it since that weekend when Livy had summoned him home. He'd almost gotten rid of it when he'd left the rodeo, but instead he'd held on to it the same as he'd held on to everything else.

Tonight he figured that had been one of the few smart things he'd done.

CHAPTER 49

Before the sun rose over the flat lands to the east, Devin had started whistling.

He hadn't whistled in years, but he couldn't help but feel his luck was starting to take a turn for the better. It was a ridiculous thought, considering his home had burned and things weren't resolved with Claire yet. But the feeling persisted despite its absurdity. After all, things were looking up.

A few hours later, he was still feeling good.

The horses were where they belonged. They'd been spooked with the smoke, but none had hurt themselves in their panic. He'd found a change of clothes in the trailer. Sure, they smelled a bit musty, but it was an improvement over smelling like smoke. And he'd found his cell phone in the barn's office when one of his former rodeo buddies called, sending the thing ringing and vibrating along the top of the desk.

His friend wanted to breed his mare with Devin's stallion for a tidy stud fee. It wasn't the same money he'd have received for the yearling, but it'd do for now. He'd just finished that conversation when he discovered one of his regulars had recommended his place to a potential boarder who was looking for a place for two horses—they'd emailed him asking about rates.

Finally, Devin could start training the colt, and quit trying to sell it.

And the best news was seeing that Claire had tried to call him—four times. Rather than call her, he decided to surprise her and see if there was anything he could help with for her show.

Yes, today things were better.

Today he'd tell Claire he loved her.

After finishing at the barn, Devin had tried to help the fire investigators, but there wasn't much they needed from him. In the end, he left them to their jobs and headed for town with his few pieces of clothing bundled. He needed to check on his mom, and he might as well use Aunt Meg's washer and dryer while he was there.

Devin continued to whistle to the songs on the radio all the way to town. His good mood persisted as he washed his clothes, ate a good home-cooked breakfast—to which Jay had also been invited—and told his mom what he knew of the fire damage. His aunt had asked if he was in shock. He grinned at her but didn't answer.

Then he hopped in his truck and struck out to find Claire. When the radio announcer introduced Shirley, Devin's good mood vanished. God, how was he going to tell Shirley about the fire? The only remaining pieces of Livy's work were the few things Shirley had and what was on display at the gallery. She'd never forgive him.

CHAPTER 50

It was still morning when Claire left the hospital. She had been unable to get hold of Devin the night before, and finally, around three in the morning, she decided that maybe that was for the best. She needed more time to talk to him about this cancer worry, and today wasn't a good time for a heart-to-heart.

This procedure, from her end, resembled the previous one. The doctor didn't have an intern with him this time. At least that was one small blessing. He said he was sending the excised cells to the lab for a more accurate assessment of the abnormal area.

Claire had listened, but she didn't want to think about it.

So this was a good day to have the procedure, because with the preparations and the gala, she wouldn't have time to think about anything else—except the pain in her abdomen kept distracting her. The doctor suggested she take an over-the-counter pain killer and call the hospital if she had any problems. The pill hadn't dulled the pain, but then again she'd just left the hospital—she wasn't out of the parking lot—so perhaps it hadn't kicked in yet.

What she should have asked was at what point the pain moved from the realm of discomfort to a place of concern. But, of course, she hadn't thought of that when she was in the stirrups.

She tried to open her car door but she was shaking too badly, making her miss the keyhole. She took a deep breath and concentrated on the lock. Had Livy gone to the hospital on her own, too? Or had Shirley gone with her? Had Livy kept it a secret from everyone? Was it to protect her family and friends? But they hadn't been protected, had they? They had been hurt. A small voice inside her head told Claire that she was doing the same thing.

No, it wasn't the same.

A minute later Claire was inside, even though her hands were still shaking. She locked the door. She didn't know why—it wasn't as if a car lock would keep the cancer and her fears away—she just did.

She should have asked someone for a ride.

Claire leaned back in the seat and closed her eyes. No, she could do this. Besides, she had tried to call Devin last night, in between entertaining her parents at that mediocre dinner and then the god-awful play they'd insisted on attending with her. He hadn't answered his phone.

It was better this way. The conversation she needed to have with Devin would require time and a clear head.

And she couldn't tell her parents; they were worried about her enough as it was. They had tried to persuade her to return to Toronto all through dinner. What if she did have cancer? Maybe it would be better to return with her parents. She wouldn't be running away this time, the problem was inside her—she'd be carrying it with her wherever she went.

No, it'd be okay. She'd be okay. The test was done and now all she had to do was survive the fundraiser. Claire took deep breaths—the kind she'd learned to do once in a beginner yoga class.

She wasn't sure how long she'd sat in the car doing her breathing but finally she felt calmer. She opened her eyes and braced her shoulders. Claire fit the key into the ignition in one try.

Driving to Morning Lake at this time of day was dead boring. She couldn't quit thinking about—well, everything. She needed a distraction.

She punched the radio to the local station and hoped for a familiar song. If she was singing, she couldn't be thinking, right? Instead, the radio announcer was talking. Claire reached out to turn the station when she stopped and realized what the man was saying.

"This morning we are happy to have a local woman on the show with us. Every week we highlight one community organization, and today we are speaking with Shirley Patterson about a local initiative to raise money for families affected by cancer."

Shirley managed to get a radio spot. Wow, that was fantastic. Claire cranked the volume.

"Good morning, Fred. Oops, I'm sorry, I mean Ted."

God, was she drunk?

"Tell us about the gala tonight and the show."

"As you all remember," Shirley said, "my daughter, Olivia, succumbed to cancer a few years ago. It was a horrible shock to all of us. You can't imagine the pain of losing your own child, your own..." Shirley's voice trailed off. A soft sob whispered through the speakers.

Claire pulled over to the side of the road.

The announcer cleared his throat. "The show is being held at a local gallery, The Red Door. The event showcases the work of local artisans who have either fought cancer themselves or had a family member affected by it." He was reading from the event flyer. "The opening gala is tonight from seven to eleven."

"My Olivia's work will be on display starting tonight until the end of the show in three weeks. She did the most beautiful butterfly—you'll be able to see it there." Shirley sniffled. "Thank you, Fr—Ted, for talking with me today. I have been the only one to try to promote this. If the show isn't a success, it is all on the shoulders of that gallery girl. But the proceeds do go to cancer charities, I checked with the gallery owner. But, if this show isn't a success, it is no reflection on the quality of Olivia's work." Oh, God, Shirley was all over the place. Claire slumped.

"And, that's—" The radio announcer tried to interrupt.

"My Olivia, her work was underappreciated. I'm here now to keep her memory and her art alive. That gallery girl is too busy screwing—" Shirley was cut off mid-sentence with a radio ad.

Claire turned off the radio and rested her forehead on the steering wheel. Had she been the architect of Shirley's latest bout of pain? If she hadn't organized the show, if she hadn't slept with Devin, if she hadn't fallen in love with him…

How many people heard that radio broadcast? Claire was the only one in Morning Lake who could be labeled the "gallery girl." Everyone in town would be curious now. They'd all be talking about her. At least the radio station had stopped Shirley from saying Devin's name.

Here was yet another reason it was good she had gone to her appointment alone.

CHAPTER 51

Devin listened to the interview.

God, he hoped Claire hadn't heard it. When had Shirley started to hate Claire? Devin shook his head. He was an idiot—of course, Shirley wouldn't want him getting close to Claire. She'd never accepted Livy's death, and believed he shouldn't either. How was he going to solve this?

Now that he'd found Claire, he wasn't going to give her up. He had to find her before she heard about Shirley's interview.

He tried her home first. She wasn't there…again.

When he arrived at the gallery, Devin rattled the door handle. It was locked. A sign was taped to the window: *Please excuse us while we prepare for tonight's gala. Regular business hours will resume tomorrow.*

That wasn't going to work for him. Devin cupped his hands and peered into the gallery window. The lights were off.

He returned to his truck and waited.

When his cell rang, Devin nearly choked on his gum. He glanced at the display. It was Jay, not Claire. Damn. He answered anyway. The kid asked if it'd be okay if he went to the farm with Melody and her parents to finish the chair. When he ended the call, Devin resisted the urge to return to the farm to help him, but Claire was more important than her chair. He had to see her.

Two pieces of gum later, Devin saw Claire's car. The worry in his chest lightened at the sight of her parking across the street, and a sudden nervousness gripped the back of his neck. He'd never felt this way. Not when he'd asked Jean-Anne, the hottest girl in his class, to the high school prom. Not when he'd asked Livy to be his wife.

Devin rubbed his palms over his jeans, then got out of the truck to wait for Claire by the gallery's red door.

She didn't exit her car immediately. She sat staring at him, with her hands tight on the steering wheel, even though she was parked. Devin resisted the urge to go to her—the look on her face told him she needed a minute, and truth be told, he needed a minute, too. But waiting was killing him. It wasn't more than a moment, but it'd felt like an eternity before Claire finally left her car and approached him.

She was beyond pale. Her eyes were filling with tears. Shit. She'd heard the interview, hadn't she? Why else would she be crying? She had her keys in her hand, and moved past him. She didn't say a word to him. When she lifted the keys to the lock, they slipped from her grasp. And no wonder, too. Her hand was shaking.

"Claire," Devin whispered. He touched her, wanting to draw her into his arms to comfort her. She stiffened and pulled away.

When she bent to retrieve the keys, she gasped and winced. She pressed her hand to her lower belly. Devin's heart stopped. Why was she grabbing herself there? Was she pregnant? They'd only ever used condoms for protection, and those weren't always reliable—particularly when you didn't follow the directions. She would have told him about a baby, wouldn't she?

God, if she was pregnant, that would be…perfect. Devin almost smiled, until his senses returned to him—it didn't take a genius to figure out that she wasn't happy to see him, and she wasn't happy about the pregnancy either.

"What's the matter? What's happened?" Would she tell him?

"You shouldn't be here, Devin." Claire squeezed her hand in a fist over the keys, as she glanced up and down the street. Shit, she was scared of being caught in public with him. This wasn't about a pregnancy.

Devin stepped closer, touching her shoulder. "Is this about Shirley?"

Claire closed her eyes. "You heard the interview? Or did you hear about the grocery store?"

"I heard the interview." Devin nodded, but Claire turned away from him before opening her eyes. She reached up to open the gallery lock, and this time managed to fit the key into the slot. "What happened at the store?"

Devin followed Claire into the gallery.

Claire sighed. "Then you realize why you shouldn't—"

"Jesus, Claire, Livy's dead. I have spent years being faithful to her ghost. Years. Isn't it time—"

His cell phone started to vibrate in his pocket. Shit. What if it was about the fire? Or insurance? Or God only knew what else. He fished the phone out and glanced at the screen. It was his mother. "I have to get this."

Claire turned from him.

"What?" Devin answered his phone more abruptly than he'd planned. He expected a reprimand from his mother, but instead she said his name softly. Oh, God, now what?

"What's happened? Did they phone about the house?"

"Oh, Devin, I…" Her voice was soft with tears. He heard her blow her nose and then sniffle. A heavy sense of doom closed over his throat. "I got a call from Norma down at the police station. It's…it's Shirley. She's died."

Devin's grip on the phone tightened. "No, Shirley was on the radio."

Claire glanced at him. He turned away from her and pressed his phone closer to his ear.

His mom took a deep breath. "It just happened. Norma said she knew she shouldn't call yet, but… Oh, Devin, Shirley had been drinking already today. They're trying to figure out what happened. Her car hit the bridge railing down by Johnston River. The car flipped over, straight into the water."

"Jesus." Devin closed his eyes. Shit. He should have seen this coming. He should have tried to do something.

Was it wrong to feel relief she was no longer in pain?

"She didn't get out of the car. It was in that water. You know how deep Johnston…" His mom's words trailed off. She cleared her throat. "She died, Devin. Shirley's gone."

When he disconnected from the call a minute later, Claire was watching him, her eyes alight with expectation. He cleared his throat, wiped a tear or two away with his thumb, then he told her what had happened.

"No," Claire shook her head. "No, that—" Her voice broke. "That can't be."

Devin crossed to her. The disbelief in her eyes was clear. "Come here."

He pulled her into her arms. She struggled at first, but he held her until she settled. She sobbed in his embrace, her tears wetting his shirt. Her slender shoulders shook. Claire was taking this a lot harder than he'd have thought. Yes, she was sensitive and caring—determined to help people with her fundraiser—but she hardly knew Shirley.

"Talk to me," he murmured. God, it was good to hold her.

He pressed his lips against her hair, wishing he knew what he could say to her to ease her distress. Slowly she stilled. He wanted to ease her pain, ease his, too. He wanted to know how to help her. He needed to tell her so much.

"I love you," he whispered. Shit, he hadn't meant to tell her like that. She tensed in his arms immediately.

"No." She pulled away from him. "Don't." He knew she had feelings for him, but… Devin looked at her again. No, he was wrong—her shoulders were slumped, she was pale, and her movements were jerky. This wasn't about her feelings.

Something was wrong. Was she pregnant? She'd tell him, wouldn't she? She'd said it was a woman's appointment—that could mean pregnancy. Was there something wrong with the baby?

Then it hit him. What if it wasn't his baby she carried? She'd gone to that appointment at the hospital way before they'd spent the night together.

That memory, when coupled with her worries about hurting him, pointed to a pregnancy that had nothing to do with him. She wasn't showing, but when did that happen? Maybe she was still early in her term.

Devin clenched his fingers. Who was the dad? Why wasn't he here with her? Devin could plant a fist right in the absentee's face. But Claire couldn't be scared of Devin's acceptance of a baby, could she? God, he'd love any child of Claire's as if it were his own. What if it was a little girl with Claire's dimple? Devin hushed the giddy rush in his blood. She'd be beautiful when she started to show more, and later when she held the babe in her arms, she'd sing those sweet lullabies he'd imagined when he first met her.

"Claire, look at me."

Claire walked away from him. "I can't. Not now."

Devin followed her. He'd love the child as much as he loved her. He had to assure her of his eagerness to share this joy with her.

Then she spun toward him, slicing her hand through the air. "Don't push me. Not right now. I can't do it. I can't do it today." Claire's eyes were filling with tears again. She blinked quickly. One tear escaped. She swiped at it angrily.

He went to her and captured her face in his hands. She looked at him, and really saw him, perhaps for the first time since she'd left the car. "Claire, tell me what to do to help you. Let me help you."

"Why? Why do you keep pushing at this?"

Her words hurt, but he knew his reaction was stupid, irrational. "Claire—"

Claire pushed at him. He tried to hold her, but she thrust him away. Her face was flushed. "Fine," Claire snapped. "I was at a doctor's appointment."

"I told you I'd take you—"

"I tried to call you. I tried. You weren't home. I got in at the last minute. They just told me yesterday."

"Shit, honey, I'm sorry." Devin nodded, encouraging her to talk. If only she could tell him, let him share some of this—

"Getting tested for the big C." She swung away from him. Her arms waved through the air erratically.

"Oh, God." Claire? Cancer? Dizziness swept over him. "Jesus, Claire, why—"

"No. Stop." Her words silenced him. "I didn't want to tell you. Not like this."

She didn't want to tell him? Just like Livy. Devin stepped away from her. Her focus on the fundraiser made sense. Jesus, how could he have made such a colossal error in his deduction? Why hadn't he pressed for answers from her when he'd seen that big red circle? Instead, he'd jumped on the answer he wanted to hear. His words from that morning rushed over him. No wonder she hadn't confided in him.

Her gaze darted over the gallery—landing anywhere but on him. "The show... I have to think about the show. It is—oh, God, the show. I have to call Peter. We should stop the show. We should..." Her lips trembled.

Despite the pounding of his heart, Devin shook his head slowly. Claire was pushing him away. He took a deep breath. What could he say? "Shirley would want the show to continue as scheduled." That was not what he wanted to say. It was probably the least important thing at the moment, but Claire didn't want to hear anything else. Not from him. Not right now.

"I shouldn't have told you. I tried to protect you. I wanted to—"

"Claire," Devin whispered. She appeared so fragile, it broke his heart. How could she think he wouldn't want to know? He crossed the distance between them and pulled her close. She stood rigid in his embrace, tension rippling through her. He caressed her back, trying to soothe away the pain and fear he'd seen in her eyes. "I told you I love you, I'm here for you."

Her sob exploded through the silence. "No, no—"

"What the hell is going on?" Peter's voice broke over them.

Son of bitch, could he have come at a worse moment? Devin ignored him. Claire started to move away from Devin. He held her in place for a moment longer, bending to kiss her forehead. "Let's go talk."

She leaned against him for a heartbeat, before stepping back, away from him. "I can't. Not now. The...the show..."

Devin wanted to throw her over his shoulder and take her away, but when she looked at him, he saw her resolve. She wasn't going to leave here. Not now. "Okay," he agreed, though it killed him to say it. "I realize this isn't the best time to talk about this, but I need you to know it'll be okay."

Peter yanked him around by the shoulder. "You made her cry?"

Devin fisted his hands. He wasn't in the mood to deal with Peter's crap today. "Stand back, you son of a bitch."

"Get out of here." Spittle flew from Peter's lips.

"Stop." Claire's voice was soft and weak. She sounded so tired. Was she really sick? She should rest. She should—

She was walking away from him.

Devin pulled away from Peter and stared at him, wondering if the man realized just how damn lucky he was that Claire was there. Then Devin left. He could do little else.

He climbed into his truck and punched his steering wheel.

He should go back in there and take her away from here.

He'd recognized it wasn't all about Shirley, and he'd pushed her. And now he knew. *Tested for the big C.* Jesus. He yanked open his truck door and vomited—right there on the cracked asphalt.

When Devin sat back in his seat again, he didn't move for a minute. His door was open, blocking part of the drive lane. A passing car honked at him. He wiped his mouth on his sleeve, then slammed his door shut. He hit the steering wheel again.

God, he hadn't even told Claire about the fire. No, he'd told her he loved her instead. He'd wanted to tell her, but not like that. He'd said it and she'd pulled away.

God, he wanted Claire, wanted to keep her safe, but he couldn't protect her from this. He was useless and she knew it.

He wanted her to let him into her life, but he knew he couldn't force her. If he hadn't pushed, would she have ever told him? Or would she have hidden it from him the same as Livy had?

God, he shouldn't have pushed her. She should have felt she could come to him on her own time. He should have respected that, but he hadn't. At least he knew now. But it was probably killing her that he knew. She'd been upset that it'd slipped out. He knew she had a lot going on—her emotions were running high, the show was stressing her, and Shirley's accident hadn't helped.

But if only she could trust him, just a little.

If only she could let him be there for her, to support her. Could she let him love her? How could he make her believe him?

Make? No, that was the wrong word. He needed to earn her trust. Earn and cherish it.

He needed to prove to her that she could trust him with her problems. Always. Cancer or no cancer.

CHAPTER 52

Claire clung to the damp rag in her hand.

"I have more to do," she argued. "More to clean. More to—"

Peter shook his head. "Claire, you need to go home and rest. It'll be a long night and you look worn out."

"But there are still things to do." She glanced around the gallery. What was left? Surely, there were a million little tasks remaining. But no, the gallery was ready. She should know, she'd worked to get it there. She had washed the floors, set up the cocktail tables and did a third—or was it fourth?—dusting of the displays. Her abdominal pain had pinged with each movement, until finally she had taken another pill. The pain didn't matter—she needed to be busy, keep moving.

"The caterers and the photographer will set up now. I'll stay with them, then I'll close up and go home for a bit myself." Peter said. He touched her shoulder. This time it didn't feel creepy. This time it felt patronizing. Anger shot through her.

"Take your hand off me."

Peter let go immediately. "Claire?"

He looked surprised and more than a little concerned. She just needed to get through the show, then she would be free of him. And, in truth, he didn't seem touchy just now. Instead he looked sincere. Claire tamped down her emotions. *Wasn't that just the story of her life?*

"I'm sorry," Claire said. "Maybe you are right, I think I need to rest."

A moment later, she had gathered her things and was leaving the gallery.

To go home? She sighed. There wasn't anywhere else to go, was there? And Peter was correct—she should rest. Her parents would badger her if she wasn't perky and smiley. Another stab of pain shot through her, smack dab in the spot that cramped each month. Except it wasn't that time. Damn it. She couldn't take another painkiller—they were sucking her energy faster than her mom's fancy vacuum sucked up dust bunnies.

A little nap would be heavenly.

Pain dogged her the whole drive home, and she found trudging up the stairs to her apartment was harder than it should be. Harder than it'd ever been before.

In minutes, Claire was on her bed, staring at the ceiling. What was she going to do? She needed to talk to Devin.

I love you.

He'd said it. So why did she want to cry?

God, her stomach hurt. She curled on her side and groaned. Maybe she'd pushed too hard today. The doctor had said no heavy lifting, but he hadn't said hibernate. Besides, the tables hadn't been *that* heavy.

She hugged a pillow across her abdomen and pushed her face into the mattress.

She'd probably feel better if she slept for a bit. She pulled the blanket over her, and its warmth enveloped her. She wished it was Devin's warmth holding her, but what would he do? This little pang was nothing compared to the pain she'd feel if she did have cancer.

How had Livy hidden it for so long? Livy must have hurt and she was alone—by choice. Now Claire was doing the same thing. God, she didn't want to be alone.

Did Devin really love her?

He knew the truth now. The hurt in his eyes had almost been enough to paralyze her, but she'd sent him away instead. The similarities between her actions and Livy's—God, what was he thinking right now? What was he feeling?

Claire swallowed the bile flooding her mouth. She'd hurt him with her lies, and now she'd hurt him with the truth.

CHAPTER 53

Jesus, why did men have to wear suits? Devin pulled at his tie for the sixteenth time. He had checked his old suit when he had stolen into the house that afternoon to see the damage for himself—it had reeked of smoke, just like the rest of his clothing. So he'd had to buy a new one. This one carried the musty smell of the store where he'd found it that afternoon. Still, store-stink was probably a step up from smoke.

The vision of his ravished home flashed in his memory—what the fire hadn't consumed, the smoke and the water had destroyed. The place was a mess. The fire inspector had changed his tune now, and he wasn't optimistic about the house being livable again.

And was he doing the right thing by Shirley? Shirley would want the gala to go forward, but she'd probably hate him for going to it.

Devin clenched his teeth and focused on the road ahead. He wasn't going to solve Shirley, the fire or the house today.

No, tonight was about Claire's gala.

A few months ago, he'd have scoffed at anyone suggesting he'd be going to Peter's gallery for some hoity-toity fundraiser, but here he was.

He swung by Claire's first, hoping she'd let him escort her. His mom was attending with his Aunt Meg, so he was on his own. His heart raced when he saw Claire's car in the driveway, but she didn't answer when he knocked. The lights were off in her apartment, though it was bright enough she may not need the lamp yet—so she could just be ignoring him.

Devin pounded on the door again and listened. Nothing. She must have gotten a ride to the gallery with someone else. Her parents were in town, so that made sense. He hoped it wasn't with Peter.

CHAPTER 54

Claire lay still, listening. Silence. She could have sworn someone had been knocking, but she must have been dreaming. Oh no, was that the time? She must have been more tired than she had thought. She should have set the alarm.

Pain sliced through her abdomen when she scrambled out of bed. She fell back to the mattress and gripped her stomach. Jesus, what was going on? She took ten deep breaths. *I'm fine. I'm fine. I'm fine.*

But she wasn't, was she? She must have pushed too hard this afternoon. Stupidity was her middle name today.

She eased out of bed, testing to see if she could straighten. Slowly, she managed it. Why was her body taking charge today? Couldn't it wait until tomorrow?

A knock at the door sent Claire's heart tumbling. Was it Devin? She'd said she'd talk to him later. All she wanted to do was crawl into his lap and hold him.

She trudged across the room, forced her muscles to relax, pasted a smile on her face and opened the door. Her parents stared back at her.

"Aren't you ready yet?" her mother scolded.

Her dad glanced at his wristwatch. "We came to take you to that thing tonight. Doesn't it start in half an hour?"

Claire nodded. "I fell asleep."

Alarm shot over her mother's face. She pressed her hand to Claire's forehead. "Are you sick? You're pale. You've never slept in the afternoon, even as a child." She turned to Claire's dad. "Doesn't she look peaked?"

"Quit fussing," her dad admonished. He cleared his throat and glanced around the studio. "Not much space in here, is there? Why don't I leave you two here to get ready for the thing. I'll meet you there."

"Mom, you don't have to—"

"Of course, it'll be fun." She slipped into the apartment, brushing a kiss over Dad's lips as she passed him. Then without a second glance, she shut the door.

She swept into the apartment and flopped to the sofa with a flourish. "I'll sit here while you have your shower, then we can chat while you dress."

Claire tried to keep the smile on her face and the hunch out of her stance, but when she turned toward the bathroom, pain stabbed through her. She gasped and grabbed for the wall to steady herself.

"Claire!" Her mom was at her side in an instance. "I knew you weren't feeling well. Why didn't you tell me?"

She let her mom guide her to a chair, and she lowered herself into it. "I'm fine, really."

Her mom didn't say anything; she just waited at Claire's side.

Claire took a deep breath. "Okay, I'm a touch sore, but I'll be fine."

"What happened? You seemed fine yesterday."

Claire closed her eyes. She didn't want to tell her mom. She had been trying for so long not to tell anyone. "I had a day—" Claire paused and looked at her mom. She couldn't tell her mom she'd had day surgery. It would freak her out. "A little procedure this morning. It's nothing. I—"

"Why didn't you call me or your father? How did you get there? What was it for?" Her mom's foot tapped loudly against the wood floor.

"It was a minor thing."

Her mom's foot kept tapping. What would any other mom do in this situation? She doubted they'd be annoyed and impatient.

"It is called a L.E.E.P. It is—"

"I know what it is," her mom said. Her stance relaxed instantaneously. "Oh, thank goodness. You had me scared."

Claire blinked at her mom. "You know what it is?"

"Of course, love." Her mom smiled and patted her on the shoulder. "I've had it done. Aunty Bev and your cousin Theresa have both had that, too. It's nothing to worry about."

Claire gulped. *Nothing to worry about?* She'd done nothing *but* worry. Some of the tension in her chest eased. She hadn't realized it was there—she'd lived with it for months. "You've had abnormal cells?"

"I'm fit as a fiddle, and you will be, too." Her mom smiled. "Have you been worrying about this? You should have told me."

Claire nodded slowly. "I didn't want anyone to worry."

"That's what friends and family are for." Her mom leaned forward. "Did you tell your boyfriend?"

Claire swallowed. She was fitting a lie around her tongue when she realized she couldn't lie anymore. "It is complicated."

Her mom sat on the coffee table in front of Claire. She reached for Claire's hand and cradled it in her own. "Oh, my poor girl. I bet it seems complicated, but…" She paused. "Do you remember my beef Wellington?"

Claire blinked. "Of course, it's great."

"It took me years to figure it out. Your father insisted that it was his favorite meal and that his mom's was the best." She poked her nose in the air. "Flip through any cookbook and you'll see it isn't an easy thing to make. Grandma refused to give me her recipe—that woman was impossible—so I figured it out all on my own. I figured out how to make the pastry light, not tough or soggy. I figured out how to make the beef melt in your mouth, not undercooked or overcooked. I did it all. And now I can do it without thinking about it."

"That's some metaphor, Mom." Claire leaned back and rubbed her aching belly. "What are you trying to tell me?"

Her mom shrugged. "The point is, whatever seems complicated is often not. What is beef Wellington but a bit of beef and some pastry? If you practice enough, nothing is complicated and it can end up being quite wonderful."

Claire tried to blink away the tears welling in her eyes. "I messed up. I think this beef Wellington is inedible."

"If it is important, don't give up."

Claire swallowed. "He thinks I lied to him."

"Did you?"

"It's complicated," Claire repeated. Unable to meet her mom's eyes, she studied her hands. Her mom waited. "He had someone die of cancer, so when I found out I needed the procedure, I didn't want him to worry."

"You've been all bottled up with this, haven't you?" Her mom leaned over and kissed her cheek. "You need to talk to him."

"I don't know how."

Her mom nodded. "That takes practice, too."

Claire brushed her tears away. "I'm sorry I didn't tell you."

"It is okay, Claire. When Grandma died, you took it the hardest. I should have seen how hard. I should have come out then and spent some time with you, talked to you. You can always talk to me, sweet pea. I wish I'd known." Her mom's words trailed off, and she tried to muster a smile. The tears in her eyes made the smile awkward, but Claire found it oddly comforting. "We need to get you ready for the gala."

Claire sat forward, and her abdomen clenched. She exhaled slowly and grabbed the arm of the chair, waiting for the pain to subside. "I think I did too much today."

Her mom brushed Claire's cheek, then tucked a stray strand of hair behind her ear. "I imagine you did. You take after your dad that way."

"Do you think it would be horrible if I didn't go?"

She smiled. "You need to do what will make you happy."

Claire blinked at her mom. When had her mom gotten so sentimental and philosophical?

"Now, don't you worry." Her mom rose and crossed to the kitchen. She set the kettle on the stove and set about making tea. Claire watched. When had her mom made her tea? She couldn't remember. It wasn't a beverage they drank when she was growing up.

A few minutes later, her mom set a steaming cup of peppermint tea on the table beside Claire. Then she kissed Claire's forehead. "You rest and don't worry so much. Everything will be okay, you'll see. Your dad and I will go over to the gallery and talk to that odd Peter fellow."

"Thank you, Mom." Claire blinked away a new batch of tears. Why was she so teary-eyed lately?

A knock at the door caught them both by surprise.

"You stay, I'll get it," her mom said.

Claire's dad was on the landing. "Are you ready?" Then he looked at his wife and pointed to Claire. "Why isn't she ready?"

"Claire needs to rest tonight. She's not quite up to snuff." Her mother smiled. "I thought you went for a drink at the pub."

He glanced between his wife and daughter, as if to assess if there was anything he needed to worry about. The smile on his wife's face seemed to appease him though, because he nodded. "Some kids dropped off a chair. I swear it looks like that old thing your grandfather made, but it's all new."

Her dad crossed the room and gave Claire a petite blue envelope. "They asked if I could give you this."

The card inside read: *Sorry about the car and the chair and stuff. Jay*

Claire smiled, and glanced to the threshold. If Jay was here with the chair, Devin couldn't be too far away. "Are they coming upstairs?"

Her dad shook his head. "Don't think so. The girl said her parents were waiting in the truck."

"Girl?"

His dad shrugged. "Melanie?"

"Melody."

"Yes, that's it. Why?"

Claire wasn't about to tell her parents that Jay and Melody had been making out in Grandpa's study—doing rather unforgettable things with the paperweights. Claire cleared her throat. "Oh, no reason."

"Okay, love, we'll head over to the gallery," her mom said. "We'll help Peter if he needs anything, but I bet you have everything all under control. It is what we Underwood women do." She winked. "Call if you need anything."

After her parents left, Claire sipped her tea and tried not to be disappointed that Devin hadn't come. Which was stupid. How many times would he keep coming back when she kept pushing him away? Was it too late?

CHAPTER 55

Every time the damn bell on the gallery door jingled, Devin expected to see Claire glide into the room. This was her big night, there was no way she would miss it. Her books were arranged on little tables throughout the gallery. He'd already bought his copy; it was tucked under his arm.

So where was she?

A harpist was in the corner of the room, thrumming her thick strings, and each note she plucked, plunked at his nerves. Servers toted trays of champagne and finger food, offering them to the growing crowd. How many times did he have to say no before they would leave him alone? And then there was Peter. He smiled smoothly and attempted to ingratiate himself with everyone except Devin.

His mom and aunt mingled with their neighbors and admired the displays. His mom's eyes went glassy with unshed tears every time someone asked about Shirley. And a few people asked about the fire, but Devin stopped the queries, saying that they didn't have any answers yet.

No one seemed to notice that Claire hadn't arrived. No one except him.

Where the hell was she?

He couldn't do this much longer. Patting his pockets for the umpteenth time and coming up empty-handed, he reminded himself again why he shouldn't chew gum at Claire's special gala. It wasn't the venue for cinnamon gum. He could do this. For Claire. He adjusted his tie again and rolled his shoulders.

Another jingle tittered through the growing din. Claire's parents entered. Devin's chest clenched and he waited to see Claire. Would she be happy he was here? The door shut behind them. No Claire. Had he missed her? He glanced around the room.

She wasn't here. Jesus, had something more happened since this afternoon? She had been so upset.

Claire's parents went to Peter's side. Jealousy cut through him. They

214

motioned Peter away from the people with whom he had been speaking. Then they bent their heads close, and it appeared they were whispering.

Damn it, what was going on?

Peter looked up then, directly at Devin. The son of a bitch scowled at him. Devin clenched his teeth. He had to get out of here before he hit that look off that ugly mug of his. Besides, he was here for Claire. If Claire wasn't coming, he would go and find her.

He was halfway to the exit when his mom reached his side and placed her hand on his arm. In one glance, he knew she had seen all of his frustration. She squeezed his arm, silently urging him to stay longer. He was about to push off, but then he noticed that she had tears in her eyes.

"Are you okay?"

"I think you should say something, honey," she said.

"No."

"It's important." She squeezed his arm again.

Devin took a deep breath. She was right, of course. He had planned to make an announcement tonight about Livy and Shirley—but he hadn't thought everyone would be so sentimental, so emotional. He didn't do sentimental. He didn't do emotional. But did that mean he shouldn't say anything? That would be pretty damn cowardly, wouldn't it? Shit.

Behind them, a soft tinkling sound caused people to hush. Devin turned to see Claire's mom tapping her wedding ring against her champagne glass.

She smiled when she had everyone's attention. Claire had her smile. Devin's heart ached suddenly—when was the last time he had seen Claire smile?

"Thank you, everyone. I wanted to take a moment to thank you all for coming tonight. As some of you may know, I am Claire's mother. She couldn't come tonight, so I wanted to say a few words."

She smiled and nodded at Devin when she spoke, as if to reassure him that Claire would be okay. But he wasn't reassured. He wouldn't be until he had seen her himself. If she wasn't coming tonight, then something was seriously wrong. His pulse roared in his ears, until it was all he could hear.

What had happened to Claire? Had she received confirmation of her cancer? It was too soon, wasn't it? Earlier it'd sounded like she was just being tested. Claire's parents wouldn't leave her alone if she'd had confirmation, would they?

"I grew up in Morning Lake," she continued, "and I'm so proud of my daughter for organizing this gala tonight. Thank you, Peter, for hosting such a wonderful event."

She smiled at Peter, and Devin felt like an idiot. Claire was right, not everything was about him. And it was good of Peter to have allowed Claire to do this. Devin couldn't have given Claire her own show and fundraiser—but it didn't mean that he had to like it. He wanted to be able to give Claire everything.

Claire's mom nodded. "Cancer has hit all of us in one way or another—whether we've struggled ourselves, or it's been our friends and family."

Claire's dad put his arm at his wife's back to offer her support. She leaned into him. Why couldn't Claire let him do that, too?

"My mother passed away a few years ago from cancer. It was how she died, but it wasn't how she lived. This…" Claire's mother gestured to the art displays. "This celebrates how we all live. Look at all of the wonderful people and their creations." She waved to the walls. "It is beautiful." She wiped tears from her cheeks gracefully. "Excuse me," she mumbled, "I knew this was going to happen." She sniffled, then straightened. "I guess I wanted to say thank you."

A few people clapped. Then a woman stepped forward, who seemed vaguely familiar. When he heard her voice, he recognized her from the convenience store where he bought gum. She had one of those voices that had been ravaged by smoking. It was weird to see her out of context.

"I agree," the woman said after she introduced herself. "This is a great thing for our community. I haven't ever been so proud to be a citizen of our small town, with so many people coming together tonight to help the people in our community who need it. It is hard when you don't have family, and not everyone does. But now, I feel I have a family of hundreds." She paused and looked down at her hands. "My neighbor had breast cancer. She died last March." The woman's voice cracked. "And I hope she knew that although she didn't have a family of her own, our community was there for her. I think this will make a difference."

Three more people spoke, sharing similar stories. His mom pressed harder on his arm. Oh God, she wanted him to speak in front of all these people. Sweat beaded along his hairline. How could this be more intimidating than climbing on the back of an angry bull in the front of a roaring crowd?

When the man beside him finished speaking, Devin cleared his throat. Everyone turned to him. His hands were wet.

"Ah…" Devin swallowed. Why hadn't he taken that champagne? "I'm Devin…ah…Trent." Jesus, he couldn't remember his own name. "My wife, well, that's her stained glass over there."

He gestured toward the window. The late summer sunlight still shone through the front window, piercing through the stained glass, sending bright colours dancing through the air. He'd avoided Livy's display all night. Now people split like the bloody Red Sea so they could view her work. Beside Livy's artwork was Claire's photo of Livy.

His chest tightened. Some part of him realized that Livy's photo didn't bother him now, not the way it had that first day he met Claire in the gallery. Beside him, his mother nudged him. The attendees were waiting for him to continue, their eyes soft with empathy. He looked up, above their faces.

"She died," Devin said, as he pulled at his necktie again. "I wanted to say that when this show is over, I'll be donating her work to the oncology ward at the Red Deer hospital, in memory of both Livy and Shirley, her mother." His words were tumbling out faster now. "Shirley passed away earlier today, and I hope they've found each other in heaven again."

Everyone was staring at him still. He could feel the weight of their gazes, even though he was fixated on a spot on the top of the wall, right where it met the ceiling.

"But I also wanted to say that no one should go through any of that alone—cancer or any other illness. Sometimes you have to ask for help. Tonight is just one night, but the feelings and the sentiments of community and helping shouldn't just be here one night of the year. Sometimes it might feel like it is too hard to ask for help, but it shouldn't be." Devin shrugged. "Um, that's it. That's all I wanted to say."

People clapped, then everyone's attention turned to the next person who wanted to speak. Devin yanked off his tie.

"That was perfect," his mom whispered. Her eyes were glistening with more tears. Then she reached up and patted his cheek. "Now, go find Claire."

CHAPTER 56

When Devin stepped into the street, fresh air slapped his face. The restaurant patios lining the sidewalk on either side of him were alive with light, laughter and music. It was suffocating.

He balled up his tie and shoved it into his pocket. Son of a bitch. His hand was shaking. He made a fist and tried to regain some control as he leaned against the narrow bit of wall that divided the gallery from the adjacent business. He glanced at the book—Claire's book—under his arm. He hadn't looked through it yet—he'd wanted to be with Claire when he did.

The gallery door opened a moment later.

"What do you want?" Devin said to Peter. Luckily, he already had his fist formed. It would feel damn good to hit the SOB once and for all.

Peter rolled his eyes. "Get over yourself, okay? I want to thank you for coming tonight."

Devin narrowed his eyes. "Pardon me?"

"We haven't been on the best terms, but it was good you came."

"Do you think my attitude could have had anything to do with you screwing my wife?"

Peter didn't look away, but a telltale red blotchiness crept above his shirt collar.

"Can't deny it, can you?"

"I loved her," Peter mumbled. Grief broke over his smarmy face, making it the most sincere emotion Devin had ever seen from the guy.

"She was my wife." Devin crossed his arms over Claire's book. It was true, Livy was his wife, but his feelings for her were nothing compared to what he felt for Claire. He had better places to be. Devin pushed by Peter.

Peter pursed his lips, then he blew out a breath. "I'm sorry."

Devin spun toward the other man. Was Peter sincere? It would seem so.

"Me, too." Devin nodded.

218

They stood silent, studying one another for a minute, then Devin stretched his hand toward the other man. Peter's eyes widened in surprise, but he shook. Devin never wanted to see the son of a bitch again, but maybe this needed to be done too—one last step on closing that part of his life. When Peter tried to pull away, Devin squeezed. Hard. "I love Claire."

Peter scowled. "You better not hurt her."

"She loves me, too." He knew it, even if she'd never said the words. Then Devin released Peter.

Peter stepped back, rubbed his hand, then he pulled the gallery door open. Claire's parents hurried out, colliding with Peter. Claire's mom smiled and started to apologize, but when she saw Devin, she stopped talking and rushed to him.

"Goodness gracious," Claire's mom exclaimed to Devin, forgetting about her apology to Peter. "What are you still doing here?" She elbowed Devin away from the gallery. "You need to go see our Claire."

CHAPTER 57

After the gallery, he'd gone straight to Claire's place. He found the chair in the back yard, but there was no sign of Claire, and her car wasn't there. The fact that she was still MIA. after he spent an hour driving each street in Morning Lake was frustrating as hell. He figured if anyone knew what he was doing, winding up and down each street, they'd think he was a stalker or a creep—but her mom had said he should go find her and that was what he was damn well trying to do.

Where was she?

Damn it. If she didn't want to be found, then he wasn't going to find her. She couldn't avoid him forever, though, but he would give up the search for tonight.

The last place he wanted to be was heading for that stuffy old trailer again. Alone. Those 140 square feet were going to feel like a cage if he didn't figure out a way to calm down. Devin unrolled his window when he got close to the farm and slowed his vehicle. It was a quiet, tranquil evening, but the pollen-clogged air still flooded his truck. The crickets were starting to sing when he turned into his drive.

His palms began to sweat the moment he saw Claire's car. Had she been here all night?

Her car was vacant. Jesus, even here at his own home he had to hunt for her. Devin called her name. There was no answer. The setting sun cast long shadows over the farm, but he could see well enough. The front entrance was still sealed over with the warning tape, so she hadn't gone inside.

He checked the barn, but she wasn't there either.

Was he going insane?

Finally, he circled the house.

Claire was huddled at the edge of the scorched grass, staring at the burnt timbers. Lingering scents of the fire filled the air. He knelt beside her. "Claire?"

She grabbed him in a hug so fast and fierce that he lost his balance and fell to the grass-covered earth. She fell over with him, not loosening her hold one little bit. He was sprawled on the ground, and she was over him. She was here. Safe. With him.

He couldn't believe the lightness stealing over his chest.

"Devin, thank God." With her face pressed into his chest, her words were muffled.

Then he realized she was shaking. He wrapped his arms around her and rubbed her back, trying to soothe her. "Claire, what's the matter? What happened?"

She pulled out of his embrace, bracing herself on her arms, and started at him with wide eyes. "Are you okay?" she demanded.

"I'm fine. Why?" Then he realized why she'd asked. Was he an idiot or what? "It's okay. The fire—"

Before he could finish—or even start—his explanation, she started rubbing her hands over his limbs, as if doing her own assessment of whether or not he had been injured. She was hiccupping now. Oh, God, was she crying?

"I saw the—" Claire waved toward the building. "I didn't know where you were. I got so scared." Her cheeks were wet with tears. He tried to pull her into his arms again, but she resisted. When she finished her check of his well-being, her hiccups seemed to ease.

Then she punched him in the arm.

"Jesus, Claire, what was that for?" He rubbed his shoulder.

"You should have told me. When did this happen? It didn't happen today, did it? That was what I was holding on to, all the time I was sitting here. I knew I'd seen you this afternoon... I knew..." Claire's words ended on a gulp, then she grabbed him in a bear hug again.

"Yesterday. It happened yesterday."

Claire eased back, then climbed off him and plopped to the ground beside him. He missed her warmth immediately. He sat and reached for her, but she crossed her arms and stared at him, silently entreating him to tell her what she wanted to know.

He took a deep breath, then explained about the fire. When he told her about the hospital, she grasped his hand. Her nails bit into his palm, but he didn't care. Tears overwhelmed her eyes. She wiped at them when the droplets were about halfway down her flushed cheeks.

"I'm okay. So are Mom and Jay and all the livestock," he said in the end. "Mom is staying with her sister. When I saw her this morning, she said she might move in there again. The house here, well, at first they thought it might be livable again, but now the fire inspector isn't so sure."

Devin paused. Why was he babbling like an old woman? He took a deep breath and refocused his thoughts. "I didn't mean to scare you. I tried to

find you. I tried to phone you last night, but I missed you. Then today…"
He let the thought trail off. A lot had happened in that one day.

"I don't know what I would have done if—" Claire shook her head, as if unwilling to finish that thought. She crawled to him again, and snuggled into his embrace. This time, she accepted his comfort, and the frantic fear that had held her earlier seemed to ebb away. "When I saw all this, I was so scared, so lost. I don't even know how long I've sat here."

Devin pressed kisses against her hair.

"Are you going to tell me what is going on with you now?" Devin whispered. She tensed in his arms, but then she nodded.

"That's why I came here," she said. "I'm so sorry." She pressed her lips to his. She tasted of the salty tears that had washed over her face. When their lips parted, her eyes were soft with regret. "I love you, too, Devin. I didn't say that earlier, but I should have. It is true. I don't ever want secrets between us again. And I know I've been the worst at that. I'm so sorry for the way I talked to you earlier. I never wanted to tell you that way."

Devin tucked her hair behind her ear. "I'm always, and will always be, here for you."

"I know," she whispered. "I think that's what scared me. I didn't want to worry you, but I was wrong. I see that now."

Claire looked at him. She didn't blink. "But what if I do have cancer?"

"I would never let you face that alone. We'll do it together."

Tears welled in her eyes again. "I'm so scared to put you through that. You still love Livy so much. What if I die? I don't want you to grieve over me like that. I don't want you to be in pain because of me."

"Claire, I'm not sure where to begin." Devin rubbed his forehead. "I never loved Livy the way I love you. I'm halfway to thinking that I was more in love with the idea of Livy than the reality. It wasn't fair to her, and it wasn't fair to me." He held up his hand. "No, don't argue with me. Let me talk here a minute. Livy had a chance at happiness, and it wasn't with me. I wish like hell she'd had the opportunity to live that happiness and the freedom to express her love. I know I want to tattoo how I feel about you on the moon so the whole universe knows."

"Livy was in love with another man?"

Devin nodded. "She let that love slip through her fingers, but I won't. I want to fight for you. I never want you to question how I feel about you. I was stupid to tell you the way I did today, and I didn't mean to put you in that position, but I—"

Claire's lips covered his in a warm, possessive kiss, stopping his words. A moment later, he broke free. He needed to tell her more. He needed to finish what he had to say. "If you have cancer, I'll be right there with you. Through every bit of it. I'll fight at your side. No matter what it is. We'll fight it together." Then he paused. He wasn't sure if it was appropriate to ask his questions now, but he couldn't seem to stop himself. "What happened today? Why didn't you go to the gala?"

Claire glanced at him then, and seemed to realize for the first time that he was in a suit. She stroked his lapel. "You went, didn't you? To the gallery." Tears welled in her eyes again. Her words were obscured with hiccups and more sobbing, but he understood when she said, "I love you so much."

The shadows on this side of the building were getting deeper, but Devin could still see Claire's face. After a few minutes, she calmed again. "I was sore, but I'm okay now." Her words were slow, as if she wasn't sure how to proceed. Opening up to him was new for her—he understood that—but she was doing it. She was trying to let him into her pain, trying to share this private and fearful thing with him. He held her tight and willed her to continue. "I don't feel any tenderness now at all."

Then the meaning of her words hit him. She was hurting.

"Are you sure? God, are you in pain? We shouldn't be sitting out here on the ground. Should we—" Damn it, he was going to the hospital again.

Then Claire smiled up at him, and the panic stampeding over his heart geared down to a trot. "I'm better now that you are here. And really, I'm okay. Trust me."

And he did trust her. Devin took a few deep breaths, then he cleared his throat. "Can you—I mean, I don't want to pressure you, and it is absolutely okay if you don't want to, but...do you think you could talk to me about it? About what's been going on?"

Claire nodded. Then, in the quiet of the late August evening, Claire started to talk to him. She told him all her fears and worries, and her hopes and her love.

Then he knew it would all be okay.

EPILOGUE

One Year Later

Claire stared at the telephone on the barn office desk. The world around her blurred, until all she could see was the tiny red light blinking in a slow and steady rhythm, indicating that the speakerphone was still on. Devin sat on the other side of the desk, but she didn't dare meet his eyes. Not yet.

She didn't want to ask, but she had to. She swallowed and wished she could figure out how to breathe. "Are you sure?"

Devin reached for her, stretching across the glossy wood surface, and she grabbed his hand. The pads of his fingers were more calloused than ever, now that they'd started to build their new home, but when he rubbed her palm his touch was soothing in its familiarity and strength.

"Yes, Mrs. Trent," the nurse said. The woman's voice, loud and tinny, broadcast over the little speakers. "Our doctor has reviewed your last set of results and says he doesn't have to see you again. You can do your regular annual exams through your general practitioner."

Claire glanced at Devin then. His eyes were watery, but happy. He squeezed her hand. Her heart was pounding. Was she free and clear? Had cancer stepped around her? Could it be over?

"Thank you," Claire said before hanging up. For a moment they didn't speak. Devin held her hand and her gaze, then he pushed back his chair. The metal legs scraped across the wood floor.

Planning the second annual fundraiser had been easier with Devin's support, but she was still plagued with many fearful moments in the middle of the night. Devin had helped with that, too. He'd loop his arm around her in the darkness and hold her tight.

Now, the paralyzing fear she had struggled with for the last year cracked and crumbled as he arrived at her side.

"I don't have cancer," she whispered. Then she smiled. "I don't have

224

cancer." This time her words were a little louder. Then she shouted them and gave a hoot after. Sure, the doctor and nurses had said that her tests were okay before now, but they kept wanting her to return for more exams—as if they weren't convinced they had removed all of the abnormal cells. And if they weren't convinced, Claire wasn't convinced. At least until now.

She sprang from her chair and into Devin's embrace, then she jumped up, wrapping her legs around his hips. He caught her easily. When he kissed her, his laughter rumbled against her lips.

"It's over," Devin murmured, his words muffled by her mouth.

"No," Claire said as she pulled away from him so she could look into his eyes. "This is the beginning."

THE END

TITLES BY LORRAINE PATON

Morning Lake Series:
Chloe's Matchmaking Terrier
Devin's Second Chance
Annie's Christmas Plan

ABOUT THE AUTHOR

When Lorraine Paton finished her master's degree, she was tempted to sign on to do a doctorate, but then she realized she wanted to write fiction more. So, by day, she works in a hectic office, and by night, she lets loose her passion for writing romance novels. She lives with two cats who hate one another and a wonderfully patient man with a sexy Scottish accent in Alberta, Canada, which is where her contemporary stories take place. A diehard romance reader and writer, her goal is to bring happily-ever-afters to as many people—*or characters*—as she can.

Connect with Lorraine on:
* her newsletter (http://eepurl.com/tYuqP)
* her blog (www.lorrainepaton.com),
* Twitter (twitter.com/patonlorraine), and
* Facebook (facebook.com/LorrainePaton.Author).

www.ingramcontent.com/pod-product-compliance
Lightning Source LLC
Chambersburg PA
CBHW022013170626
46808CB00001B/388